Heavenly
Blues

The Amish Classics Series

For a complete listing of books, please visit the author's website at
www.sarahpriceauthor.com.

Heavenly Blues

SARAH PRICE

Waterfall
PRESS

Text copyright © 2017 by Price Publishing, LLC
All rights reserved.

No part of this book may be reproduced, or stored in a retrieval system, or transmitted in any form or by any means, electronic, mechanical, photocopying, recording, or otherwise, without express written permission of the publisher.

Published by Waterfall Press, Grand Haven, MI
www.brilliancepublishing.com

Amazon, the Amazon logo, and Waterfall Press are trademarks of Amazon.com, Inc., or its affiliates.

ISBN-13: 9781503942875
ISBN-10: 1503942872

Cover design by Shasti O'Leary Soudant

Printed in the United States of America

No matter how old a person is or the type of cancer a person has, it's scary to walk into the Chemo Cocktail Lounge for that first time . . . and second . . . and third. But fear is a relative thing. Sometimes it takes a special person to help you realize that. One person's pain is another person's salvation. So I dedicate this book to Lori Ann Zayatz, my chemotherapy nurse, who taught me that valuable life lesson and somehow made chemotherapy (and cancer) just a little less scary. Thank you, Lori Ann, for sharing your story with me and planting the seed for this novel.

PROLOGUE

If there were ever an award given for the most stressed teenager in Jacksonville, Florida, Laura knew that she'd win it. Hands down.

It wasn't just because she was seventeen and waiting to hear from the numerous colleges she'd applied to. Joanie Frey had already received three letters, two of which were acceptances. And Sammie Linnear had received two responses, both of which had positive news.

And it wasn't that her brother had just brought home another less-than-stellar report card. He was basically flunking math and science. The fact that he didn't seem to care bothered Laura more than the fact that his grades were in the toilet. Sure, that contributed to her stress, but that wasn't what really bothered her, either.

What was weighing heavily on her mind and causing her chest to tighten each time she took a deep breath was that her mother was, once again, insisting on hosting a holiday party. At the house. Catered. And Laura knew what that meant.

When Laura had gotten home that afternoon, the first thing she saw was the note. It was written in elegant script handwriting, of course, and set on the counter where she would have no chance of missing it. She hadn't needed to even pick it up to read before she began to panic. She knew what it was: a to-do list. And Laura still had to study for her exam later that week as well as finish a research paper for history.

Clearly, all of that was on hold now.

Her mother was a detail freak. Everything *had* to be perfect. And since Sonya worked a full-time job, that meant she delegated a lot of the preparation work to Laura. The list her mother had left for her on the kitchen counter that morning had included everything from cleaning out the coat closets and organizing the pantry to polishing the silver and washing windows. Sonya Driscoll had left no stone unturned.

Now, as she reread the list, Laura felt her chest constrict, the pressure so heavy that she had to hold on to the counter to steady herself. With her eyes shut, she counted to ten slowly, matching each number with a deep breath to slow her racing pulse.

"Hey there, Kitten."

Startled, Laura looked up as her father walked into the kitchen and planted a soft kiss on the top of her head. She knew that he was oblivious to her panic attack.

"Hey, Dad," she managed to say.

He tugged at his tie with one finger as he set his laptop bag onto the counter next to her. His eyes traveled to the piece of paper in front of Laura. "What're you doing? Homework?"

As if, she thought.

"Not yet," she said, forcing a smile. "Just got home from the hospital."

Her mother had found her the job at the hospital gift shop. When Laura first started working there, she had been excited, looking forward to helping people find the perfect gift for whomever they were visiting. She quickly learned, however, that even though she asked questions about what they needed, most people were content with scooping up a trinket or the first card they looked at.

It made the job less than exciting for Laura.

"So what's that?" Her father pointed to the paper in Laura's hand.

"Instructions. From Mom."

Her father chuckled and, without even giving the list a glance, he gently squeezed her shoulder.

That was *always* his reaction. An amused chuckle and a reassuring gesture of support. Only it never provided Laura with support or comfort. In fact, she thought bitterly, his blasé indifference usually did the opposite. Just once she wished that Mr. Switzerland would stand up to Sonya.

"Before you dive in to all of that," he said, producing an envelope from behind his back and presenting it to her with great fanfare, "I thought you'd want to open this."

The plain white envelope with the big red letters in the upper left-hand corner stopped her from thinking about her mother or the chores. Rutgers School of Nursing. The color drained from her face as Laura's gaze moved from the envelope to her father. "What is that?"

"You have to open it to see." He wiggled the letter in the air.

"I . . . I can't." Her lungs felt heavy, as if they were suddenly filled with cement. She couldn't breathe as she stared at the envelope. All of her hopes and dreams depended on the letter inside it. "You open it."

But her father thrust it at her. "No way, Kitten. This is your moment, not mine."

"Dad . . ." Reluctantly, she took the letter and weighed it in her hand. "It's so light. It's definitely a rejection."

He leaned against the counter. "Don't be negative like that."

"But it's already decided, and until I open it, I can still hold out hope." She stared at him, her brown eyes wide and frightened. "I mean, it's one of the best nursing schools in the country."

Her father smiled. "I know that."

"Or at least it's the best nursing school that we can afford . . ."

At this, her father frowned. "Are you still worrying about that?"

But Laura ignored him. She stood up and carried the letter to the window. It was not quite dark outside, and her mother would be home soon. Supper was already in the slow cooker, the robust smell of the beef stew filling the kitchen with the comforting scent of winter. Besides her mother's long list, all Laura needed to do was set the table. There was no reason to *not* open the letter now. However, if it was a rejection, she knew that her evening would be ruined.

"Open it," her father coaxed one more time.

Sighing, Laura flipped over the envelope and slid her finger under the back flap, the noise of the paper ripping causing her to breathe faster. *This is it,* she thought. *No turning back now.*

Please God, she prayed. *Please! I have to get into this school. I need to get away from this house. This town. This state.*

She had selected Rutgers because it was on the East Coast—she had been to California once and earthquakes terrified her—but was far enough away from Jacksonville. Her mother couldn't insist that she come home for weekends or school breaks. Plus, Rutgers was near Philadelphia and New York City, both of which offered a little more excitement than Jacksonville, not to mention great employment opportunities for a nurse graduate.

But if she didn't get accepted, she'd be stuck attending the University of Florida or the University of Gainesville, if she was accepted at one of them. That had been the compromise. She could apply to local colleges and one out-of-state college. Her mother loved to play little manipulative games like that. You can have this or that, but only if . . . The problem was that *only if* never seemed to work out for Laura's benefit.

Perhaps this time, Laura thought. She held her breath as she pulled out the single sheet of paper. It was folded in three, and as she unfolded it, she started to feel light-headed. Her heart was pounding so fiercely, she feared she might faint from nervousness.

Dear Laura Driscoll,
We are pleased to inform you that your application to
Rutgers School of Nursing has been accepted . . .

Her fingers flew to her mouth, covering her lips as she reread the letter. Pleased. Accepted. The words practically jumped off the page at her.

"Kitten?"

Before she could answer her father, she heard the sound of the garage door opening. Seconds later came the too-familiar noise of her mother's Mercedes.

For a moment, Laura wanted to wait so that she could tell both her parents at the same time. But then she remembered her mother's reaction when Laura had announced that she wanted to pursue a nursing career. The last thing Laura wanted was for her mother to be the first to know and ruin the moment.

So Laura turned her face toward her father and whispered, "I was accepted."

Edward rose from the kitchen chair and crossed the room. "That's wonderful, Laura!" He embraced her, rocking her back and forth. "I knew they would accept you!"

"What's going on here?"

Laura looked over her father's shoulder and saw her mother standing in the doorway. She didn't look pleased. Shutting the door behind her, Sonya crossed the room, her high heels clicking on the tile floor like high-pitched gunshots.

Her mother ignored the loving scene of a father sharing a joyous moment with his daughter. And rather than inquire what the celebration was about, Sonya glanced at the piece of paper on the counter. "Laura, I hope you started working on that list I left for you."

Laura's shoulders sagged under the weight of her father's arm.

Sonya walked over to the kitchen counter where she had left the list that morning and reached down for the piece of paper. First, she pulled off one earring and then the other, holding them in her hand as she scanned the paper. "You didn't check anything off." She looked at Laura. "Please tell me you at least started the silver. You know how important this dinner party is."

Her father kept his arm around Laura's shoulder. "Dear, I think you should hear Laura's exciting news."

"Mom, I got accepted at Rutgers."

For a moment, Sonya paused. In Laura's mind, she saw her mother open her arms and hug her. It would be a tearful embrace, with her mother telling her how proud she was. She would say how much she would miss Laura and how she would come to New York City so they could meet for dinner. Maybe even a play. Her treat.

But that wasn't what happened.

"That nursing thing?"

Those three words sent a chill up Laura's arms.

Sonya dropped her hand, the paper making a crinkly noise against her leg. "Honestly, Laura. Is that all you can think about?"

Her father cleared his throat. "I think you meant to say 'Congratulations,' right?"

"Yes, congratulations on being accepted to Rutgers, Laura." Sonya sighed as she tossed the paper onto the counter. "Perhaps I'd be more enthused if it was law school or medical school." She turned toward her daughter. "*Real* medical school."

Laura pressed her lips together.

"The real money is in being a doctor, Laura. Nurses are little more than secretaries with a stethoscope." She started to walk into the family room, but before crossing the threshold, she turned back. "And those horrible blue scrubs!"

"Sonya . . ."

"Don't Sonya me!" she snapped at her husband, her dark eyes blazing. "I haven't been killing myself all these years, working and saving so that my daughter can be nothing more than a glorified janitor to a physician! Bed pans, blood pressure, and temperature taking." She turned to Laura, pointing her finger directly at her chest. "That's what your future as a nurse will be like, young lady. You think doctors will respect you? The patients will appreciate you? I see it every day, Laura. Everyone knows that nurses are nothing more than medical school wannabes."

"Mom . . ."

But her mother ignored her. "And with your grades? Why, you could easily have made it into med school."

"I don't care, Mother." She lifted her chin, just a little, as a small act of defiance. "I want to be a nurse."

Her mother scoffed. "Clearly. But I *do* care." She leveled her gaze at Laura. "I see it all at the hospital. The long hours. The stress. The burnout. Do you think I want that for you?" Her chest rose and fell as she took a deep breath and exhaled. "I know what it's like to be the person taking orders instead of giving them. I've been there and it's exhausting, Laura. Don't you think I want better for you?"

That was always her mother's argument. Be the boss, not the lackey. And yet, at home, there was no chance of anyone except her mother assuming the top tier of the hierarchy. After all of these years, Laura knew, just as her father and brother did, that there could only be one leader in the family. The irony that, in fact, her mother had groomed her to be an order taker and not an order maker was not lost on Laura.

Sonya raised her hand to her head and shut her eyes. "I need to lie down for a bit. I feel a headache coming on."

And then she was gone.

For a moment, in the silence of the room, Laura tried to remember a time when her mother hadn't been in charge, then averted her gaze away from her father. She wasn't certain for whom she felt more embarrassed: herself, for never measuring up to her mother's ivory-tower ideal, or her father, for never standing up to his wife's paradigm of perfection.

"She doesn't mean to sound so critical, Kitten," her father said after her mother was out of earshot.

Laura suspected that wasn't true. The sad look in her father's eyes made her heart hurt just a little bit more. So she did the only thing she knew how to do: she pretended. "I know, Dad."

"It's just her way."

"I know that, too." It was true. Her mother had always been like that. She was driven and ambitious, joining the workforce when women were still secretaries, fetching coffee and listening to sexist comments without any recourse. Not Sonya. After years of being one of those women, she had managed to claw her way to the top.

"She works really hard. It's been tough for her to climb through the ranks like she has." Laura's father squeezed her shoulder one last time. "You don't get to a position like your mother has by accepting mediocrity in people."

But I'm not people, Laura wanted to say. *I'm her daughter.* And there was nothing mediocre about being a nurse. Just because nursing was beneath her mother's ideals of a worthy profession didn't mean that it wasn't valuable. In time, Sonya might come around and find a way to be proud of Laura. If not, Laura would survive. She always had and she always would.

When her father left the kitchen, probably to go upstairs and calm down his wife, Laura hurried over to Sonya's purse. She unzipped the side pocket and pulled out a small orange bottle. Carefully, she pressed down on the white lid and turned it, just a little in a clockwise direction. She peered inside and saw that three pills were left, two fewer than she'd seen that morning.

Laura glanced over her shoulder as if to make certain that no one had quietly returned, then dumped the pills into the sink. She reached out to turn on the faucet and let the cold water run. The steady stream of water quickly dissolved the pills down the drain. Laura snapped the lid on the now-empty pill bottle and slid it back into her mother's purse.

CHAPTER 1

Even though it was Monday morning, it was going to be a great day. At least that's what Laura told herself as she finished applying her makeup in the small bathroom that she shared with her husband, Eric.

He was still in the shower, the steam clouding the mirror. Occasionally, she'd take a cloth and wipe away the fog. But she was almost finished, and her morning routine was simple enough that she didn't mind not seeing her reflection clearly. With a quick glance in the small area she had just swiped clear of mist, she assessed herself. Hair pulled back into a sleek ponytail. Foundation and blush applied. And a nude-colored lipstick applied to her lips.

"Meet you in the kitchen." She didn't wait for Eric to answer as she hurried out of the bathroom.

As she made her way down the hallway of their ranch house toward the kitchen, she could hear *Sesame Street* blaring from the television.

"Morning, girls," she sang out.

Neither of her daughters answered. Instead, they sat at the table, shoveling Honey Nut Cheerios into their mouths, their eyes riveted to the blue Muppets counting sheep as they jumped over a fence. The noise filled the room, and Laura reached for the remote control on the counter and pointed it at the cable box to lower the volume. Simultaneously, both girls turned their heads to stare at her.

"Mom!" the older girl cried out. "We were watching that!"

Laura set down the remote and wrapped her hand around her coffee mug. "Breakfast is family time, Becky. Besides, it's too loud. I couldn't hear myself think," she said to her daughter in a kind but firm voice. "And, Emily, you're dribbling milk all over the table."

"Sorry, Mommy."

Sparing her six-year-old daughter a smile, Laura grabbed a dish towel and tossed it toward the table. Becky reached out to grab it in midair, grinned at her mother, and then handed it to her younger sister.

"Mommy, are we still going shopping for Halloween costumes after school?"

Laura shook her head as she sipped her coffee. "Oh Becks, not today. I'm sorry."

"You promised!"

"No. I said maybe. Maybe doesn't mean definitely."

Becky groaned. "Halloween's next week!"

Fortunately, the sound of footsteps in the hallway interrupted the conversation, temporarily distracting Becky as both she and Emily turned their heads toward the doorway.

"Daddy!" Emily cried out, forgetting about the spilled milk as she pushed back from the table, the legs of the ladder-back chair scraping against the hardwood floor. She ran to greet her father as he entered the kitchen.

"Eric, coffee?" Laura called out. She glanced over her shoulder in time to see Emily jump into his arms. "Easy, Em."

"Of course!" he called out, as Emily tucked her head into his shoulder and burrowed into his neck. With his crisp white shirt peeking out from his black suit jacket, Laura couldn't help but think that Eric was as handsome as the day they had met over twelve years ago. Perhaps a little thicker around the waist, and with graying hair, but still good-looking. In her mind, she saw him as the athletic rugby player who after each game sang bawdy songs at the local college bar. As she poured him a mug of coffee, she wondered if he still remembered the lyrics.

Eric set Emily down on the counter and playfully tugged at her shoes while she giggled. With their heads bent together, Emily's dirty-blonde hair falling over her face and brushing against her father's head, Laura couldn't tell where one began and the other ended.

"Uh-oh," Eric said, holding Emily's two feet in his large tanned hands. He inspected them with a quizzical look on his face. "What's this?"

Laura peered over her shoulder to see what had attracted his attention. "Emily Reese! Are you wearing two different shoes?" She couldn't help laughing, especially when the expression on Emily's still-cherubic face changed from joy to panic.

"I like them both, Mommy. I couldn't decide."

Laura glanced over Emily's head, her dark eyes meeting Eric's. As usual, they were sparkling. Maybe it was because they were blue, but he always appeared more vibrant when he was around his two daughters. He adored his girls and it showed. For Laura, he reserved a different kind of love.

When Eric gave an amused shrug, Laura acquiesced. *What did it matter?* she thought. Turning to Emily, she tugged at one of her daughter's ponytails. "Just for today. Then you can decide which one looks better."

With a big grin and a clapping of hands, Emily cheered.

Laughing, Eric scooped her back into his arms and planted her onto the floor. "Go on now. Finish your breakfast and then brush your teeth. We'll leave in ten minutes."

Handing him his coffee, Laura leaned against the counter, careful to avoid a drop of the beverage that had spilled when she had poured it. She didn't want to stain the front of her blue scrubs. "I can take them today, sweetheart," she said as she reached for a sponge and wiped the spill.

He raised the coffee mug to his lips, peering at her over the top of the rim. The steam that rose misted his eyeglasses, and he reached up with his free hand to remove them. "You sure? I don't mind."

The school was only a few miles from the hospital where she worked. She could easily drop off the girls and still make it to the hospital in time for her seven o'clock start. They paid extra to have the girls in both before- and aftercare programs to accommodate Laura's always-fluctuating schedule. This year was easy, since both girls went to the same elementary school, but next year, Becky would be at a different school for third to fifth graders. Laura had no idea how that would work out when she had the day shift.

"Don't you get the new schedules today?"

She looked at him for a second. It amazed her how Eric stayed on top of everything. Even *she* had forgotten that today was when Gillian, the nurse supervisor, distributed the new schedules for the next month. They normally were distributed earlier in the month, but Gillian was new and the schedules were delayed.

"I guess it is."

Setting down his coffee mug, Eric walked around the counter and placed his hands on her shoulders, bending his knees so that he was eye level with her. "Now, you know that whatever happens, you have to keep your cool. It'll be OK. Right, Laura?"

She nodded but avoided looking into those blue eyes. She hated that look, the one that reminded her so much of her father. *Take it easy, Laura. It'll be OK,* he'd always told her whenever she had gotten upset or stressed. Laura shook her head as if, in doing so, she could erase the memories from her childhood.

But as usual, Eric saw through her.

"Laura?" He placed a finger under her chin and tilted her face so that she had no choice but to meet his gaze. "You understand that, right?"

"I know, I know." She broke away from him, averting her eyes as she started fiddling with her napkin. When he stared at her with such intensity, almost as if he could read her mind—and she suspected that he could—she always felt uncomfortable. She didn't want him inside her head; it was crowded enough in there without him. "It's just that she's so infuriating. I . . . I don't know what I did that caused her to dislike me so much."

That wasn't necessarily true. She remembered far too well the confrontation she had with Gillian just the previous week, after Laura challenged a doctor who prescribed a patient medicines that counteracted each other. If there was one thing Laura had quickly learned about her new supervisor, it was that she did not like conflict between doctors and nurses. Her staff was supposed to leave all management issues to her and *not* handle confrontations on their own.

"I'm sure that's not true. She can't *dislike* you." Eric gave her one of those looks. Patronizing. As if he were her father, not her husband. "You just have to get used to her, Laura. What has it been? Three weeks?"

"Is that it? It feels like she's been there for years!"

Eric almost laughed.

"And so far, all she's done is turn everything upside down. All she cares about is the hospital, not the patients. 'The bottom line. The bottom line.' You know how she is," Laura continued in a mocking voice. "I don't care about the bottom line when I have patients in pain and doctors who won't return messages to increase their pain meds! That Dr. Olson is the worst. You *know* how he is."

Eric leaned forward and planted a soft kiss on her forehead. "I know how he is and I know how she is, but I also know how *you* are. And you are what concerns me, not them."

She forced a smile.

"You don't need more stress, Laura."

There it was once again. The fatherly tone in his voice. When they had first started dating in college, she'd found it attractive. Finally, someone who was looking out for her best interests! Now, however, she found herself resenting it.

"I'll keep my cool, Eric."

"Promise?"

Reluctantly, Laura nodded, hearing her father's voice in her head: *That's my girl.*

"Good." He reached down and playfully patted her backside. "On to other matters then." Retrieving his coffee mug, he leaned against the counter. She watched as he inhaled the steam and shut his eyes. "You make the best coffee."

She smiled, even though he wasn't watching.

After taking a sip, he opened his eyes and looked at her. "Oh! Don't forget I have that late meeting today. You'll have to pick up the girls from aftercare."

Laura took a deep breath. She had forgotten. She had wanted to run some errands after work and come home for a few minutes to unwind. But Eric didn't ask her to pick up the girls very often. It was the least she could do. "Five o'clock. Got it."

"Four o'clock, Mommy!"

She glanced at Emily, who gave her a pleading look. Her daughters hated the after-school program, probably as much as Laura dreaded the monthly departmental meetings. Schedules. Changes. New procedures. Even when everything changed, it always stayed the same. "I'll try, honey. But it's hard to get out of the hospital early." Especially when her boss liked to throw more work at her just as she was walking out the door, or even worse, ask her to stay on because someone else was running late. "No promises."

Becky groaned and rolled her eyes. "Just don't be late like last time."

Laura bit her lower lip as she looked away, busying herself with packing up the girls' lunches and snacks. Why couldn't Becky just forget about the last time? "Well, let's hope there's no traffic today, OK? I can't control everything."

Eric glanced at his cell phone. His eyes seemed to scan something. A text message, no doubt. And from the way a shadow moved across his face, it was clearly not a message that brought good news.

Abruptly, he shoved the phone into his pocket and sighed. "I need to get going."

"Problem?"

He shrugged. "Donald arrived early and the receptionist isn't there. He's locked out, and that means I'll have my own bear of a boss to deal with." He slid the coffee mug down the length of the counter toward the sink and hurried over to brush his lips against hers. "Keep me posted about the meeting and the scheduling. And don't forget to pick up the girls." Eric started to head toward the door and then, as if on second thought, he returned to give both of his daughters a kiss on the top of their heads. "Be good for Mommy today." He gave Laura a wink before leaving the house.

"Aw, I'm always good." Emily pouted.

Becky made a face at her. "Except when you're wearing two different shoes."

"So?"

Laura clapped her hands. "You heard your father. If you're finished with breakfast, go brush your teeth and get your backpacks." She watched as they scrambled from the table and ran down the hallway, Becky forcing her way past Emily. "And take it easy. No fighting." She leaned around the corner, watching the girls scamper to the bathroom.

When they were out of sight, Laura paused. Mornings. The start of a new day that always brought the promise of good things, and yet those new beginnings always left her feeling exhausted. She glanced at the clock and hesitated before she reached for her purse. Digging inside, she unzipped an inner pocket to make certain she had her ChapStick. When her fingers touched a cylinder-shaped object, she withdrew it.

It wasn't her lip balm. Instead, she held an orange prescription bottle. Xanax. Just two weeks earlier, her doctor had prescribed it for Laura's anxiety. One a day as needed, James had told her.

So far, Laura hadn't taken any. She hadn't even wanted to *fill* the prescription, but James had insisted, encouraging her to have it on hand "just in case." Well, Laura was doing her best to make certain that *just in case* never happened.

Shoving the bottle back into her bag and making certain to zip up the pocket—she didn't want the girls finding it, or Eric for that matter—she peered inside but didn't find what she was looking for.

"Becky! Did you take my ChapStick again?" she called out.

"No, Mommy."

Glancing at the clock, Laura exhaled and shook her head. Darn it! That was the third tube of lip balm she'd lost in less than a month. She'd have to stop at the gift shop for some ChapStick, then. She didn't have time to stop at the pharmacy.

"Girls? You ready?"

She heard them running toward the kitchen, their voices loud enough for her to know that they were arguing but too soft for her to know about what. The fighting between the two girls seemed increasingly worse. She didn't know what to do about it. They were too young to always be at each other's throats. She made another mental note: talk to Susan about how to deal with the constant bickering between two young daughters.

"Girls!"

"Coming, Momma!" Emily practically bounced down the hallway, her pink ballerina backpack trailing behind her. She tripped on the edge of the runner and fell to her knees.

"Clumsy." Becky stepped around her younger sister.

Laura sighed. "Help her, Becks, OK?"

With a contemptuous look in Laura's direction, Becky reached down and helped Emily back to her feet.

"Thank you." Laura gestured toward the door.

"But you said we had more time," Becky whined as she guided Emily through the kitchen.

Laura took a deep breath. It was hard to remain cheerful and positive when she felt second-guessed. "Well we don't. Let's get a hustle on, OK?"

Reluctantly, both girls took their lunch bags from the counter and made their way to the front door. Becky grabbed her plaid backpack and slung it across her shoulder. The matching pencil case slid out and crayons spilled onto the hardwood floor. Laura sighed, bending down to scoop them up.

"Sorry, Momma."

Another forced smile. "No problem, baby. Just help Em into the car, OK?"

Both girls ran out the door and Laura could hear them chattering as they chased each other down the front walk toward the car parked in the driveway. Standing, Laura picked up her keys and glanced in the mirror that hung next to the front door. With her brown hair pulled back, a hint of gray peeking through at her roofline, and the dark circles under her eyes, she already looked more tired than she had earlier. How could her energy have been sapped so soon?

Running her hand over her face, she sighed. Another day, another dollar. Wasn't that what her father had always sung as he roused her from her bed in the mornings? It had been charming then. Now? Not so much. Laura wished her father had warned her that another day and another dollar came with such responsibility. His singsong morning wake-up call hadn't prepared her for the reality of work, marriage, parenthood, bills. Always the bills. And yet her parents had always seemed to keep it together. Why couldn't she?

Taking a deep breath, Laura grabbed her purse, then opened the front door, slowly starting to relax as she convinced herself that today would be different. Today was a new day, and she would do more than just survive; she would thrive.

CHAPTER 2

"Now, Mr. Monroe, you really need to take your medicine."

Laura stood next to the patient, an elderly man with thinning white hair and thick, bushy eyebrows that almost masked his closed eyes. She glanced at the student nurse at the foot of the bed, her arms crossed angrily over her chest as she met Laura's gaze.

"I told you," she whispered to Laura.

Laura held up her hand to quiet the young woman and kept her attention focused on the patient. "The doctor prescribed this medicine to help you get better, Mr. Monroe," Laura coaxed. "Believe me, you do *not* want your incision to get infected." She paused. "Fever. Pain at the incision site. Swelling. Not fun, let me assure you."

He grumbled something inaudible and turned his head toward the window.

The student nurse made a scoffing noise and threw her hands into the air.

Laura ignored her and sat down in the chair next to the bed. She lowered her voice as she leaned toward the patient. "Mr. Monroe," she said softly. "Help me out here, OK? You've been giving this student nurse a hard time, and if you don't take this medicine now, you're going to make me look bad."

She noticed that he frowned as if contemplating her words.

"And, you see, we have a new nurse supervisor and she's been really reading us all the riot act. I'd hate for her to hear that I couldn't get a patient to take his medicine. Why, I might get put on probation or even fired!"

The man turned his head to stare at her.

"That's right. Dereliction of duty."

She thought she heard the student nurse snicker, but it was quickly covered up by a cough.

"So do me this favor, Mr. Monroe. Please? I have two little girls to feed. I can't afford to be unemployed. And you really can't afford an infection."

The older man grumbled but nodded his head, taking the white cup of pills from her. Laura gave him a warm smile as she stood up. She handed him another cup, this one full of water. "Thank you, Mr. Monroe. You really know how to save a damsel in distress."

Outside in the hallway, the student nurse grabbed Laura's arm and started to laugh. "That was amazing, Laura!"

She didn't have time to answer. She could see several people heading for the nurses' break room. Laura glanced at the round clock on the wall. It was almost time for the meeting.

"I gotta go," she said to the student nurse. "Don't forget to change room 311's bandage and make certain that room 313 has eaten all of her breakfast. Apparently, she refused to eat yesterday. Doctors want to know everything she's eaten."

"Hunger strike?"

Laura walked backward and laughed. "No. Says the food stinks here."

The break room was almost full, but Laura managed to squeeze through a few nurses. There was an empty chair near the front of the room where Gillian stood. Clearly, no one wanted to sit in the front. Laura didn't care so she made her way to the empty chair, watching as their new nurse supervisor appeared to scan the faces of the nurses who were both seated and standing in the too-small break room. Unfortunately, there was no other place to meet. However, with the floor being almost unattended during these meetings, that usually meant that Gillian kept them brief.

Small blessings, Laura thought.

"Let's make this quick, people," Gillian started as she reached up to pat down her perfectly coiffed brown hair. "Night shifters want to leave and the rest of you have patients to tend to."

The room quieted.

"I know there've been a lot of changes recently," Gillian began. "Between Marsha retiring and two temporary supervisors until now, there has been a lot of loosey-goosey going on around here. Just last week, we had two shifts uncovered because people *thought* they had it covered." She shook her head and held up two fingers. "Twice. That's two times too many."

Laura fought the urge to turn around and glance at her friend Monica.

"So there will be no changes to the schedule." Gillian's eyes darted around the room. "None."

Laura fought the urge to grimace. *She* had never missed a shift. In fact, she was usually the one who was willing to cover other people's shifts. Their former nurse supervisor, Marsha, would have known that. But Gillian was new and it would take time for her to figure out who were the reliable nurses on the floor.

"The floor has to be staffed. That's my job," Gillian continued. "Missing a shift hurts more than the patients. It hurts the rest of the staff and, ultimately, the hospital as a whole. So, no swapping of shifts. Period. And that includes for the holidays." She reached for a pile of papers beside her and handed the stack to a nurse seated in front of her.

The noise of passing paper filled the room. The woman seated next to Laura handed her the schedules. Laura took one and passed the rest to the nurse to her left.

"And as for vacation requests for the holidays . . . ," Gillian said. As the papers continued being passed out, she paused and waited until every eye in the room was staring at her. But it took longer than usual as the nurses glanced down at the schedules. "There have been a few changes."

Immediately, the energy in the room shifted.

Laura glanced down and quickly read the schedule. She took a deep breath and tried to calm herself down. Two swing shifts, two night shifts, and only one day shift. *Thank you, Gillian.* Her sleep cycle would be completely destroyed by the time December rolled around.

And then her eyes fell to Thanksgiving.

No, no, no, Laura wanted to scream.

Before Marsha had retired, she had asked for everyone's holiday vacation requests. Laura had submitted hers right away. Marsha had assured her that she'd get off for Thanksgiving. Eric and Laura planned to travel to Boston to visit his parents and take the girls on a day trip to Plimoth Plantation on the Friday after the holiday. His parents had arranged for tickets. It would be the first Thanksgiving spent with Eric's family in five years, and everyone had been looking forward to it.

Great. Laura shoved the schedule into her purse. Besides Eric being furious, Laura could only imagine how crestfallen the girls would be. *Just great.*

Murmurs filled the air. Other nurses must have done the same exact thing: reviewed the regular schedule first and then looked at the holiday week. Clearly, Laura wasn't the only one disappointed to find that she was scheduled to work that day.

"And I don't want to hear any complaints about it. The good news is that some of you will work twelve-hour shifts that day and get overtime."

One nurse spoke up. "But I put in my request over a month ago!"

"You and a dozen other people." Gillian's expression remained unchanged. "Now, if there's nothing else to bring up . . ."

Out of the corner of her eye, Laura saw Monica and that new nurse, Chelsea, raise their hands, which surprised her. Chelsea had only just started that past week when another nurse, Mary Mason, had left on maternity leave.

". . . that doesn't have to do with holidays or vacation time or schedules . . ."

Down went both hands.

Laura slumped in her chair.

"One last order of business." Gillian held up her hand and looked away from the onslaught of nurses grumbling to one another. She waited until the room quieted once again. "I've noticed a lot of complaints from doctors about being second-guessed in regard to pain medicine. I want to remind you that doctors prescribe the medicine. Nurses administer it."

"They're underprescribing pain medicine!" one of the nurses in the back of the room shouted.

Gillian snapped her gaze in the direction of the voice. "Let me repeat that. Doctors prescribe. Nurses administer."

Laura knew better than to speak up, especially after the issue with Gillian last week. But the other nurses began to talk at once about this ongoing problem.

Monica spoke up. "These people shouldn't have to be in such pain."

"If you don't like it, you should've gone to med school." Gillian glared at her.

"It's the insurance companies' fault," someone else offered. "They cut corners everywhere."

"Yeah, well, the doctors are the only ones who can force the issue."

Gillian held up her hand. "People, please. Just do as you are instructed." Once again, the nurses grew quiet. Gillian scanned the room, her eyes piercing as she looked at each member of her team. "Otherwise, it creates problems, ladies and gentlemen. Problems for me and that means problems for you."

While Gillian avoided looking at Laura, everyone else was. Laura stared straight ahead, but she felt certain Gillian was referencing the incident from the previous week. It had been the talk of the entire floor when Dr. Olson had prescribed a medication for a patient that Laura realized counteracted another medicine. She had felt it was her duty to point this out to the doctor, and the entire situation had blown out of control. Before the end of the day, Laura had to deal not just with Gillian but also Human Resources. Dr. Olson had filed a complaint about Laura not following proper protocol. She was supposed to notify Gillian, not him directly, with any questions. In the meantime, the patient received both medicines even though Laura had been correct. Fortunately, there had been no adverse reaction, but there were quite a few noses pushed out of joint.

"The doctors, not you, are responsible for the protocol of the patients' care. It's our job to ensure that their instructions are followed. To a T. Any issues, you come see me, and only me. Is that understood?"

A few heads nodded but the room remained silent.

"And finally, keep your workstations clean and charting up to date. Anyone with incomplete charts at the end of their shift needs to make sure they are completed *before leaving*. Period. No overtime for incomplete work." Gillian started to collect her things. "It's your job to finish your work, even if it means staying late."

After Gillian dismissed her team like an army general sending the troops to the front lines while she retreated to the safety of her office, Laura glanced around at the collateral damage. Several of the nurses complained to each other as they rose from their seats and slowly moved toward the door.

"I put in my request a week before the deadline," one of the nurses grumbled.

"Two weeks for me!"

Laura tried to shut her ears to their grousing. She'd feel sorry for them if she didn't know how furious her own husband would be. And rightfully so. This would be the third year in a row that Laura had missed Thanksgiving with her family, never mind missing out on spending it with Eric's. Third year! And, despite being new to the floor, Gillian was well aware of that fact. Marsha had left everyone's requests in a special folder for her successor. Clearly, Gillian was punishing Laura for last week's confrontation. And Laura was well aware of *that*.

As she walked out of the break room, Laura felt that all-too-familiar tightening in her chest. Quietly, she counted to ten and took several deep breaths, but the pressure in her chest continued to mount. How would she tell Eric? The girls? Why hadn't Marsha finalized the schedule *before* retiring? And what, exactly, did Gillian think she was doing by forcing the more senior nurses to work on the holiday? Didn't she realize that she wasn't winning over any fans among her own nursing staff?

The resentment built and Laura had to take several long breaths to calm down.

Ahead of her, she overheard three of her colleagues grumbling about the vacation schedule decree, but Laura remained silent. The last thing Laura needed was for Gillian to catch wind of her complaining. That would only add more fuel to the fire.

No. It was time for Gillian to find someone else to target for a change.

"You all right?"

Startled, Laura looked up and forced a smile at Monica. "Yeah, sure."

"You didn't get your vacation request, did you?"

She shook her head. "Nope."

"How early did you put it in?"

"Two months ago. Marsha had promised me I'd get it."

"Ouch." Monica shook her head in empathy, her short blonde bob brushing against her cheeks. "I hate when new managers do this. Total power play."

Laura couldn't agree more. "And she put me on weekends. Swings shift on Saturdays and days on Sunday." That was probably additional punishment for the Dr. Olson fiasco. With only Wednesdays and Fridays off, she'd have no time to spend with her family when the new schedule started in two weeks. Sighing, Laura prayed that Gillian took it easy on her for the Christmas holidays. "Why did they transfer her here?"

Monica laughed. "I've started praying that they transfer her back. Does that make me a bad person?"

"Not in my book!" Laura motioned toward the restroom and slipped inside, making certain to shut and lock the door behind her.

For a long moment, she stood at the sink and stared at her reflection. She needed to catch her breath and calm down. She usually got along so well with everyone. She worked hard and felt rewarded for her efforts. But ever since Gillian had started, every day seemed to bring on a new battle. Gillian seemed to complain about everything. If it wasn't about Laura's charts being illegible, then Gillian was complaining that her rounds took too long. All of which Laura knew was just a bunch of baloney. The harder Laura tried to set things right, the harder Gillian cracked down on her, especially since the previous week.

Laura knew that she wasn't the only one in the target range. Most of the nurses shared similar complaints about their new supervisor. Still, Laura wasn't used to having such conflict with anyone, never mind with her supervisor. She always did her job and helped others. No one had ever complained about her performance before. At least not until now.

You'll be sorry, her mother had told her when Laura decided to pursue a nursing career. *You'll never have a normal schedule. Not like doctors. They make their own hours. You'll be at the beck and call of the hospital.*

That voice that echoed in her memory caused Laura to squeeze her eyes shut and will it away.

Despite her mother's lack of support—and her father's lack of a backbone—Laura had stayed true to her chosen career. What her mother never seemed to understand was that there was more to life than having two little initials after one's name. And why would Laura want to be an MD anyway? They were all business and, unlike nurses, hardly got to spend any time with the patients.

No. That had never been for Laura. She wanted to nurture people, not breeze into and out of the room, scribbling orders on charts or telling nurses how to do their jobs. That was too militant. Too much like her mother.

After taking a few deep breaths, Laura opened her eyes, turned on the faucet, and splashed cold water on her face. The cool sensation against her skin helped her calm down. Just a little, but not enough. She reached for a brown paper towel and dabbed at her cheeks and forehead before tossing it into the trash. Gillian was working Laura's shift today, and that meant she would be hypervigilant to point out each and every mistake made by the nurses. While Laura was always diligent and attentive to her patients' care, she wasn't used to someone looking over her shoulder all the time.

Already, Laura's nerves were shot.

Taking a deep breath, she placed her hands on the edge of the porcelain sink and stared at her reflection. Eric was going to be furious. Just the thought of telling him put her stomach in knots. If there was one thing she hated, it was disappointing him.

Someone knocked on the door.

"Just a minute," she called out as she reached for her ChapStick. After applying it, she shoved it into the front pocket of her blue scrub shirt and turned to unlock the door.

She'd have to tell Eric the news, and the sooner the better. Still, she decided to wait until he got home. No text or email would suffice. This was something she'd have to do in person. He'd be disappointed, for certain, and possibly angry because not only would her absence put a damper on the holiday, especially for the girls, but he'd have to manage without her. Dealing with two young children for several days was enough to try anyone's patience, even Eric's. But what could Laura do? She was a nurse and patients needed care. They'd just have to understand.

CHAPTER 3

When she arrived at work the next day, Laura threw her purse under her workstation, not caring that it was in plain sight. No one would steal from her. Frankly, there was little of any value in her bag. Just her cell phone and one credit card. Not even lipstick or ChapStick. Once again, she had forgotten to take her ChapStick out of her scrubs yesterday, only realizing that after finding it had melted all over the clothes in the dryer that morning.

Another great start for what wasn't looking like a great week. Laura had been so hopeful that she could turn over a new leaf. But the previous day's meeting with Gillian had thrown a wrench in her gears. And it hadn't helped that Laura hadn't picked up the girls until a quarter after five, late as far as they were concerned, which Becky certainly didn't let her forget. Her explanations about having to finish her charts sounded feeble when she realized she was talking to a six- and an eight-year-old. What did *they* know about work-related responsibilities? And then Eric hadn't arrived home until after eight thirty. Both girls had already been tucked in, and Laura was reading a book in bed, exhausted from a typical crazy Monday.

He had never asked her about the schedule or Thanksgiving for that matter. At the time, Laura had been relieved. The last thing she had wanted was to have a confrontation when she was winding down for the night. Fortunately, he seemed to be preoccupied with his own work-related problems.

But when Eric hadn't inquired that morning, Laura realized that he just presumed she had gotten the time off. She had sipped her coffee, watching as he juggled checking his emails and eating breakfast with the girls. Why would he think she *wouldn't have* gotten the time off? After all, in his world, nobody worked on holidays. People didn't need financial advice on holidays, and both stock markets and banks were closed. In Eric's world, work hours were predictable and when there was too much work to do, it could be carried home in a briefcase.

Now, as she stood by her chair, Laura rubbed her face with both hands and sighed. She was working the swing shift today, which normally put her in a good mood. It was certainly better than the night shift, which always messed up her sleep cycle. However, the fiasco with the laundry and the melted lip balm had sidetracked her from the list of errands she had wanted to run that morning before she started her shift. Namely those Halloween costumes she hadn't yet found time to buy.

But even her workday wasn't looking as if it was off to a good start.

She had just been briefed by the day nurse about her patients for this shift and was told that they were awaiting a patient from recovery. He should have been up two hours ago. And that always made Laura worry.

She picked up the phone and dialed the recovery floor, growing irritated when she was put on hold right away. It took almost five minutes for the woman to come back on the line.

"Status on the arrival of Raymond Stewart? He was due in post-op two hours ago."

Laura could hear the shuffling of papers and then the clicking of a keyboard. Impatiently, she tapped her foot as she waited.

"He hasn't awoken yet."

She felt a sudden surge of worry. "Is everything OK?"

"Yeah. Sure. But his surgery took longer than expected."

Laura wondered why the day nurse hadn't called for an update. "Well, keep us posted." She hung up the phone and said a quick prayer that Mr. Stewart would be fine. She knew from the charts that he'd had surgery to remove a tumor from his colon. Given that the surgery had taken longer than expected, Laura could only hope that didn't mean the cancer had spread.

"You all right?"

Laura dropped her hands and glanced over her shoulder to see her friend Susan standing behind her. "Right as rain," Laura said with a smile.

Susan raised an eyebrow. "I hate rain. Almost as much as I hate snow."

"And I hate snow almost as much as I hate Halloween."

Susan reached over and grabbed a pen from the desk. "Oh, yes. I remember those days. Dressing up the little ones to go beg for candy that kept them wired for hours only to find myself raiding their loot after I finally got them to bed."

Laura laughed.

While she tried to keep to herself at work, and usually avoided socializing with the nurses outside of the hospital, Susan and Monica were two colleagues that she considered friends. While Monica was Laura's age (and still unmarried), Susan was entering the stage in life where both of her daughters were independent. As Laura tiptoed into the surf of approaching hormones and preteen years, she often relied on Susan's sea of experience as a lifeline.

"So what do the little monkeys want to be this year?" Susan lowered her glasses, which had been propped atop her head as she glanced through her charts.

The question caught Laura off guard. What did they want to be? She didn't even know. Last year, they were both Disney princesses. This year? Well, at the rate Laura was going, they'd be lucky if they didn't reuse last year's costumes. "It's a stupid holiday, isn't it? Who came up with the idea anyway?"

Shutting a file folder, Susan peered over her glasses at Laura. "Depends. Either those ancient Celts or Pope Gregory the Third. Either way, I agree with you." She tossed the pen back onto the desk. "Although I do like Milky Ways."

"I'll remember that on November first."

"Ladies, please!" Gillian's voice from behind interrupted them. "The last time I checked we have patients to attend to!"

Susan pursed her lips and rolled her eyes as she turned and walked away toward one of her patients' rooms.

"Any word on your new admit, Laura?"

"Still in recovery."

Gillian scowled and glanced at the clock on the wall. "Taking their sweet time, aren't they?" Without another word, she stormed over to a phone, dialed an extension, and turned her back to Laura.

Laura had worked at the hospital for more than twelve years and knew there was good reason to be concerned when a patient—especially an elderly one—took longer than expected. While she had spent several years working in maternity and then another five in the emergency room, she had found her happy place in post-op. In the maternity ward, patients wanted nothing more than to be left alone with their newborns. And when Laura had worked in the emergency room, she mostly dealt with stabilizing patients who were only there for a few hours or trying to soothe their hysterical family members. On the post-op floor, Laura was able to do what she'd always wanted to do: help nurture patients back to health.

She had learned about the opening on the post-op floor three years ago and, after much deliberation, she had applied. The interview process was grueling—the nurse supervisor had a tough reputation. And the post-op floor was rumored to be hard on the nursing staff. But when she was offered the position, Laura had jumped on it as her chance to really engage with her patients.

Some days, however, she wondered if she had made a mistake.

Like today.

"Would it have been so hard for you to have called recovery to find out why he's delayed?"

It took a minute for Laura to realize that Gillian was talking to her. "I did."

"Then would it have been so hard for you to have informed me of that?"

Here we go, Laura thought. Her weekly dress down. "I'm sorry, Gillian. I didn't think . . ."

"No you didn't. And that's the problem, Laura," Gillian snapped. "I shouldn't have to think for you. You're one of the most experienced nurses here. I expect more from you."

Laura frowned as Gillian stormed away. Her hands began to tremble and she clenched her fists a few times, hoping to stop the wave of anxiety that washed over her. She *had* called recovery, just like she *always* did. But to be chastised for not informing the nurse supervisor about why a patient was delayed?

"Hey, don't sweat it."

Laura hadn't realized that Monica was standing there, holding a pink plastic bin filled with gauze. "She's always after me about something," Laura said.

"Correction. She's always after all of us about something." Monica gave her a smile of encouragement. "Hey, I need to change a dressing in 314. If Dr. Paterson calls, I must talk to her, OK?" She emphasized the word *must*.

Laura nodded.

"Oh, and your patient in room 302 was calling for you," Monica added as she walked away.

Laura glanced up. Room 302. Heart bypass. "Thanks."

She hurried down the hallway.

"Oh, Laura!"

She turned in the direction of the voice that called her name. "Yes?"

It was Gillian, standing outside of the nurses' station and staring at the large whiteboard on the wall. "Room 304's waiting for a blood transfusion. Can you find out what the holdup is?"

"Got it."

So. That was how the afternoon was going to be . . . Gillian breathing down her neck. Again. Marsha had known which nurses she didn't need to micromanage. Clearly, Gillian was still uncertain or simply didn't trust her team yet. Like Eric had said the other morning, it would take time for Gillian's management style to sync with the rest of the team.

Laura sighed as she poked her head into room 302, not surprised to see her patient staring at the television screen. He was a news junkie. Always switching from MSNBC to CNN to Fox News and then back to MSNBC.

"Everything all right in here?"

The man hit the "Mute" button. "There you are. I wanted to find out if the doctor OK'd the increased pain meds. My chest is killing me."

Laura shook her head. From her morning briefing, she knew that the night nurse had called Dr. Jacobs about forty-five minutes ago, just before Laura had arrived. "Not that I'm aware. I'll give him a call again in fifteen minutes if I don't hear from him."

"Please. I can't take it much longer." Without another word, he pressed the "Mute" button again, the sound immediately filling the room, and turned his attention back to the screen.

Laura had been around the block enough times to know that the patient was milking the system. Legal narcotics on the insurance company's check. More than likely, his "pain" would continue for a lot longer than his actual recovery. Undoubtedly, his doctor would keep him on Percocet until it became embarrassing. At that point, Mr. Chest

Pain would have a choice to make: quit cold turkey or start ordering drugs from Canada over the Internet.

Laura guessed that he'd have to go the cold-turkey route.

But she never would know the answer.

She moved next door to room 314 and greeted the young woman with a smile. "Ready to get that dressing changed?"

"Again?"

Laura laughed. "I bet it feels like it was just an hour ago, but it was almost four! We need to keep that dressing clean and dry. Sorry."

The woman sighed. "It's just that it hurts, you know."

Yes, Laura knew. She had seen the tears in the woman's eyes earlier when she had to change the bandage. But, unlike Mr. Chest Pain, this woman did not ask for more painkillers. In fact, she had questioned whether she really needed to take them at all.

"I'll be gentle. I promise."

There were some joys in nursing. Patients like this woman were one of them. It was why Laura had become a nurse, to care for people in need. Genuine need. And despite the stress of juggling shifts, medicine, doctors' orders, and patients' needs, Laura had never regretted for one minute her decision to become a nurse, even when it meant working on holidays.

Of course, this holiday was an exception. She'd arranged it far enough in advance to make sure she could be with her—and Eric's—family this year. What made Gillian's decision even harder to swallow was that some of the nurses—herself included—had already sacrificed so many holidays in the past. Of course, Gillian wouldn't have known that, but what upset Laura was that she apparently hadn't even inquired. Or, even worse, simply didn't care. Marsha had always made a point of rotating holidays and taking into account special family or travel circumstances when she could.

Laura's attention to care was unmatched by any other nurse. She never said no to working late or picking up extra shifts. She never left early and would always stay until the next shift was ready to take over. And her charts were *always* accurate and complete.

No, Laura knew that Gillian should have given her Thanksgiving off. Nurse burnout was too real, and with so many new nurses on the team, Laura was one of the few experienced ones that Gillian shouldn't risk losing. Susan was another one. The fact that neither one of them had been given time off for Thanksgiving irritated Laura, and she found herself dwelling on it far too much.

By the time Laura returned to the workstation to call Dr. Jacobs for Mr. Chest Pain, almost thirty minutes had passed. She left a message with his office and glanced at the clock.

"Everything OK?" Susan asked as she walked around the corner and dropped her charts on her own work area.

Laura kept her hand on the receiver, even though it was in the cradle. "The patient in 302 wants more pain medicine, and I can't get Jacobs to call back."

"That bad?"

At first, Laura didn't know whether Susan was referencing the patient's pain or the doctor's neglect. But one look at Susan's face and she realized it was the former, not the latter. "I doubt it. I think he's another pain med opportunist."

"Ah."

Laura watched as Susan reached for her purse and began fishing around for something. "How's your afternoon going?"

"Fine." Susan peered inside her bag and riffled through her things again. "A blood transfusion, dressing change on a double mastectomy, and a new admit that I didn't know about until five minutes ago. I already have a headache."

Laura understood Susan's frustration. Admits meant more paper-work. Frankly, it seemed that *everything* meant more paperwork. Laura sometimes felt that she spent half of her shift charting information about the patient—when medicine was administered, how much urine they expelled, how much food they ate, what they were complaining about—and the other half entering that into the computer system. Of course she knew that it only *felt* that way because she still had to physically make her rounds every hour.

At least Laura had finished the paperwork for her new admit. She just needed him to arrive from recovery. "Need a Tylenol? I have some right here."

But Susan shook her head and pulled out the familiar white bottle with the red cap. She wiggled it as she said, "I've got some. Thanks." She popped the white caplet into her mouth and tilted her head backward. "Six patients. Can you believe it? Bad timing for a headache."

Six was unusual. Typically, the nurses took care of four patients. Five at the most. With hourly visits, charting, and following all of the different orders from doctors, that was about the maximum that any nurse could handle. Six patients meant being spread too thin, less than ten minutes per hour per patient, which was impossible to handle. That was typically when mistakes were made.

However, if a person called in sick, the patients still needed care. Laura wondered which nurse had blown off her shift.

"Let me know if I can help with anything," Laura offered. She genuinely liked and respected Susan—her work ethic, her compassion for the patients, and her ability to juggle everything. She was a great nurse and an even better colleague.

"Thanks."

With her head bent down over her paperwork, Susan appeared to tune out everything around her. Laura watched her with a mixture of curiosity and awe. How could she keep it all together? Laura knew that if *she* were the one receiving a sixth patient, she'd begin unraveling. Susan, however, tended to switch on to autopilot and focus on getting the job done. It was a skill that Laura envied and tried to emulate. But sometimes holding it all together was hard, especially when she was on overload.

"Hey, Laura." A young nurse intern stood in front of her workstation. "Patient in 302 is asking for you. His pain meds?"

Laura sighed and stood up. "I'm on it." Only she wasn't "on it" because Dr. Jacobs still had not returned her call. In the meantime, she would be on the firing line with Mr. Chest Pain, not only about his pain but likely also her incompetence with regard to getting ahold of the doctor. Sometimes there was no way to please everyone. Laura had learned that lesson long ago.

All in a day's work, she thought as she hurried toward his room.

CHAPTER 4

The candle flickered on the white linen–covered table while Eric topped off Laura's glass of red wine. She watched without saying anything. He knew that she never indulged in more than one glass of wine, and even that was on rare occasions. But apparently, tonight was one of those nights.

She had worked the day shift, and even though they rarely went out on Thursday nights, with her new upcoming schedule, she knew that they needed to take the time whenever they could in order to spend an hour or two alone together.

"Everything working out for Halloween?" Eric set down the bottle of wine.

Laura laughed.

"What's so funny?" he asked, smiling.

She gave a silly shrug. "Here we are, a nice restaurant, two grown adults, fancy food, candlelight, and you're asking me about Halloween?"

He gave a little chuckle. "I guess that's what happens when you've been married for so long with two kids."

She sipped her wine and finally responded to his question. "Yes."

"Yes what?"

"Yes, everything's ready for Halloween. But I'm working that afternoon and evening. Swing shift."

"No worries. Just make certain I know who is wearing what before I take them trick-or-treating."

Laura loved that about him. He didn't mind stepping up whenever her job called for her to be away from the family.

"So," Eric started as he leaned back in his chair. "I forgot to tell you that I ran into Ryan at Kings earlier."

"Why were you at Kings?" Laura spread some butter on a piece of still-warm bread. "I just went food shopping two days ago. And Kings is totally overpriced." Whenever he went to the grocery store, she felt as if she had failed him. That was *her* job, to make certain the family had everything they needed at home.

"That's not the point," he laughed.

"Still . . ." She waved her butter knife at him. "You're the finance guy," she teased. "You know what the word 'budget' means."

"Yeah, yeah." He smiled as he lifted his glass and took a sip of the wine.

"So? Why were you there?"

"The girls wanted Oreos."

Laura feigned shock. "Why doesn't *that* surprise me?"

"That they wanted Oreos?"

"No. That you took them!"

They both laughed. Neither one of them needed to point out that Becky and Emily had their father wrapped around their little fingers. Whenever he picked them up from after-school care, they would try to cajole him into stopping for candy or soda or, when it was warmer, ice cream. Clearly, today had been a cookie day.

"So, as I was saying," he began again. "I ran into Ryan at Kings . . ."

"Ryan?" She blinked, unable to think of whom Eric meant. It wasn't as if Eric hung around with a large circle of friends. In fact, he barely went out at all. Their social circle was limited to work colleagues and a few old college friends. "Do I know a Ryan?"

"Weaver."

It took Laura a minute to recognize the name. One of the men whom Eric had golfed with a few times over the past year. Her expression changed from confusion to distaste. "You mean that client from the country club?"

He didn't appear to notice the shift in her demeanor. "That's right. You met his wife at the breast cancer fund-raiser, remember?"

Laura wanted to tell him that she most certainly did remember, especially the part about meeting Debbie Weaver. Between the constant name-dropping and judgmental comments that hinted at a tireless effort to climb that social ladder, Debbie Weaver represented everything Laura avoided.

"How could I forget such a momentous night?"

He must have thought she was joking because he laughed. "Oh, come on. She wasn't that bad."

"Not that bad?" Laura made a face at him. "She got drunk at a charity event!"

Eric chuckled. "She wasn't drunk."

"Eric! She could barely stand!" Laura didn't want to remind him that too much alcohol not only had caused Debbie to lose her balance but her judgment. By ten o'clock, she had wrapped her arms around Eric and clung to him, talking far too loud about how the country club needed more good-looking men like Eric Reese and why didn't they join the club? To say that Debbie Weaver left a bad impression on Laura was putting it mildly. Eric, however, had thought the whole scene endearing, an adjective that Laura would not have used as she'd peeled Debbie's arms off her husband.

"He asked how you're doing."

Laura took a bite of her bread. "I hope you told him that I still have a leash on you for fear that you might run into his crazy wife."

Another laugh. "Now, Laura, you should feel flattered that other women find me attractive."

She made a face. "Apparently not as flattered as you felt."

Truth be told, she had never once questioned Eric's faithfulness to her. Their marriage was as solid as the Rock of Gibraltar. While she had some girlfriends, Eric was, without a doubt, her best friend. Laura hadn't worried about Eric in the least at that—or any!—party. Still, she had been offended by Debbie's boozy flirtations.

"They aren't *that* bad." Eric lifted the wine bottle and poured some into her glass before refilling his own. "She just had a little too much to drink that night."

"Well, that was not the night nor the place for an intoxicated display of unsophistication."

He chuckled at her caustic remark. "The Weavers are not 'unsophisticated.' She just had a bad night." He set down the wine bottle and lifted his own glass to his lips, peering at her over the rim. "A charge we're all guilty of from time to time, no?"

She averted her eyes.

"So, about Ryan . . ."

Inwardly, Laura groaned.

"I meant to tell you that he invited me to come look at the club."

For a moment, his words seemed to hang in the air between them. Had she heard him properly? "Excuse me?"

Eric traced his finger along the bottom of his wineglass and avoided looking at her. "You know, the country club. He invited me to come check it out."

There they were again. Words that hung in the air. If she looked hard enough, she probably could have visualized them. "For the purpose of what, exactly?" she said, motioning with her fingers for him to divulge more.

"Joining, I suppose."

Silence replaced the words "country club," and Laura sat back in her chair, just staring at him. What on earth was he talking about? Joining a country club? A golf country club? "You suppose?"

Eric leaned forward and lowered his voice. "Look, I'm just going to meet with some people, check it out, and see what the story is."

"You know how I feel about country clubs, right? You remember who you're married to, correct?"

He gave a nervous chuckle. "Laura, just because your mother—"

"Lived and breathed social mobility?"

Eric sighed. "It's not the same thing, Laura. This is for work."

"You do realize how expensive country clubs are, right? It's basically a year's tuition to just walk in the front door and at least half that in annual dues every year after that." Many of the doctors belonged to different clubs in the area, and Laura knew only too well how the rest of the staff merely rolled their eyes whenever the doctors compared notes on which golf course was better or discussed an upcoming member-guest golfing event.

"Well, I think the company would put up the bond. I mean, it *was* Donald who invited us to the breast cancer fund-raiser and gave me Ryan's account. It's one of the largest for the firm."

Laura took a deep breath. "Why would they put up the bond?"

"Well, you know," he said in a low voice, "a lot of business is done on the golf course, Laura."

She reached for her wineglass. "Sounds like a lousy sales pitch if I ever heard one."

"It's true. And if the company pays the bond, I can probably get them to pay for some of the annual dues."

"We have two daughters, Eric." She shook her head. "Two. That's two proms. Two college tuitions. Two weddings. It's a bad idea. And just another reason to not like the Weavers. He's planting seeds in a field that doesn't have enough fertilizer to sprout a crop!"

"The girls are young, Laura," he said softly, a look of reprimand in his eyes. "We have plenty of time to save for college."

Laura wanted to argue with him that they were barely making do as it was with the mortgage, overinflated Morristown taxes, after-school care, and other bills. Since she handled the bills, she knew exactly what was in the girls' college account so far, enough to barely pay for textbooks for one semester. "And when, exactly, do you intend to play on this golf course? The weekends?" Laura remembered when she and her younger brother, Rodney, became socially orphaned by their parents when *they* had joined a golf club in Jacksonville. Now Eric wanted to make her a golf widow?

"Just think about it, Laura, OK? It'd be good to expand our circles, anyway. I mean, we hardly socialize anymore. Between your work schedule and mine—"

"And our daughters," she added abruptly.

He nodded emphatically, and she wondered if he had misunderstood her. "And the girls, yes. They'd benefit, too."

Clearly, Eric had misunderstood.

"Our schedules are so busy, Laura. We don't have a lot of time for making friends. And you'll love the pool in the summer. So will Becky and Emily. There are lots of young girls their age."

"That's not what I meant, Eric." She leveled her gaze at him. "Frankly, I don't like this idea at all. You know how I feel about trying to keep up with the Joneses."

Oh, she knew all about that from her own childhood. Everything had revolved around what people would think and how her mother could improve their social standing, even at the expense of her family.

"Why aren't you wearing your new dress, Laura? I bought it just for tonight's dinner."

Laura winced. *"I'm twelve, Mom. Not nine. That's a little girl's dress."*

"It's from Saks! Go put it on. I don't want the club people thinking we have no class!"

"Well, I'm meeting up with Ryan one day next week anyway." He gave her a half smile. "Free lunch, right?"

"There's no such thing as a free lunch."

Fortunately, their conversation was interrupted as the server brought over their meals. Laura leaned back in her chair, her eyes following the plates as he set them down, hers first and then Eric's. Hoping to salvage the evening, Laura managed to smile at him, even though she had lost her appetite.

With his fork in hand, Eric stabbed at his pasta. "Hey, you never told me about your November schedule. Everything good to go?" He took a bite. "My parents are thrilled, by the way."

She froze. "You confirmed everything with your parents already?"

"Why wouldn't I?"

Laura's shoulders slumped. "Gillian put me on the schedule for Thanksgiving."

His glass appeared to hover over the table as he stared at her. A shadow fell over his eyes as he digested what she had just said. "She did what?"

"You heard me."

His eyes narrowed. Laura could see he was angry. Angry and disappointed, both of which made her feel even worse.

"Go talk to her."

The tone of his voice made her pulse quicken. She could feel her chest tighten, and she had trouble breathing for a moment. She lifted her hand to press against her chest.

"What do you mean you didn't make the debate team, Laura?" her mother had said when Laura told her the news. "You know you need that on your application to get into med school. Didn't you talk to the coach? What's her name? Coach Monroe?"

When Laura didn't respond fast enough, her mother must have realized the answer to her question.

Lifting her chin, her mother had narrowed her steady gaze as she ordered her daughter to "Go talk to her."

"Are you OK?"

Laura managed to take a deep breath and she looked at Eric, wondering if he meant the question figuratively or literally. "She won't change the schedule."

"Did you ask?"

Laura pressed her lips together, feeling the weight of having failed him, even though she knew it wasn't her fault. "She said the schedule is set. No changes will be made."

Abruptly, he put down his wineglass and shook his head. "That . . ."

"Easy, Eric," she whispered, her eyes scanning the room to make certain no one was listening.

But he was fuming. She could see that much from the way he yanked off his glasses and pinched the bridge of his nose. "You've worked every major holiday this past year and haven't had Thanksgiving off for four years—"

"Three years," she corrected in a soft voice.

"Three years then. Either way, it's not fair."

Suddenly, she felt as if she were dealing with a third child. But she didn't want to give him her usual "life isn't fair" speech that she used with Emily and Becky when they were arguing. Instead, she offered a defeated shrug. "It is what it is."

"How can you take that, Laura?" He leaned forward and lowered his voice.

"Come on, Eric. Please." She reached for her water glass, but he stopped her hand, laying his over hers.

Eric wasn't about to give up. "This is about family. It's important that you spend the holiday with us. Remember what you always told me? Family first. Your family?" He paused. "My family."

She yanked her hand free. "I understand your disappointment, Eric. But you know how the hospital works. It's the downside to being a nurse."

"The downside? Tell me then . . ." He released her hand and sat back in his chair, his fingers drumming on the tablecloth. "What, exactly, is the upside?"

She glared at him. The last thing she wanted to do was to fight with him. Not tonight and certainly not over this. "Let's start with the paycheck, shall we? Unfortunately, unlike the Weavers with their fancy golf country club and vacation homes and nannies, *your* wife has to work." She thought she saw him wince and immediately regretted having said that. "Look, Eric," she said, lowering her voice. "I love my job."

He gave a short laugh. "You hate your job."

"I don't hate my job."

"Well, you definitely don't love it."

She could feel the wave begin to wash over her. Her heart started racing again and her vision became cloudy around the periphery. Tunnel vision, she called it. As if dark shadows were closing in. "I seem to remember that you were attracted to me because of my nursing career. What was it you always said?" She held a finger to her temple as she feigned thinking. "About nurses being so nurturing?"

He didn't look amused. Instead, he raised his eyebrows and stared at her with those blue eyes.

"Maybe it's time you transferred your desire to nurture to your family instead of strangers."

Her mouth opened, her hand instinctively rising to her chest once again. Those heart palpitations. Couldn't he hear them? The black cloud tightened and all she could see was Eric. "Are you saying that I put work before my family?"

"It sure seems that way. You've been late picking up the girls, you procrastinated about Halloween, and now you're missing Thanksgiving. Sometimes I wonder if you're not turning into your mother."

And there it was.

Somehow she managed to exhale, all of her breath whooshing out of her mouth, and she stood up, her linen napkin falling from her lap to the floor. Her hands shook and she looked around for the nearest exit. For a moment, she felt as if she were dreaming, floating above the restaurant and watching a scene play out. Except that she was the main character and everyone else was staring at her, watching her, judging her.

"What are you doing?" Eric hissed.

She motioned with her hand for him to stay seated as she tried to find her voice. "I . . . I need some air," she managed to whisper in short, clipped words. Before he could get up, she hurried around the other tables and past the hostess desk near the front door. It didn't matter that it was late October or that she wasn't wearing her coat. She pushed through the door and embraced the cold night air.

For what felt like several minutes, she gulped the air and leaned against the front of the building with her eyes shut.

One . . . two . . . three . . . But she couldn't slow her heart. *Maybe it's not a* panic *attack,* she thought. *Maybe* this *time it really is a heart attack.* Maybe James had been wrong when she had visited him last month about the way her chest felt and her heart raced at times. But she was a nurse. She knew she wasn't going into cardiac failure or having a stroke, even if it felt like it.

James.

Just the thought of him made her remember the prescription in her purse. She dug through her bag, unzipped the inner pocket, and pulled out the bottle of Xanax. This was why he had prescribed it. For panic attacks. And this was definitely a full-blown episode.

No matter how much she had wanted to avoid this moment, she knew that she had to return inside, go back to the table. And she couldn't. Just couldn't. Not right now. But if she took a Xanax, just one, it wouldn't make her a bad person, not like her mother, who used to pop Valium two to three times a day.

One.

Just one.

Laura tried to muster up enough saliva to swallow the small blue pill. Thankfully, it practically dissolved on her tongue, the bitter taste filling her throat as it slid down. She counted her breaths again as she waited for something—anything!—to change: her breathing, her heart, her vision.

Slowly, she began to feel the cold and knew that she had no choice but to return to the table. Shivering, she turned to the door and reached for the wooden handle, reluctantly opening it and stepping back inside. As she walked back toward where Eric sat, his eyes staring at his cell phone, she felt the beginning of a new sense of calm. The pill was doing its work.

"You all right?"

She sat back in her seat. "Sorry. I . . . I just needed to catch my breath."

"Look, I'm sorry, Laura. I didn't mean to go there."

"I'm sorry, too." She didn't know why she was apologizing.

"It's just so disappointing. Don't you think you could at least ask her?"

Talking to Gillian would achieve nothing. Laura knew that, but she wanted the conversation to end. "I guess I could approach her. Although remember what happened the last time."

"Sometimes I wish you'd apply for a transfer to another floor with a steadier schedule."

It wasn't the first time that Eric had mentioned that to her. The problem was that Laura liked working on the surgical floor. She didn't see a lot of death, something her floor did not encounter on a regular basis, unlike a lot of other departments, such as the cancer or geriatrics floor. However, even if she did transfer to one of those floors, her schedule would still be unpredictable and, most likely, include weekends and holidays. Of course, she could transfer to radiation or oncology, but that wasn't her passion. Caring for postoperative patients was where her heart lay.

"We'll see." Sometimes it was better to just put Eric off. Most likely, after the holidays, he wouldn't mention transferring again until next November, and that was a whole year away. Plenty of time for things to change. And as for the country club issue, she'd add a prayer that Eric's company might refuse to pay the bond, because, if they didn't, she'd have a hard time convincing him what a terrible idea this was.

CHAPTER 5

All morning, Laura couldn't stop thinking about the previous night's dinner and her argument with Eric. She told herself that he hadn't *meant* to crack down on her about her work schedule. It wasn't as if she had *volunteered* to pick up the Thanksgiving shift. Besides, that was part of being a nurse. Working holidays.

But try as she might to forget it, she kept returning to his terse comment that she was turning into her mother. Why had he said such a thing? It hadn't been fair, but once spoken, words could not be erased. And even though she had calmed down after taking that Xanax, she now found herself rehashing his harsh comments, dwelling on his tone of voice and choice of words.

It wasn't like Eric to hurt her. One of the reasons she had fallen in love with him was how supportive he had been of her chosen profession, something she hadn't received from her mother. And Eric was a family man. In some ways, he reminded her of her father, or, rather, her father whenever Sonya wasn't around.

Sure, Eric had been looking forward to enjoying the long Thanksgiving weekend at his parents' with his wife and the girls. Laura knew that they rarely had time to visit his family anymore with her erratic, constantly changing schedule. He had a point that there didn't seem to be any real payoff for the long days and overtime. The money wasn't even that great, especially when she considered the stress and inconvenience of the hours. But nursing was what she loved to do. Taking care of people. Eric had married her because of—not in spite of—her career, admiring her competence as well as her desire to help people.

Sure, when the kids came along, they'd had a major adjustment. Juggling jobs and new babies wasn't easy for anyone. But they had managed to survive those first grueling years until both Becky and Emily were in school and they said goodbye to day care and regular babysitters for good.

Unfortunately, right when things should have been stabilizing, Laura's nurse supervisor had retired, throwing *her* job into a new level of chaos. And Eric's job was becoming more demanding, too. Something was up with his boss, Donald. Inviting them to fund-raisers, pushing the country club, giving Eric new accounts. Far too many nights, Eric was coming home after she had put the girls to bed. She knew it was a compromise to make up for the days when he had to leave on time because she was working the swing shift, but those long nights were growing increasingly frequent.

For a man who insisted that his wife should put family first, he was sliding down a path that smacked of hypocrisy.

Twirling around in her chair, Laura glanced through the open doorway of a patient's room at the windows. It was rainy and gray outside, which didn't help her mood. She tapped her fingers against the arm of the chair and contemplated calling Eric. She'd already done her rounds and had a few free minutes. With her mind continually pulling her back to Eric, she couldn't concentrate on charts or anything else.

Though she was still a little sore about his attitude toward the country club and his comments about her job, she reached for her phone and dialed his cell phone number.

"Hey honey," she said when his voice mail answered. "I just wanted to check in, see how your day's going." She paused, glancing down at the front of her blue scrubs. There was a stain where the ChapStick had melted earlier that week. "And, you know, to say I'm sorry about dinner last night."

"Laura!"

She glanced over her shoulder as Susan approached the workstation.

"Gotta run." She hung up after adding a quick "I love you."

"You have a minute to help me with a patient?" Susan leaned against the counter. "I need some help changing his dressings on his back."

Shoving the cell phone into her purse, Laura nodded and stood up. "Lead the way." She followed Susan down the hall toward the patient's room, pausing once when another patient called out to her as she passed his room.

"Give me a few minutes," she said with a smile. "I just have to help with another patient, OK?"

By the time she came back to her workstation, an hour had passed. After helping Susan and returning to that other patient, she had been stopped by a student nurse who had questions about changing a catheter, and then another patient called her regarding his pain medication. Distractions were par for the course for any nurse, especially one who worked on the post-surgery floor.

"Girl, your phone's been blowing up!" Monica gave her a look. "I almost went into your purse to shut it off."

"Oh gee!" Quickly, Laura grabbed her bag and dug out her phone. "Sorry. I forgot to put it on vibrate."

"Clearly." Despite Monica's dry tone, Laura knew that she wasn't angry with her. "Good thing Gillian didn't walk by."

"Yeah. Good thing." Gillian had a strict rule about cell phones on the floor: if a nurse wasn't carrying it on her, the phone had better not ring. Laura didn't know why she hadn't switched it to vibrate. It wasn't like her to forget.

Plopping down into her chair, Laura looked at the phone. Eric had called. Not once but twice. And left two text messages telling her to call him. For a moment, she panicked that something was wrong with the girls. But then she knew that the school would have contacted her first, and there had been no other incoming calls.

She dialed his number and pressed the phone against her ear. It rang three times before she heard his familiar voice say, "Hey, baby!"

"What's up? Everything OK?"

"More than OK. You'll never guess what just happened . . ."

From the jubilation in his voice, Laura could tell that he was in a good mood, their argument from the previous night just water under the bridge now. That's how it rolled with Eric. They didn't argue often, and he was quick to move right along. She loved that about him. "Tell me."

"Donald's retiring."

Something caught in her throat. "Your boss?"

She heard him laugh. "Of course! You know what that means, right?"

She didn't know what that meant. And she didn't know why Eric was so happy. He liked working for Donald. When he had first arrived at AES Financial, Donald had promoted a few of the junior analysts to more prominent positions, Eric among them. Donald had only worked at AES for eight years. Now he was retiring from an upper management position?

"I imagine it means you'll have a new vice president."

"Wrong. AES will have a new vice president, not me."

She frowned, trying to decipher what he was saying.

"Baby, they've offered me the position."

For a long-drawn-out second, Laura didn't know what to say. Images of her mother flooded through her mind, and she found herself unable to speak.

"Laura. Rodney. Your mother has something to tell you."

It was the beginning of November, just before Thanksgiving. The family sat around the supper table, Laura on her mother's left, and Rodney on her right. Laura craned her neck to stare at her mother, wide-eyed. The last time they'd had this talk, her mother had announced that she was pregnant. But tonight her mother didn't have that same smile on her face, the one that spoke of a wonderful secret that, six months later, resulted in a small crowd standing around an even smaller casket.

Laura had only been seven and never really understood why her mother had never brought her baby sister home from the hospital. And her mother refused to mention the missing baby. After the funeral, when Rodney whispered questions to Laura, Laura shushed him, promising that he'd understand it later when their mother explained to them what had happened.

But Sonya never did.

"You aren't going to have another baby, are you?"

Laura shot her brother a fierce look.

Her mother ignored the question.

"Children, you're both old enough now to take care of yourselves," her mother said in a strained voice.

Laura felt as if her heart had fallen to her feet.

Rodney must have sensed the same apprehension. "Are you getting rid of us, too?" he asked, wide-eyed and his lower lip trembling.

"Rodney!" Their father shook his head at his son.

Sonya frowned at her son before she continued talking. "I've gotten a job." When neither child said anything, she added, "At the hospital."

"Who will watch us after school?" Laura asked.

"Oh Laura! Please!" Sonya pressed her lips together and shook her head. "You're old enough to look out for yourselves for an hour or so after school."

"For how long?" she whispered.

"How long what, Laura?" her father asked gently.

"How long will Mommy be working?"

There was a moment of silence and an exchange of glances between the parents. Finally, it was Sonya who answered.

"I have an opportunity to do more, Laura. I need more than just . . ." She gestured toward the kitchen, her hand making haphazard circles in the air. "Just this. I want to prove myself and succeed in my career."

Edward shot Sonya a stern look and then gave his attention to Laura. "What your mother means is that work can be very fulfilling for adults. And the extra money she brings home . . . well, we'll all benefit, yes?" He tried to force a smile. "Family vacations. A new television."

Rodney cheered and Laura wished she could kick him under the table.

"See?" Her father reached out and tousled Rodney's hair. "There's a good side to this news, right?"

But Laura's eyes searched her mother's face. Even at nine years old, Laura knew that there was something else going on. Maybe her mother's sudden desire to work had to do with the dead baby girl. Stillborn. That was the word Laura had heard whispered at family gatherings during the year after the funeral. Maybe being at home just reminded her mother of all she'd lost.

"Just think how this will change our lives, Laura!"

Laura forced herself to push aside the memory of her mother's promotion, the one that had changed *their* lives.

"That's . . . great, Eric." She swallowed again, too aware that her mouth was dry. "I'm . . . proud of you."

"It won't take effect until after the new year, not officially anyway." He sounded like a little boy on Christmas morning.

"Did you know he was thinking about retiring?"

She heard a squeaking noise over the phone and suspected that he had leaned back in his leather chair. Unlike her, Eric had a private office with a window and a view. Now, he'd probably be moving to Donald's larger office at AES's headquarters in Newark, with a better view. Once, Eric had taken her to Newark, introducing her to Donald. Though Laura had feigned admiration for the swanky surroundings that day, she was distracted by the memory of her mother's self-satisfaction about her own private office at the hospital after her promotion.

"Not really. I mean he's almost seventy, so I guess I shouldn't be surprised." He gave a soft laugh. "And he's been taking a lot of time off. I thought something was wrong with his wife, frankly." In the background, someone must have entered his office. "Hey baby, I have to go. I'll tell you more later and we can celebrate this weekend."

When Laura hung up, she sat at her workstation and stared at the screen saver on her computer monitor. A promotion? To vice president? She didn't know how to feel about this news. On the one hand, it meant that their financial situation would improve. Goodbye to strict budgets and hello to a few impulse purchases. During their marriage, Laura had never enjoyed the luxury of buying things "just because." Even better, it would be wonderful to take a proper vacation with the girls. Laura had always hoped that, one day, she and Eric could take them to a Caribbean resort getaway. And now that might even be a real possibility.

But a cloud of doubt lingered over her head. A promotion to upper management would mean changes to their lives. Eric would have to entertain more clients and attend more functions. Surely she would be expected to attend some of them, too. Unfortunately, fancy dresses and high-heeled shoes were not her thing, and she always felt anxious in those situations. Sometimes her palms would sweat just from the idea of meeting new people. Especially people like the Weavers. What was she supposed to talk about? Politics? The economy? She knew nothing about any of those things and even less about the world of finance and accounting. All she knew was nursing and caring for her children.

A weight pressed against her chest, and Laura laid her hand over her heart. She could feel it pounding. *Not again,* she thought. She took a few short breaths, inhaling through her nose and exhaling through her mouth. It didn't help. She felt as if the walls were collapsing around her, creating an unseen pressure that made her blood feel as if it were trembling. Too much was happening too quickly. Promotions. Advancement. While most people would consider these events to be wonderful and life changing, to Laura they were nothing more than fresh reminders of everything she had worked so hard to forget.

With such a long day ahead of her, Laura made a quick decision. She couldn't deal with a whole day of patients, charting, doctors, Gillian, and more charting, if she was in the middle of a panic attack.

After the previous evening, when she had finally succumbed to taking one of the Xanax, she wondered why, exactly, she had fought it for so long. It had only taken a few minutes for a new sense of calm to wash over her. When was the last time she had felt so serene? Had she really been so tightly wound for so long that she'd forgotten what calm felt like?

Now, Laura found herself reaching for her purse. She dug through it until her fingers touched the pill bottle. She hesitated, hoping that her panic would dissipate without taking the medicine. When it didn't, she gave in and opened the bottle.

The pill practically dissolved on her tongue, both bitter and sweet at the same time. She shut her eyes and focused on her breathing. Slowly, her mind began to clear and the pressure disappeared. What did it matter if she had to go to a few fancy dinners.

Yes, Laura convinced herself, maybe she *could* hold her own at those events. A small smile crossed her lips as she imagined turning up at an event dressed in nursing blues complete with a dangling plastic name tag and stethoscope hanging around her neck.

"What's that smile for?"

Laura opened her eyes and saw Monica watching her. "Nothing."

"Uh-huh?" Monica made a face at her, her bright-red lips pursed as she suppressed a teasing smile. "Looks to me like you were thinking about that hunky husband of yours." She winked at Laura.

"What?" Confused at first, Laura blushed as she realized what Monica was insinuating. "Oh, no! Nothing like that."

"Well, whatever you're thinking, I bet it's not about your new admit that's coming up in thirty minutes." Monica dropped a chart on Laura's lap and walked around the nurses' station toward the small kitchen.

A new admit? She already had four patients. Laura sighed and glanced through the chart. An abdominal hysterectomy patient. She'd be a short stay, probably two days at the most.

Laura heard her cell phone vibrate against the side of her computer and she reached for it. Eric had texted her.

Maybe you could talk to Gillian about Thanksgiving again?
I'd love for you to be there when I tell my family.

Laura took a short, quick breath and held it. Hadn't they already gone through this? Didn't he realize the pressure he was putting her under?

No, Laura was certain that he did not.

Yet, even though she did *not* want to talk to Gillian about Thanksgiving, Laura suspected that she would. Eventually. After all, it wasn't like Eric to drop something like this, not without a fight. Unfortunately, when there *was* a fight, Laura too often found herself on the front line while Eric remained comfortably safe in his own little sheltered world. If only he understood that with every fight, there was collateral damage, and she was beginning to feel that her sanity was the unintended victim.

CHAPTER 6

On Tuesday, as she stood in the parking lot of Woodland School, Laura shivered beneath her black North Face jacket as she waited for the children to march single file through the front doors for the annual Halloween parade.

Laura couldn't be happier that she had to work and would miss the annual evening of trick-or-treating with the girls. She hated the cold weather. Growing up, Laura had enjoyed Halloween. Her father had usually been the one to accompany her and Rodney to the neighbors' houses. But that had been in Florida where the October evenings were still warm. Here in New Jersey, it was too cold to go trudging through the darkness from house to house. Yes, she was more than happy to have an excuse not to brave the cold night air this year for trick-or-treating with the girls.

And yet, even with a legitimate excuse, she still felt a touch of mommy guilt.

Laura remembered far too well how her own mother had never attended anything, and how disappointed Laura had felt. She had vowed to never do that to her own children, even if it meant standing in the cold, like right now, to wait for the school's little Halloween parade.

Behind her, she could hear two men talking as they, too, waited. "Patrick is the quarterback for the Wildcats," the one father bragged.

"Quarterback, eh?" The other man sounded impressed.

"Coach said he's a natural," the father said. "If he stays with it until eighth grade, Coach will try to get him on the high school team."

Laura rolled her eyes as she shifted her weight from one foot to the other, trying to get warm. So many roads lay ahead of these children. Who knew what they would want to do in six years? She was far too aware that time changed childhood dreams into reality. And what the parents wanted wasn't always what the children eventually did.

"Oh! Here they come!"

Thank goodness, Laura thought as she glanced over her shoulder at the young mother who practically squealed with delight as the doors opened and the principal, dressed like Waldo, led the parade outside. Laura felt her mood change, shifting from irritated to a bit more relaxed, as she watched the pirates and princesses and teddy bears and Disney characters march behind their teachers. Music blasted from an outdoor speaker as the children walked around the circular driveway, each one scanning the audience for their parents.

When Laura saw Becky, dressed as a cowgirl, she smiled and waved. Becky tried to hide her smile, being a second grader and clearly too cool to wave at her mother. But, to Laura's delight, Becky snuck in a raised hand as she walked by. Emily, on the other hand, wearing Becky's princess costume from last year, was more than happy to wave to her mother.

"I take it that's your little girl?"

Laura turned to the woman next to her. "Hmm? Oh, yes." And then, as parental protocol dictated, she added, "And yours?"

The woman pointed to a little girl dressed like an angel. "She isn't, trust me."

Laughing, Laura returned her attention to the parade.

"She's my youngest. I have four."

"Wow. It's hard enough with just the two girls. I can't imagine four."

The woman gave a cynical chuckle. "Just wait. These are the easy years."

From her jacket pocket, Laura felt her cell phone vibrate. She withdrew it and saw that it was Susan. Politely extricating herself from the crowd and the noise, Laura moved toward the sidewalk where she could hear better.

"What's up?"

"Any chance you can get here early? Monica just left for a family emergency."

Laura caught her breath. "Everything OK?"

Susan must have been rustling papers at the desk. "Something about her father."

Something about her father.

Just those four words caught Laura off guard and she felt her heart begin to race. The muscles above her breasts twitched, and she tried to take deep breaths to ward off the beginning of a panic attack.

Was it already seven years since she, too, had received such a phone call? Only it hadn't been *something* but the *big thing*. A heart attack at home while weeding the garden on a Saturday afternoon.

"Laura, your father died."

For a moment, Laura held her phone in one hand while resting a fidgety one-year-old Becky against her hip. She had been cooking supper when the house phone had rung. "Mom?"

"Of course it's me!" Sonya snapped. "Who else would call to tell you about your father?"

"I couldn't hear you," Laura said as she stirred the vegetables. "Becky's teething and fussing up a storm."

There was a split second of silence and Laura wondered if her mother was still on the other end.

"I'm at the hospital, Laura. Your father died."

Suddenly, everything around Laura seemed to stop. She felt a pressure in the room, and yet, at the same time, it felt as if all the air had been sucked out. Carefully, she stepped away from the stove and edged her way along the counter toward the table. She didn't trust herself to hold Becky, and she needed the security of a chair.

"Mom, no. Please."

It wasn't supposed to happen this way, *Laura thought. Not her father first. He hadn't been a perfect dad, but he had tried to balance her mother's focus on professional excellence and drive for upward social mobility. Given how calm and even tempered he was, Laura had never thought for a moment that he wouldn't age gracefully, cruising well into his eighties.*

But life had an insensitive way of reminding people to not take anything for granted.

"Mommy! Mommy!"

"I'll get there as soon as possible," Laura told Susan before she slipped the phone back into her pocket and turned around, just in time to find the arms of a pretty, pretty princess wrapped around her waist.

"You came!"

Laura did her best to calm her racing heart. She forced a laugh and knelt down before Emily. "Of course I came! How could I miss this?" She motioned with her hand toward the chaos of children trying to find their parents in the audience now that the parade was over.

"Are you taking us home now?"

Becky pretended to canter over to them, reining in her invisible horse. "Whoa girl!"

Laura's breath seemed to come easier. She said a silent prayer of thanks that she hadn't needed a Xanax to calm down.

Smiling, she reached out to tap the edge of Becky's cowboy hat. "Hey cowgirl!"

Becky grinned at her. "Can we go trick-or-treating in Morristown?"

Immediately, Laura felt the palpitations again. It was at moments like these when she had to count to ten, sometimes twice. Wasn't it enough that she had shown up for the parade? That she had even found the time to get Becky's costume? Take in the hem of Emily's dress? Why wasn't any of it ever enough? But instead they always wanted more. She often wondered why they only ever noticed what she didn't do and not everything she did. She knew that it was all part of being a mom, but it didn't ever really get easier.

I can't do it all, she told herself. But the mommy guilt was still there.

"Girls, you know I have to go to work," she started slowly, trying to breathe deeply through her mouth. Sometimes that helped.

Becky scowled. "Jenny's mom is taking her!"

"Well, good for Jenny and her mom."

Emily made a face at her sister. "Maybe Mommy will take us to Morristown before Daddy takes us trick-or-treating tonight."

But Becky shook her head. "Mom has to work, goose. That means aftercare for us."

Emily groaned.

"Excuse me," someone said from behind Laura. "Mrs. Reese?"

Laura looked at the woman in her black yoga pants and brand-new sneakers. Her shoulder-length hair was tied back in a sleek ponytail, and her skin glistened. Clearly, she had just come from working out.

"I'd be happy to take the girls." The woman smiled at Becky. "Jenny would love the company."

Before Laura could refuse, Becky jumped up and down while a little girl dressed as a mermaid joined her. She could only presume that was Jenny.

"I don't know." Laura felt put on the spot. "I wouldn't want to inconvenience you . . ."

"Oh, no bother at all!" The woman smiled as she extended her hand. "I'm Allison Tucker, by the way. Nice to meet you."

Laura shook the proffered hand, which she noticed was perfectly manicured, the nails painted soft pink. While Laura didn't know this woman, and she wasn't certain about leaving the girls in her care, she knew Allison Tucker wasn't going to *kidnap* Becky and Emily. And she really didn't want to create a scene. If she refused Allison's kind offer, both girls would probably begin to cry and *that* would add to her already-building mommy guilt.

"Well, I guess if it's not too much bother . . ." Giving in, Laura forced a weary smile. "My shift starts at three, and they just called asking if I could get there a bit earlier. Their father will be able to pick them up from your house after work." She glanced at Emily, who was twirling around, watching her princess costume poof out. "Remember, he'll take you trick-or-treating in our neighborhood later."

Emily gave her a grin.

Returning her attention to Allison, Laura couldn't help but ask, "Are you sure you don't mind? All of this seems like an awful lot."

Allison waved her hand dismissively. "Don't think twice about it. It's Halloween, after all! All about the kids, right?" She gave a short laugh and rolled her eyes.

The thought crossed Laura's mind that, under different circumstances—if she had time to develop new friendships—she might actually like someone like Allison Tucker.

"I'll make certain they have some supper, and don't worry about picking them up. I'll bring them home in time for trick-or-treating with Dad." Allison leaned forward and whispered, "I find if they trick-or-treat on a full stomach, they eat less candy and go to sleep earlier."

"Makes sense. Less sugar before bedtime, less spice at bedtime."

"Exactly." Allison laughed. "I'll have to remember that one." Then she turned her attention to the girls. "Any mermaids, cowgirls, and princesses want to head uptown to treat-or-treat?" She motioned for them to follow her.

Laura watched as Allison walked off with Becky and Emily in tow. She wondered if less sugar might be the trick to getting less spice from Gillian when she finally gathered enough courage to approach her about Thanksgiving.

Somehow she doubted it.

CHAPTER 7

On Wednesday, Laura sat in the break room, ignoring the hot coffee in front of her. Why had she bothered to pour it? She was too nervous to drink more caffeine; her hands were already trembling. Eric had reminded her, yet again, that she needed to speak to Gillian about Thanksgiving. Laura didn't see what the point was. Thanksgiving was less than three weeks away.

Laura had meant to approach Gillian last week on Halloween, but she had been slammed with patients. By the time she could catch her breath, Gillian had left for the day. Now that the new schedule had started, this was the first opportunity she had to speak to her supervisor, especially since Gillian had taken off a few days the previous week. Laura knew it was a long shot; too much time had gone by since the schedules had been circulated. Still, she knew she had to at least approach her supervisor, even though Laura suspected it would be a waste of her time.

How many nurses had gone into Gillian's office after she'd announced the November schedule? Laura had overheard at least five complaining about how they had begged her to reconsider. Even that new nurse, Chelsea, had requested off, although Laura wasn't surprised that *she* had been shot down. As a temporary transfer to the floor, Chelsea didn't have any seniority.

But Laura did.

Only two other nurses, Susan and an older woman named Margaret, had worked on the floor longer than Laura. Neither one of them had younger children, and only Margaret had been given off for Thanksgiving.

Sure, Laura knew that patients didn't go away simply because it was a holiday. But Laura also knew that the post-op floor had a high turnover rate of nurses. And, if Gillian continued reminding everyone who complained that *this* was what nursing was about, Laura suspected several might transfer to other floors or even doctors' offices where nine to five was the norm.

Most nurses who worked in post-op would be bored to death with the revolving door of patients with colds, flu, and depression. Just take the blood pressure and temperature, scribble a few notes on the file, and pass it over to the doctor to write the script.

No. Post-op nurses usually didn't apply for *those* jobs because *those* jobs lacked logistical chaos, medical troubleshooting, and in-depth interactions with the patients. Nurses on the post-op floor tended to be type-A go-getters, people who thrived in a stressful environment.

With a sigh, Laura stood up and carried her coffee mug to the sink. She watched the liquid as she poured it down the drain. Her break was almost over, and she figured that she needed to tackle her discussion with Gillian sooner rather than keep procrastinating.

Standing outside of Gillian's office, she smoothed down the front of her shirt. That morning, Laura had made certain to wear freshly laundered and ironed scrubs, hoping that a tidy appearance might help her cause. Then, after taking a deep breath, she reached out and knocked on the partially open door.

Gillian looked up and peered at her over the top of her glasses. "What is it, Laura?"

"May I come in?"

The office was small, barely enough room for the desk and chair. On the wall was a whiteboard where Gillian wrote notes. Laura could see the names of several nurses under the heading "Thanksgiving." She tried to focus on Gillian, not the names.

Gillian nodded, her eyes flickering quickly to the clock on the wall. "Did that new nurse, Chelsea, show up yet?"

It was almost three o'clock, time for the swing shift to start.

"I haven't seen her yet, no."

Gillian inhaled and mumbled something under her breath.

Laura knew that Chelsea still had ten minutes to show up before she was officially late. However, since the new schedule had started, Chelsea kept arriving late for her shifts. With Chelsea being new to the floor, Laura would've thought Chelsea would arrive exactly on time or even early. She had never been late for the night shifts. But now that Gillian had given her a few day and swing shifts, Chelsea's act was falling apart. That sure didn't bode well for her future on the post-op floor.

"So, what did you want to see me about?"

Laura snapped out of her fog and focused, once again, on Gillian. "I . . . I wanted to talk to you about Thanksgiving, Gillian."

The stout woman leaned back in her chair, leveling her gaze at Laura. "You're the sixth person to approach me since our last meeting."

"I'm sure." She felt her heart begin to race and, hoping to calm down, she squeezed her hand shut, clenching it as tight as she could. She could feel her fingernails dig into the flesh of her palm, the sharpness causing a momentary distraction.

Gillian raised an eyebrow. "So why, exactly, are you here then?"

"I'd . . . I'd like you to reconsider."

Immediately, Laura saw a hint of an acrimonious expression cross Gillian's round face.

"I'm sure you would," Gillian said in a flat voice. "But I'm not going to."

Despite the sense of dread that she felt, Laura lifted her chin. "I haven't had a major holiday off this whole year. And I've worked the last three Thanksgivings."

Not one hint of compassion showed on Gillian's face. Instead, she almost appeared smug when she replied, "The schedule is set, Laura. I can't change it now." Gillian reached for a pencil that was on her desk and began to tap it on a pile of papers. "I have to staff the floor."

The noise of the papers irritated Laura. It sounded ten times louder in the silence of the small office. In her mind, she could hear Eric chastising her again, complaining that she hadn't fought hard enough.

"What do you mean you didn't ask for extra help?" Her mother scowled at her. "These are your grades, Laura. It's your job to do well at school so you can get into college."

At least her mother hadn't said "med school," although Laura knew that her mother was still dead set on her becoming a doctor. "It's just one test," Laura countered, although she knew her response sounded weak.

So did her mother. "'One test'? 'Just one test'?" Sonya repeated. "When are you going to learn that you have to fight harder? This isn't about a test but your future!"

Gillian tapped the pencil against the side of the desk and Laura found herself staring at the woman's fingers. Her nails were painted in a French manicure. Like Laura's mother's.

"A whole year," Laura repeated softly. "I'd like to spend a holiday with my family."

"Unfortunately, Laura, patients don't take holidays from their medical issues."

Inwardly, Laura winced. She felt her muscles tense, especially in her neck. "Lisa had both Thanksgiving and Christmas off last year, and I had neither. I have small children, Gillian. We're taking them to their grandparents outside of Boston. They haven't seen them for a holiday in almost two years."

Gillian remained silent.

"I'm entitled to vacation time."

"Indeed you are."

Laura clenched her jaw. She had to force herself to stop and calm down. "I don't need to explain myself."

"Easy there, Tiger."

"Sorry, Dad."

"I'm entitled to sharing holidays with my family."

"I'm sorry, Laura," Gillian said, although her voice indicated that she was anything but sorry.

In fact, the way that Gillian's eyes fixated on her infuriated Laura. Her sardonic tone added salt to a very gaping wound. Laura wanted to scream at her. She wanted to yell, *Are you sorry? Are you really?* But she knew that doing so would only jeopardize her future at the hospital. No one cared that Laura had missed so many Thanksgivings, or that her husband was getting a big promotion and she wanted to share the moment when he told his parents. No. Despite Gillian's words, Laura knew that she was most certainly *not* sorry.

Gillian cleared her throat and folded her hands in front of her, letting them rest on the desk. Suddenly, Laura felt as if she were sitting before the principal at elementary school, being taught a lesson on why students weren't allowed to have more than one dessert at lunchtime.

"As I said, my job is to staff this floor," Gillian said in a slow, deliberate manner. Clearly, this speech about the duty of a nurse supervisor was rehearsed, a sermon that Laura suspected Gillian had prepared in anticipation of so many people complaining about the new schedule. "Part of nursing requires sacrifice in order to tend to the patients. There are a lot of people who aren't happy about missing Thanksgiving with their family. I don't see why you should get special treatment."

Laura fought the urge to raise her voice. "I don't want special treatment. Just fair treatment. And the same people keep getting time off while others . . ." She let her voice fade.

With a blank expression on her face, Gillian stared at her, her fingers still playing with the pencil. Tap, tap, tap.

"I don't want to go to the union rep," Laura said at last, her eyes meeting Gillian's fierce stare. She hadn't meant it as a threat, but realized that it sounded that way. And as soon as the words left her mouth, she realized that she did not want to involve her union rep. Doing so would mean interviews and reports and a growing wedge between her and Gillian. Laura knew that would only mean more crappy shifts and lost weekends. No. She really did not want to involve the union rep.

To her surprise, Gillian smiled. Only it wasn't as much a smile as a smirk. "By all means, Laura. It's your right to contact your rep." She reached for some papers on her desk and stood up, an indication that the meeting was over. Slapping the sides of the files on the edge of the table, Gillian glanced toward the door. "Now, if that will be all . . ."

Back on the floor, Laura hurried to her workstation. She didn't have to do her rounds for another fifteen minutes, and she needed that time to cool down. The other nurses were talking, standing near the kitchen area. Laura reached for her purse and grabbed her prescription bottle. She didn't even care if anyone saw her flip off the white cap and tip the orange bottle into her hand. The way that her heart was racing, Laura knew that she needed to calm down.

Tipping the bottle into her palm, she slid one pill out.

She popped it into her mouth and tossed the bottle back into her purse. Eric would absolutely flip when he heard about Gillian's response. Laura wasn't certain which was worse: dealing with Eric or dealing with Gillian. If she called the union representative and filed a formal complaint, chances were that Gillian would put her on the Christmas schedule. However, if she didn't call the union rep, she'd never hear the end of it from Eric, and Gillian would know she had been bluffing.

"Hey!" Monica sat down in the chair next to her. "Saw you were in with Gillian. How'd it go?"

Laura shot her a weary look. Monica had already had her own fair share of run-ins with Gillian. Recently, she had been lying low and, therefore, stayed off Gillian's radar. Laura wished that she had enough presence of mind to follow Monica's lead. Not only did she not solve her Thanksgiving problem, now she had to worry about the possibility that Gillian might retaliate with an even worse schedule for December.

But Laura expressed none of that to Monica. "How do you think it went?"

Monica pressed her lips together and shook her head knowingly. "Let me guess. She gave you the nurse supervisor lecture?"

Laura nodded.

Monica exhaled loudly. "I don't understand why God's not listening to my prayers," she said in a flat tone.

For a moment, Laura didn't understand. And then she remembered their conversation and realized that Monica was teasing. Somehow Laura found the strength to laugh. "Well, don't stop praying for that transfer, OK? Maybe he's busy dealing with some other horrible person, and when he's finished, he'll work on it."

"One can only hope." Monica started to walk away. "At least you'll be in good company on Thanksgiving. Right, Susan?"

Laura glanced over her shoulder.

Susan approached and patted Laura's arm. "I take it Gillian said no. So, what're you missing this year?"

"Missing?"

"You know. For Thanksgiving."

Laura felt stupid for not having made the connection. The conversation with Gillian had thrown her off her game. What was she missing? Family. Peace. Justice. "Right. Eric and I wanted to take the kids to visit his parents outside of Boston. We have reservations for the Plimoth Plantation tour on Friday, too. Do you even know how hard those tickets were to get over Thanksgiving?"

"I'm sure." Susan gave her an empathetic look. "I always wanted to do that. Go to Plimoth for Thanksgiving. I never did though."

"Looks like I won't be doing it, either."

Susan chuckled. "You like them, right?"

"Who?"

"Your in-laws," Susan said.

She did. Patricia and Ed had always been kind to her, and they were very good to the girls. "I sure do. It's *my* mother that I have issues with."

Susan grabbed a chart from the in-box and flipped through it.

Laura didn't need to read over her shoulder to know that it was release paperwork for one of Susan's patients. And while there was always a sense of joy to sending a patient home, it was short-lived. An empty room was quickly filled with another patient. Laura knew that the hospital needed to make money and that the name of the game was keeping the rooms filled. Sometimes she wondered what would happen if, just once, there was a day when not one new person was admitted to the hospital. She could imagine heads exploding at the lost revenue.

"So what's up with your mother?" Susan asked as she shut the chart.

Speaking of heads exploding . . . "Where do I start?" Just the mention of her mother made Laura feel anxious. She took a deep breath and exhaled through her mouth. "I rarely see her. She still lives in Jacksonville."

"Florida?"

Laura nodded. "That's where I grew up."

Susan made a noise. "I never knew that."

"I moved north for college and never went back."

Susan raised an eyebrow. "You voluntarily stayed in New Jersey over Florida?"

Laura gave a little chuckle. "New Jersey winters aren't half as bad as Florida summers," she said, even though she knew that seasons had nothing to do with why she hadn't returned to Jacksonville. "My mother worked at the hospital, in charge of Human Resources."

"So that's where you developed a passion to be a nurse."

"No." Laura sighed. "In fact, the irony is that she never supported me being a nurse at all."

"Oh gee." Susan exhaled and shook her head. "Let me guess. She wanted you to be a doctor."

"How'd you know?"

Susan laughed. "I've been working in the hospital for a lot longer than you, Laura. I'm used to the stereotypes about nurses being slaves to the doctors as well as the patients."

"Yeah, well, that's just one of many ways I disappointed her. No matter what I did, it just wasn't good enough." She scratched the back of her neck, and her eye twitched. She hoped that the Xanax would kick in soon. "Nothing was ever good enough," Laura mumbled more to herself than to Susan.

"So why'd you choose nursing anyway?"

Laura looked up, almost surprised to see Susan still standing there. "Huh?"

"Nursing? Most of us have a story about why we chose nursing as a career. What's yours?"

Laura sat in the waiting room of the hospital. It had been over two hours since the doctor had escorted her parents into Rodney's room. Two long hours of Laura sitting alone and wondering what was happening with her twelve-year-old brother.

She felt abandoned. It was as if they had forgotten she was there, waiting. All she knew was that Rodney had been gasping for breath and her mother had been hysterical.

In the empty waiting room, Laura leafed through every People, National Geographic, *and* Vanity Fair *magazine, barely reading any of the words or seeing any of the photos. Most of them were outdated, and a few were missing pages. But Laura didn't care. Flipping through the pages helped refocus her mind.*

"Hey. You by yourself?"

Laura looked up and saw a nurse in green scrubs leaning against the door frame. With her dark hair pulled back into a loose ponytail and the hint of blush on her cheeks, the woman looked young, maybe twenty-six at the most.

"Kinda." Laura glanced at the clock. It was almost one o'clock in the morning. "I mean my parents are in there." She pointed in the direction that the doctor had led them. "With my brother."

"Driscoll? Rodney Driscoll?"

Laura nodded.

The nurse walked over and sat down beside her. "Has anyone come to talk to you?"

Laura shook her head.

"I see."

Something crossed the nurse's face, a dark cloud that shadowed her eyes. Laura wished that she knew what that meant.

"Is . . . is he going to be all right? He was turning blue."

Immediately, the nurse's expression changed. "Oh yes. He's fine. He just . . . well, your parents should be telling you this." Another frown and she seemed to be contemplating whether or not to divulge information to Laura. But she quickly gave an irritated shake of her head. "It was just a bad asthma attack."

"My father woke me up," Laura said softly, a lump forming in her throat. She blinked, trying hard to push back the tears along with the memory of her brother on the gurney being rolled to the ambulance. "My mother was going to just leave me at home." With a blank expression, Laura stared at the nurse. "I would've woken up alone with no idea what happened."

The nurse reached for her hand and held it between her own. "Well, I'm here. For as long as you need."

"My brother had a severe asthma attack. He couldn't breathe," Laura said softly, focusing her gaze on Susan. "I always took care of him because my mother worked at the hospital. You know how that goes."

Susan nodded. "And how."

"No one told me what was going on and, because I was fourteen, I had to stay in the waiting room. Alone."

"Ouch."

That one word comforted Laura. Finally, someone who understood. "Looking back, I think I felt guilty. I mean, it was my job to take care of him and he was sick. Couldn't breathe. I had no idea what was going on. For hours. It's like they forgot about me, which only made me feel worse." A soft smile crossed her lips as she remembered the nurse. Marion Reilly. That was her name. "But this one nurse saw me there. She sat with me until my parents returned. Almost an entire hour she sat there in the waiting room, just holding my hand and praying with me."

"I think all of us have one of those stories." Susan reached out and gave Laura's arm a gentle squeeze. "We realize the difference we can make, not just with the patients but with their families, too. It takes a special kind of person to be a nurse. A lot of work goes into caring for these patients, and we sure don't get the glory—or the pay!—that doctors do. But it's in our blood. Maybe that's why we work holidays, even when we'd prefer to be with our families," she said, a resigned expression on her face before she walked away.

Despite Susan's kind words, Laura didn't feel resigned. What she felt was disappointed. And not just with Gillian. While she didn't mind working, she did mind having to tell Eric. He'd be furious. And she hated that because it was just one more reminder that she had let him down. She was also disappointed that she would be missing family time with the girls as well as her in-laws.

Her thoughts were interrupted when her cell phone buzzed. Reaching for it, she touched the screen. Eric.

Good luck with Gillian. Stay firm.

Groaning, Laura flung her phone onto the desk and covered her eyes with her hands. Her head felt compressed, as if someone were squeezing it. The pain went throughout her body, from her head to her toes. *Impossible,* she thought. Life was impossible. No matter how hard she tried, she simply couldn't please everyone.

Without giving it a second thought, Laura reached for her purse and dug for her prescription bottle. If she were going to get through the rest of the day, she knew that she needed to calm down. Another Xanax would help. That was why James had prescribed it for her after all, wasn't it?

CHAPTER 8

It was five thirty when she pulled into the driveway. After her shift had ended, she had run a few errands in Morristown, stopping to pick up Eric's shirts from the dry cleaners and running into ShopRite for a few essentials to tide over the family until she could do her next big grocery run.

Turning off the car engine, Laura placed both of her hands on the steering wheel and stared out the windshield.

When Eric learned about the meeting she'd had with Gillian, he'd be enraged. On the one hand, Laura couldn't fault him; she, too, had wanted to explode when Gillian sat there, so smug, safe, and secure behind her desk, and declared that no changes would be made. And while he would rant and rave about it, Laura knew that it wasn't necessarily an attack against her. But it would feel like it. And she would feel helpless that she couldn't do anything to make the situation better.

On the other hand, she was still smarting over his cutting remarks at the restaurant from the previous week. It was bad enough that Eric was disappointed—she was, too!—but she needed his understanding right now, not more pressure.

Reluctantly, she got out of the car and made her way to the front door of the house. She fumbled in her coat pocket for her house keys.

To her surprise, the door opened.

"Well, hello there!" Eric greeted her with a big smile.

"What are you doing home so early?" Laura felt that familiar tightening of her chest as Eric pulled her into his arms and kissed her. He was so happy, still on cloud nine about his promotion.

When Eric released her, he pulled her into the house and kicked the door shut. "Thought I'd surprise you."

"Surprise," she said drily.

He laughed.

She set her purse on the floor and slipped out of her coat. The house was warm compared to outside, but she still felt chilled. With the gray overcast sky, everything felt cold, including her mood. Maybe that was why she hadn't noticed his car parked on the road in front of the house. Their driveway was too small for both cars, and like a true gentleman, he always let her park there.

Eric glanced behind her. "Where're the girls?"

Laura froze. "What?"

"The girls? You know, our daughters?"

She groaned. "I thought you were picking them up." Hadn't she asked him to? She thought she had told him she needed to run some errands.

"Aw, come on, Laura." Eric gave her that look, the one that reminded her so much of her father. "What's going on with you these days? You *know* you always pick them up when you work the day shift."

Taking a deep breath, she reached for her coat that she had just hung up. She didn't want to fight with him. Not over this. If she had screwed up and forgotten to ask him, so be it. "Right. Got it."

As she stooped for her purse, Eric snapped, "Never mind. I'll do it." He sounded as irritated as she felt.

"Don't be a hero, Eric. I don't mind."

"A hero? It's called being a parent." And with that, he pushed past her and went out the door.

She leaned against the shut door and banged the back of her head against it twice. Darn it, darn it! How could she have forgotten? She could picture the girls in aftercare, waiting for her to pick them up. In her mind, she saw the disappointment on Becky and Emily's faces whenever the door opened and it was some other mother or father who walked through it to pick up their child. How could Laura explain to a small child that her day had gone from bad to worse? That she had been more focused on dealing with Eric than on picking up her children? Of course, Laura knew that they couldn't understand that. Had she understood when *she* was a child? When her mother failed to follow through on promises?

The only difference was that Laura hadn't meant to forget. Her mother simply hadn't meant to remember.

Ever since they had moved from their old ranch house to the new, fancy Mediterranean-style home in a gated community outside of Jacksonville, Laura often found herself sitting on the stairs. The novelty of the new, big house—two stories at that!—hadn't worn off yet. Tonight, she sat on the stairs, her chin resting on her hands as she waited for her mother. Her eyes watched the pendulum of the grandfather clock as it swayed back and forth.

It was almost seven o'clock. Where was her mother?

When she heard the familiar clicking of high heels on the kitchen tile, Laura perked up. "Mom? Is that you?"

"Of course it's me!"

"Where've you been?"

The clicking grew louder as her mother left the kitchen and crossed the foyer to the bottom of the stairs. "Why isn't supper ready?"

Laura pressed her lips together. Her mother had forgotten!

"Why are you sitting there with your jacket on?"

Laura felt as if someone had reached into her chest and squeezed her heart. Hard. "We're supposed to go to the movies tonight. Remember? Titanic?"

Laura loved Leonardo DiCaprio. She had been waiting weeks to see the movie. Tonight was the night. Her mother had promised.

But her mother hadn't remembered.

With an overly dramatic sigh, Sonya set her purse on the foyer table. Slowly, she slipped her arms from her coat and draped it over the Queen Anne–style chair that no one ever sat in. "Please Laura. I don't need this tonight."

"You promised!"

Immediately, her mother's eyes narrowed and she glowered at Laura. "Are you really so selfish? I'm exhausted, Laura! Exhausted! Do you ever think about that? Or are you so preoccupied with yourself that you simply cannot think about me?"

Laura glared at her.

"I work day in and day out for you people!" Her mother's voice was rising and that was not a good sign. "And I get absolutely zero appreciation from any of you. Not your father, not your brother, and certainly not you!" It rose another octave higher. "No one ever thinks about me! About the sacrifices I make! And you keep piling on demands for more?"

Laura started to stand up. Her mother was getting hysterical and Laura wasn't about to take the grenade on this particular guilt trip. Demands? she wanted to scream back. Spending quality time with your daughter was a demand? A sacrifice?

"Whatever," she mumbled and stomped upstairs. But even when she shut her bedroom door and flopped onto the bed, she could still hear her mother's ranting from downstairs. With no one to listen to it, for her father had taken Rodney out for pizza, her mother eventually quieted. Laura crept to the door and cracked it open, shocked to hear the sound of soft weeping coming from the landing on the stairs.

Laura shook her head, trying to erase the overwhelming guilt that she still felt over that evening. Maybe she should have gone to her mother, wrapped her arms around her, and consoled her.

But she hadn't.

In hindsight, Laura knew why she hadn't made that effort. At fifteen years old, Laura had never heard her mother cry before. Simply put, she hadn't known what to do. And yet, the older and wiser Laura also knew how manipulative her mother could be. Not just that evening, but in general. While she had accused the rest of the family of making harsh demands and forcing terrible sacrifices from her, the truth of the matter was that her mother had been projecting her own behavior.

It hadn't been Laura or Rodney or even their father who asked Sonya to work so hard and make sacrifices. It had been Sonya who demanded the sacrifices from her family.

Her career had taken over all other priorities in her life. Work came first. Family came last. Everything else fell in between.

And for what?

A career that occupied all of her time? A new house that was bigger and better than a typical Florida ranch house? The country club membership that had isolated the family from their former neighbors and friends?

But Laura wasn't like her mother. She wasn't striving for more. She was happy in *their* contemporary ranch home, and she had thought Eric was, too. They didn't live above their means and, despite her crazy schedule, they spent more time together than other families she knew.

It worked.

And yet, Laura had messed up. She had *forgotten* to pick up the girls. She had *thought* that Eric had made the offer. And now he was angry with her.

Well, what's done is done, she told herself, trying to ride past the wave of guilt that she felt. She'd make a nice supper and have the table ready for everyone. Maybe spaghetti with fresh bread (straight from the Pillsbury can) would make up for her lapse. The girls loved spaghetti.

Laura hurried into the kitchen and threw a pot of water onto the stove. After grabbing some hamburger meat from the freezer and popping it into the microwave to defrost, she began chopping garlic and onions. If nothing else, the house would smell good when the three of them returned. By the time she started cooking the garlic in olive oil over medium heat, her nerves felt wound up in knots. She reached into the refrigerator for a Corona to try to calm herself down. After she had finished half of the beer, she began to feel herself unwind. Just a little. It wasn't exactly a Xanax, but it was better than nothing.

The front door flew open and Emily charged into the house.

"Mommy!" She dropped her backpack and ran across the living room into the kitchen, her arms flung wide open as she attached herself to Laura's legs. "What happened to you?" Emily asked in her cherubic voice.

Becky appeared in the doorway and scowled. "Yeah, Mom! We were the last kids there. Again."

"Please, Becks. I'm sorry."

Becky leaned her chin on the counter and stared up at her. "Right."

"Hey, now," Eric said. "Let's give Mom a break, OK? It's not easy healing sick people all day."

When Laura looked at him and he winked, she breathed a sigh of relief. The short drive to the school must have been enough time for Eric to cool down. She mouthed *Thank you* to him and he smiled.

Emily's eyes widened as she peered at the stove. "Is that spaghetti?" She grinned. "Oh, wow!"

Laura reached out and tweaked her nose. "Maybe it was worth it, having to stay an extra few minutes, eh?"

The little girl nodded and grinned, exposing a gap in her front teeth.

Laura gasped and knelt down before her. "What's that?"

For a second, Emily looked confused but then a look of understanding crossed her face. "I lost my tooth!" She pressed her tongue against the spot as if to prove it. "See?"

"I do! I really do!"

Becky rolled her eyes. "During lunch. She bit into an apple and it stayed behind."

Laura stood up and reached for her beer. "That must have been something."

"Yeah. It bled and all the kids screamed."

Emily giggled and nodded. "I had to go to the nurse. She made me bite down on a wet cloth and I got a sticker." She pointed to her chest where there was a little sticker of a smiling tooth. "And I got to sit out for gym."

"Dodgeball again?" Laura asked.

Emily made a face. "Yuck."

"That was never my favorite, either." Laura glanced up at Eric. He was watching her from the doorway, his arms crossed over his chest and a slight smile on his face. "Why don't you girls go put the tooth under Em's pillow and get cleaned up. Play for a little bit. Supper will be another thirty minutes, OK?"

When the two girls disappeared down the hallway to their rooms, Laura finished her beer, threw out the bottle, and went for another. This time, however, she pulled out two beers and handed one to Eric. "I'm sorry, Eric." She watched him open the bottle and take a sip. "I just had a really bad day. I had a lot on my mind and I forgot."

He nodded his head. "I get it. No problem." He set the bottle down on the counter, the noise ringing in Laura's head. "So I forgot to ask about Gillian. What did she say when you spoke to her?"

"I . . . uh . . ." She couldn't finish the sentence. She just could not say the words that she knew would upset him. But she also knew it was better to just get it out in the open, like pulling a Band-Aid off a wound. Any hesitation would just make it worse. For both of them.

"Let me guess. You forgot that, too?" His biting tone did not go unnoticed.

"No, I didn't forget."

Eric blinked and stared at her. "I see. And . . . ?"

Inwardly, Laura cringed. She wanted to tell him what had transpired and explain that Gillian couldn't make exceptions for one nurse without the rest of them screaming about it. She felt that familiar clamping sensation around her heart and hesitated.

Her silence answered Eric's question.

"So I take it that means she said no."

Hoping to defuse the situation, Laura let her shoulders slump. "She said no."

"That woman!" He ran his fingers through his hair as he scowled. "Why does she have it in for you, Laura?"

His question surprised her. In the past, Eric had always been her champion. He might get angry but never *with* her. Recently, however, she had noticed a change. "I don't think she has it in for me . . ."

"Oh, come on!" Pushing off from the doorway, he crossed the room and sat on a stool behind the counter. "You've been complaining about how she's constantly on your case since she started. No one does that without just cause."

"Eric!"

"Or maybe you didn't even really ask her." He raised an eyebrow. "Did you?"

His words stung. She had never given him any reason to call her a liar. And even though she might have contemplated lying from time to time, she never did. And she knew why. There were two things in the world that she hated: liars and thieves. And her husband darn well knew that.

"I'm not even going to answer that question," she snapped.

The hurt look in her eyes must have been evident because immediately Eric softened his tone. "I'm sorry, Laura. Really I am. I wasn't thinking."

But she wasn't ready to so quickly let him off the hook. "Guess that makes two of us tonight."

He gave a soft, forced chuckle. "Touché."

When he leaned over as if to kiss her on the cheek, Laura pulled away.

"Be that way," he mumbled before turning to walk down the hall toward their bedroom.

Instinctively, Laura reached for her purse and began digging through it for her pills.

CHAPTER 9

On Friday morning, Laura pushed her medication cart into her patient's room.

"Good morning, Geri!"

The elderly woman was in bed, *The View* playing on the television that hung from the ceiling. But her eyes were barely open, and Laura couldn't tell if she was watching or had dozed off.

"You look better today than you did on Wednesday, that's for sure!" Laura left the cart near the door and walked over to the side of the hospital bed. She reached out and brushed some graying hair from Geri's forehead. Laura gave her a big smile. "But I suppose it's more important how you feel." She raised an eyebrow inquisitively. "So? How do you feel?"

She had specifically requested to take the woman's case during her shift. It was the fifth time Geri had hit the surgical floor after a bad fall on the ice last winter, which had resulted in a broken hip and, consequently, several surgeries to repair it. She was only seventy-five, but life had clearly not been too kind to her. She looked and acted almost fifteen years older. Just yesterday, she had had her hip replaced, hopefully for the last time.

"Horrible." Her voice sounded raspy and thick. The skin surrounding the IV catheter in the back of her right hand was black-and-blue.

"Well, let's get that taken care of." Returning to the cart, Laura took the hand scanner and stretched it over so that she could scan Geri's wristband. "You're due for your pain medicine."

"Can you make it a double?"

Laughing, Laura shook her head. "Unfortunately, we're not given the liberty of dispensing medicine." She winked at Geri. "But oh, if we could!"

"Darn it."

That was one of the things that Laura admired about Geri. Even though she was in pain and had a long road of physical therapy ahead of her, she managed to keep an upbeat attitude and joke around.

"But I think this should do the trick." Laura scanned the bar codes for the medicines that the doctor had ordered for Geri. "A little Percocet will take that pain away and, hopefully, help you get some sleep."

"More sleep? Bah!"

"Oh now, Geri! The more you rest, the faster you will heal." She handed Geri a small white paper cup with the assorted pills. While Geri eyeballed them, Laura poured some water into another cup and stood ready to hand it to her as well. "Or, if nothing else, a little nap will pass the time quicker. Unless, of course, you're a fan of *The View*."

"I hate it." Geri tossed back the pills and reached for the cup of water. "I just can't find that darn remote to change the channel."

Laura walked over to the sink and grabbed Geri's eyeglasses. She dangled them from her fingers. "You need these?" She didn't wait for Geri to answer. Instead, she put them on top of the tray table so that Geri could reach them. "See if that helps, OK?"

"Thanks, dear."

This was the part of the job that Laura loved. Interacting with the patients, tending to their needs, and solving the many problems that arose while they were under her care.

"How'd you sleep last night? You had a long day, didn't you?" Laura checked the IV drip while she talked.

"Terrible. Whoever that night nurse was . . ." Geri grimaced. "Her bedside manner needs some work."

Laura frowned. "What happened?"

"She came in like a wrecking ball, banging the cart against the bed and turning on the big lights. I thought a herd of elephants had barged through and God was taking me home!"

Despite Geri's story, Laura couldn't help but laugh at the way she told it.

"A small little whip of a gal," Geri said.

Why wasn't Laura surprised? Only one nurse fit that description.

"That must be Chelsea. She's new here."

Chelsea hadn't been working for too long, but already people were complaining. And not just the patients. Family members of the patients, too. She was curt and abrasive in dealing with them. Several nurses had begun to talk about it.

Laura laid a gentle hand on Geri's arm. "I'll speak to her about it. Can't have you thinking you're seeing the divine light before your time, can we now?"

"Goodness no! It'll come soon enough," Geri quipped and wagged a finger at Laura. "For all of us."

She'd have to leave a note for Chelsea since she didn't know when her next shift was. Or, perhaps, she should just alert Gillian. And then, on second thought, she immediately dismissed that idea. The less she had to do with Gillian, the better. At least for the time being.

Laura looked up to see Susan pop her head into the room and roll her eyes. "We have a situation in room 305 with Mr. Heinz. Can you give me a hand?"

Laura nodded. "Sure, I'll be right there." She knew Mr. Heinz was difficult and was glad that she wasn't assigned as his nurse. *At least there's that,* she thought as she followed Susan out the door.

Just then she felt her cell phone vibrate. She glanced at it and saw a text from Eric. He rarely bothered her when she was working, and for a moment, she panicked that something was wrong with one of the girls.

"Hang on, Susan. Text from home."

"Everything OK?"

Laura shrugged. "I hope so."

She leaned against the wall and opened her texting application.

Quick question. Did you figure out Christmas cards yet?
We need to add the Weavers to the list.
E.

Her lower left eyelid twitched and she pressed her lips together. He knew that she was at work. Why was he was texting her about Christmas cards, never mind the Weavers?

Laura could only imagine what had triggered that. *Count to ten, Laura,* she told herself. No sense getting into a fight with Eric if she could avoid it, especially over something as benign as this.

"Laura?"

She shoved the cell phone into the front pocket on her blue scrubs and looked up at Susan, who was poking her head out of Heinz's room. "Yeah?"

"Everything good at home?"

"Yup. Just perfect," she lied. No reason to air her dirty laundry, she reasoned.

Susan motioned with her hand. "Then can I get your help?"

Pushing off from the wall, Laura hurried into the patient's room. She'd deal with Eric later. For now, she needed to help Susan with her patient.

"Now, Mr. Heinz," Susan was saying when Laura entered the room. "You need to take these pills."

The elderly man glared at her. "I'm not buying into that pharmaceutical crap! Just solve everything with a pill. Probably what put me in here to begin with!"

"If you don't take the pills, we'll have to put in an IV." Susan's patience impressed Laura, but she could tell that the end was near.

"I know my rights! You're not sticking me with no IV and forcing me to take medicine that I don't need!" He waved his hand at Susan. "It's all a conspiracy!"

Susan gave her a pleading look and Laura sighed. Time to step in and help out.

"Mr. Heinz," Laura started slowly. "I can understand your concern and we can happily explain all of these medicines to you. I can assure you that there's no conspiracy. These are antibiotics, and you need them to fight off infection at the incision site. Do you understand that?"

He narrowed his eyes. "You're not a doctor!"

She felt her pulse quicken and bit her tongue to keep from saying something that would only make the situation worse. Instead, she nodded. "You're right, I'm not a doctor," Laura managed to say. "But I am a nurse and it's our job to follow the doctors' orders. And your doctor wants you to take this antibiotic."

She reached out for the white cup of pills that Susan held. Then she moved closer to his side and peered into the cup. "What's this? Two pills?" She raised her eyebrows. "Such a fuss over just two pills? Why, I thought there must have been a dozen in here!"

It was a strategy that sometimes worked.

She tipped the cup in front of him. "They aren't even that big." She gave a little laugh. "Do you really want us to contact your doctor about not taking these two small pills? Then we'll have to put in an IV drip, and that seems an awful lot worse than two small pills."

Slowly, his resolve broke and he took the medicine from her.

"Thanks for that," Susan said after they left Heinz's room.

"What? That in there?" Laura gave her a funny look. "Please. You'd do it for me."

Susan nodded and mumbled, "Darn Internet. Everyone thinks they're a medical expert. The worst are the conspiracy theorists. Pharmaceutical companies taking over the world, insurance companies denying care because they want people to die, doctors keeping people sick in order to always have patients."

Laura laughed. "Sometimes I feel that way about the insurance companies."

"And it's up to us, the lowly nurses of the world, to juggle managing the doctors' orders, insurance regulations, and patients' care, all without forgetting one single obscure instruction and while hearing how easy we are to replace." Susan shook her head. "I'll never understand why I love such an impossible job."

"Congratulations, Laura!"

At least her father appeared genuinely happy. And why shouldn't he be? After all, it was her college graduation.

"Thanks Dad." She let him embrace her, surprised to feel how thin his arms were. Between college and her part-time job, she hadn't had many opportunities to go back to Florida in the last four years. There was also the issue of dealing with her mother, who felt compelled to blame her for Rodney's decision to become a computer programmer, not a lawyer.

"Well," her mother said as she strode up to her. She wore a black dress suit with a black silk blouse. In addition to looking very corporate, it also made Laura think of a funeral. "You did it, didn't you?"

For a split second, Laura thought her mother was praising her. The way her mother stood before her, Laura even expected a hug. She almost made herself believe it. But when there was no hug, she knew that it had not been praise.

"And you really insist on working up here in New Jersey?" Sonya sounded as if Laura were going to work in a third-world country.

"Well, I have a job here in New Jersey," Laura replied, *forcing herself to remain calm, despite the way she felt trapped. Her eyes scanned the arena where the graduation ceremony had been held. Red exit signs were everywhere, but there were hundreds of people between her and them. Suddenly, she felt hot. Her red polyester graduation gown was making her sweat.*

"You never even asked me, Laura. You know I could have gotten you a job in any department at the hospital. It's not like you're a doctor. Nurses are easy to place." *Her mother leveled her gaze at her.* *"And replace. Remember that as you begin your nursing journey."*

Somehow Laura managed to take a deep breath and respond pleasantly. *"Thanks Mom. I'll remember that if it doesn't work out here."*

But Laura knew that she would never return to Florida, and she would never work in any hospital where her mother worked. Even with the horrid winters, New Jersey was paradise compared to any state where her mother resided.

"Hey. You all right?"

Laura looked up, surprised to see Susan a few paces ahead of her, staring in her direction. "Huh?" She realized that she had stopped walking. Frozen in place. "Oh. Yes. I'm fine." She shook her head and caught up with Susan. "I was just thinking about something. That's all."

But Laura knew that it *wasn't* all. And she knew that she *wasn't* fine. She felt as if she were spiraling out of control, heading down a dark well where all she could see was the shrinking light of the opening overhead. As the frequency of her panic attacks increased, so did their intensity. She was beginning to feel as if she might be going crazy, and the only thing that was helping her was Xanax. The last thing she wanted was to be anything like her mother, relying on medicine to keep her calm. But how much longer could she deal with an unhappy family, a demanding job, and increasing panic attacks?

CHAPTER 10

Tuesday was Laura's day off. But after working the night shift, it didn't seem like much of a day off. By the time she had returned home, it was almost eight o'clock in the morning and she was exhausted. Without even changing out of her scrubs, she collapsed into bed and slept until almost two o'clock.

The ringing of her cell phone awoke her.

She tried to ignore the annoying ringtone—Becky had changed it to sound like chiming bells—but when it began to ring for the second time, Laura reached out and felt along her nightstand for the phone.

"Hello?"

"Are you still sleeping?"

Laura lifted her free hand to her head and covered her eyes. "Hello, Mother."

"Let me guess. You worked the night shift again?"

This wasn't the way Laura wanted to wake up. Ever. "Only on Mondays, this month. It's not so bad."

Her mother scoffed. "Please, Laura. You work all night, sleep all day. You're like a raccoon, for crying out loud, and probably with the dark circles under your eyes to prove it!"

Laura almost laughed.

"So." Just that one word said it all. Right down to business. "I'm calling you because of your brother."

Just once Laura thought it would be nice if her mother called to check in and *not* because there was a reason.

"I'm worried about him."

Immediately, Laura sat up. "Is he OK?"

There was a momentary hesitation on her mother's part. "Well, yes."

"So what's wrong?"

Another long pause.

"Mom?"

"He lost his job. I think he's depressed."

Laura shut her eyes and sighed. "I'm sure it's nothing serious." Still, there was a bittersweet irony to her mother's concern that, in Laura's opinion, was twenty years too late.

"Well. Yes. I guess." She heard her mother sigh. "Anyway, I've tried talking to him. I told him I could speak to the hospital here in Jacksonville and get him a job in the technical support department. But he won't listen to me. He never has."

But Laura knew that was wrong. It was her mother who had never listened to Rodney. "He's established in Atlanta, Mom. His friends. His girlfriend."

Her mother scoffed.

"I'm sure he's fine, Mom."

"Maybe you could call him, Laura. Talk to him about getting a job here."

So that's what the phone call is about.

Over the phone, there was a faint noise of a door opening and birds chirping in the background. Laura suspected her mother had stepped outside. Of course. It was November. November in Jacksonville was nice. Unlike New Jersey. The thought of green trees and bright skies made Laura suddenly long for Florida weather.

"I'll call him."

Her mother remained silent.

Laura sighed. "I promise."

After hanging up with her mother, Laura sat on the edge of the bed and stared at the wall. She tried to still the ensuing panic attack. She wasn't certain whether it was because of her mother's phone call or the fact that not once during the conversation had her mother asked anything personal of Laura. While she knew better than to be surprised, she was disappointed all the same, especially since her mother was so concerned about Rodney.

Getting up, Laura made her way across the room to the dresser where she had set her purse. No sense in getting to the point where she couldn't breathe again. She took a Xanax and then wandered down the hallway toward the kitchen.

The light from the coffeepot was still on. Even though she knew the coffee would taste burnt, she poured herself a cup and stood at the sink, gazing out the window.

The trees were bare and the sky gray. It looked dismal, exactly how Laura felt at that moment.

In the house where she was raised, a house that was once filled with love, a place filled with the warm, doughy smell of homemade oatmeal cookies and nightly bedtime stories, Laura had lost a baby sister. And while she had never met the sister, for she had been born four weeks too early and unable to catch her first breath, Laura knew that was the moment when everything had changed, the moment when the heavenly blue skies and warm sunshine of her childhood had turned into a permanent winter for the Driscoll family.

"Edward," Sonya said as she marched through the door. "I've got wonderful news to share."

Hello to you, too, *Laura thought bitterly as she sat at the kitchen table, across from her brother, working on her English essay.*

"The hospital has offered me a promotion! Director of Human Resources!"

Laura watched as her father stood up and crossed the room to embrace his wife. "Congratulations! That's great!"

Laura noticed that her mother barely returned the gesture. Pushing away from her husband, Sonya stood there in her tailored suit and jacket with her three-inch-high heels that made her look taller and more sophisticated than Laura knew she was. Her mother lifted a perfectly manicured hand—French manicure, never any color—and touched her hair.

"Honestly, Edward. Is that all you can say? 'Congratulations?'" Her mouth twisted and Laura wondered if her mother knew how unattractive she looked at that moment. "'Congratulations,'" Sonya mocked. "As if I just won a spelling bee or school debate. This is bigger than just 'congratulations.' The increase in income alone will change our lives."

To Laura's horror, her mother's eyes fell upon her.

"And will help pay for Laura's med school."

Laura bristled at the comment but knew that arguing would be futile. It was a battle not worth fighting. Not yet anyway.

Sonya had never been the same after the stillbirth. Laura knew that, even though it had been several years now, her mother continued mourning the daughter who'd died. But what Laura never could understand was why her mother hadn't been able to love the children she did have. Even now, twenty-plus years later, Laura couldn't understand her mother's driving need to prove her value in the workplace while ignoring her maternal responsibilities.

An hour after Laura hung up with Sonya, an hour that gave Laura enough time to muster up her *own* long-lost maternal support for her sibling, she called. It rang twice before he picked up.

"Rodney?"

"Hey, Sis!" He sounded happy. He was always happy when they spoke, which made Laura feel guilty that she hadn't called him recently, especially now that she knew about his job loss. She had been too involved with her own life.

"Everything OK?"

"Yeah. Sure. Why?" He hesitated. "Let me guess. Did Mom call you?"

Laura leaned her head back on the sofa. "Yes."

He mumbled something incoherent.

"So? What's going on, Rodney?"

"Nothing." The happiness had disappeared from his voice. "Nothing that needs family intervention. If anything, it needs the opposite."

Laura didn't need to ask what he meant. She knew.

Distance. Less interference.

"I heard about your job."

He made a noise. "Yeah, well, that's life."

"Mom's worried about you. Says you're depressed."

This time, he laughed. "Seriously? She's not worried. She just wants someone to move back to Jacksonville to take care of her. Plus she wants to be able to control my every move."

"I don't think it's about control . . ."

"Did you grow up in the same household that I did? At least *you* stayed in the medical field. I turned out exactly as she predicted I would. A big, fat disappointment."

Laura exhaled. "That's not true . . ."

"I agree with you. Unfortunately, that's not *her* perception and we both know *her* perception is the only reality that matters."

"I'm sure that's not it," she heard herself say, even though that wasn't entirely true. "Besides, there *are* benefits to working at the hospital. And it's not like you'd have to live with her or anything," Laura added.

"Thanks, but no thanks."

"Well hey, I tried."

Rodney laughed again. "I knew she'd put you up to pushing that on me." There was a slight pause and it sounded as if he had shifted the phone to his other ear. "So how's everything going up north?"

"You know," Laura started. "Work is always crazy. I have a new nurse supervisor. She reminds me of Mom." She thought she heard Rodney chuckle. "And it's always something at the hospital. Doctors never prescribe enough medicine for pain management and . . ."

Rodney interrupted her. "What about the girls?"

"The girls?"

"Becky. Emily. You know, your daughters. My nieces."

Laura flinched. "I know who you meant, but I was telling you about work."

"I don't really want to hear about work right now."

This time, Laura felt the heat rise to her cheeks. How foolish of her to talk about work when he had just lost his job. "Sorry."

"Look, I need to go. But don't worry about me. I'll be fine, Sis. I'm not a kid anymore. You raised me well!"

She smiled at his joke, which they both knew was half true. "I know you'll be fine. Just keep looking for a new job—one that you'll really enjoy. Get up and put one foot in front of the other," she said.

He chuckled on the other end of the line. "OK, Mom," he quipped.

"I'm not like Mom."

"You're more like her than you think. You just don't know it yet."

After the conversation ended, Laura sat there in the silence of the living room, Rodney's words echoing in her head. No. She was nothing like their mother. In fact, she worked extra hard at *not* being like their mother. He was wrong. Dead wrong. She finally got up, knowing that her time was limited for completing household chores.

Hoping to clear her head of the haunting echo of his final words, Laura pushed Rodney's remarks into the shadows of her mind. Why on earth should she take anything that Rodney had to say seriously? He had no children and lived too far away for frequent visits. What could he possibly know about anything?

CHAPTER 11

"Room prep for 303."

One of the nurses dropped a folder onto Laura's desk. It plopped onto more folders and sent a lightning bolt of anxiety through her veins.

Another admit? This late? She hadn't counted on that. It was early Wednesday afternoon and she was scheduled to leave in two hours. She already had five patients. Between making her final rounds, updating her charts, and preparing her shift report for the next shift, she had enough to do. The last thing she needed was the addition of a new admit and all of the paperwork *that* entailed.

But Laura wasn't about to complain. Her time on the post-op floor had taught her that complaining didn't change anything. Patients still needed care. Somehow she'd find a way to get it all done and without shortchanging her patients of attention.

Laura merely sighed as she picked up the folder. "Thanks."

"She's coming up from surgery in another hour so you better get hustling."

An hour?

Laura pushed back from the desk and grabbed the folder. A quick glance told her all she needed to know. Post-op from a double mastectomy. She looked at the age of the patient and winced. The patient was only forty-two, the fifth young woman to hit the post-op floor to recover from breast-removal surgery that month. It was as if breast cancer were as contagious as the flu.

And while Laura hated seeing such pain—both physical and emotional—in the eyes of the women, she always thanked God that she dealt with their recovery and not their ongoing treatment. Often she wondered how many of her mastectomy patients made it to the five-year survivor mark, how many survivors did not make it to the sixth year.

Those were questions for which she suspected that she didn't want to know the answers. How anyone could be a nurse on the oncology floor was beyond Laura's comprehension. She had enough stress dealing with worrying about her patients' care. She couldn't imagine dealing with the level of stress that undoubtedly found its way on to the Chemo Cocktail Lounge or how those nurses could cope with the emotional loss when patients didn't get better.

A man hovering near the nurses' station tapped on the counter. "Excuse me?"

Startled from her thoughts, Laura looked up and smiled at the man. He was middle-aged and wearing a suit. Except that his tie had been undone and the first button of his shirt was open. From the worried look on his face, Laura knew he was a husband who was concerned about his wife. She had seen that look many times before.

"May I help you?"

"My wife? She's due for her pain medicine." He frowned at her and then glanced at the clock hanging on the wall. "Overdue, in fact. Could someone see to her?"

"Which room?"

"Room 310."

Laura forced a smile. It upset her when a concerned family member approached her about another nurse's patient. Though it would have been simple for her to reference the chart and assist their loved one, protocol forced her to defer to the assigned nurse unless it was an emergency. "I'll get her nurse."

The man rubbed his stubbly chin. "That's the problem, you see? I asked someone over thirty minutes ago. My wife is in a lot of pain." He sounded irritated. "Couldn't you help her?"

His eyes spoke of his worry, and Laura felt a strong wave of compassion. But still, her hands were tied. Hospital rules needed to be followed. "Unfortunately, that's not how it works. It has to go through her nurse," Laura explained with as much sensitivity as possible. She knew how it felt to see someone suffer and not be able to do anything about it. It was something she witnessed at least once a day on the post-op floor. "However, if she's unavailable, I'll see what I can do about getting something for your wife."

The man frowned, clearly unhappy with her response. "Please do."

As he stalked away, a wave of sorrow washed over her. She knew that each patient was the most important to *their* family, which made it hard to instill in the families that each nurse had more than just one patient to manage during a shift. It was equally as hard to feel torn between patients when they all needed the nurse's attention.

Laura glanced at the board and saw that Chelsea was covering that patient. Laura hadn't gotten to know her very well yet. From what little Laura could tell about her, Chelsea was a loner, one of several nurses on the floor who kept to themselves.

"Hey, you seen that Chelsea around?" she asked one of the nurses. The only response she received was a jerked thumb in the direction of another patient's room.

Quickly, Laura headed in that direction.

When she entered the room, Laura saw that Chelsea was changing a dressing on a middle-aged man. There was a distant look on her face, a complete disconnect with her task. Immediately, Laura felt bothered. She had seen that look before. Some nurses merely went about their tasks leaving out the most important part: actually *caring* for their patients.

"Chelsea, you need to head over to 310."

"Yeah, yeah. I know."

No emotion in her voice.

"Her husband's getting antsy."

Chelsea rolled her eyes. "I know that, too. He's been up my butt all day."

Laura glanced at the patient, relieved to see that he was sleeping, totally out of it, and hadn't heard what Chelsea just said. "Want me to finish up here?"

"Be my guest!" Chelsea tore off her gloves and tossed them into a garbage can. "I can't wait to get back on the night shift!" she mumbled as she walked by Laura without so much as a glance.

Laura shook her head, the bitter taste of distrust filling her mouth. She turned to the patient and, even though he was sleeping, she pressed her hand against his shoulder. "Don't you worry," she whispered. "I'll take good care of you."

Fifty minutes later, after finishing with Chelsea's patient and making her own rounds, Laura headed back to her workstation. She needed to update her patients' charts and get ready for that new admit who was due at any minute. But, for just one brief moment, Laura sat in her chair, trying to catch her breath. She hadn't even had time to visit the bathroom yet, and she really needed to pee.

"Hey! How about a nice pumpkin spice?" Susan called out as she approached the workstation carrying two coffee cups.

Laura greeted her with a smile. "You're here early for the swing shift."

Susan shrugged and handed her a cup. "Had nothing better to do."

Cradling the Starbucks in her hand, Laura inhaled the fresh aroma and shut her eyes. "You're a godsend."

"Nope. Just a nurse," Susan teased.

"Same thing." Laura sipped the drink, enjoying the warm, spicy taste of her favorite coffee as it slid down her throat. "Hmm. Good stuff."

"So, what'd you do yesterday?"

"Slept. What else?" Laura gave a small smile.

Susan set down her coffee and lowered her voice. "I'm sure you heard about the fireworks between Monica and Gillian."

Now this was news, indeed! "I've heard nothing."

Susan gave a soft chuckle. "Figures. You do tend to keep your head down when it comes to floor politics and gossip."

Laura wasn't so certain that was true, but she didn't bother to counter Susan's claim. Better to leave people thinking that, anyway. "What was it about?"

"Monica had it out with Gillian over the holiday schedule."

Laura squinted. "What? Still going on about Thanksgiving?"

"Not Thanksgiving. Christmas. Gillian distributed the Christmas schedules."

Laura groaned. Was that yesterday? Already? She had forgotten about it. "Don't tell me. I landed good old Christmas morning?"

Susan pretended to scowl. "Oh ye of so little faith." Then, with a laugh, she added, "No."

"Christmas Eve?"

"Wrong again. But let me save you from striking out. You're only on the schedule for Christmas night!"

Laura's mouth dropped. It took her a minute to comprehend what Susan had just told her. As a rule, everyone worked one of the three main—and dreaded—Christmas shifts: Christmas Eve night, Christmas morning, or Christmas afternoon. If Laura wasn't scheduled for any of those shifts and only had to work Christmas night, she wouldn't have to miss any of the holiday celebration with her family. *That* was a first.

"I'm shocked!"

Susan glanced over Laura's shoulder before whispering, "So were a few other people. I think you're the only one who missed the big three of Christmas."

Immediately, Laura tensed. "I didn't request off for any of those shifts," she said in a soft voice, secretly hoping that Susan would tell the other nurses. The last thing she wanted was for the other nurses to gossip about her or, even worse, be angry with her. Angry teammates meant that they wouldn't do their job as well, forgetting to change bedpans or leaving catheters to be changed. It was a passive-aggressive approach to punishing one another for breaking the unspoken code of nursing camaraderie.

"Don't sweat it. No one's said anything."

Still, the cloud of worry hung over Laura and she felt fidgety. Taking a few quick breaths, she tried to push away her anxiety and asked, "What about you? What did you land?"

"Christmas Eve." Susan shrugged. "It's no big deal. Our celebration is on Christmas Day so I'm happy. But, apparently, Monica landed Christmas Eve day and Christmas afternoon. She hit the roof. Especially since she's scheduled to work on Thanksgiving, too. She literally exploded at Gillian right there in the middle of the floor. They had to call security and Human Resources."

A chill went up Laura's arms. Goose bumps. "Security?"

Susan nodded. "Right or wrong, Monica overstepped her boundaries. Started screaming at Gillian in front of everyone."

"Patients?"

"And visitors, doctors, you name it."

Laura began to gently rub her arms. "So what happened?"

"Not sure. Probably got written up. Put on probation. Who knows?" Susan reached for her coffee and took a quick sip. "One thing I do know is that Monica definitely needs to stay off the radar for a while."

Laura glanced over Susan's shoulder, making certain that Gillian wasn't lurking nearby. "Not bad advice for all of us."

"Well, at least Eric should be happy with your Christmas schedule," Susan said, changing the subject.

The smile faded from Laura's face and a dark cloud seemed to pass over her. "Oh, sure. He'll be thrilled."

Susan tilted her head to one side as she studied Laura's expression. "*You* don't sound thrilled. Everything OK?"

For a split second, Laura almost forced a smile and said that everything was just fine. She wasn't used to sharing personal information with anyone except Eric. Yet, she knew that it was building up inside. Her panic attacks had been coming fast and furious over the past two weeks. If it wasn't her racing heart or constricting chest, it was her breathing. Sometimes her throat would close and she found herself gasping for air. And try as she might to not rely on the Xanax, it was beginning to be the only thing that calmed her down.

"I told you about Eric's big promotion, right? Well, he's going out tonight with a client, the one his boss handed to him two months ago. His client is trying to convince Eric to join one of those swanky golf and dining clubs."

"Something tells me you aren't pleased."

"Please!"

Susan laughed. "Yeah. I don't see you as country club material. You're not superficial enough."

Laura suspected that Susan was right.

Her mother stormed into the house, her cell phone still plastered to her ear as she tossed her Louis Vuitton onto the counter. "And I don't want to hear another word about that woman," she said angrily into the receiver. There was a moment of silence, and Laura suspected that whoever had been getting an earful from her mother was talking. Finally, her mother spoke. "Just get rid of her."

"What's wrong, Mom?" Laura asked when her mother finally ended the phone call.

Her mother turned, looking at her as if seeing her for the first time. "Nothing. Just club politics."

Laura cringed. Not the country club again. Fortunately, her father came into the room from his office.

"I thought I heard your voice, Sonya." He greeted her with a smile and a kiss on the cheek. "You sounded upset."

Her mother gave a heavy sigh and put her hand on her hip. "Of course I'm upset. That Meier woman is trying to start a domestic violence fund-raiser!"

Edward laughed. "And that upset you?"

Sonya's eyes narrowed. "First of all, you know that I'm the chair of the Events Committee."

How could anyone forget? Laura thought.

"She never even submitted a plan to the committee. She just booked the event. What nerve! And they aren't even golf members."

Laura shut her eyes and wished that she could just disappear from the room. Please God, she prayed to herself. Not another one of those tirades.

There was a hierarchy at the country club. To Laura, it sounded like the feudal system with landowners at the top and peasants at the bottom. And in her mother's eyes, anyone who wasn't a golf member was a peasant.

"And secondly, I run the breast cancer fund-raiser. Everyone knows that."

Despite the tightening of her chest, Laura heard herself speak. "Why can't you have both?"

From the way her mother's expression changed, Laura immediately knew she must have said something terribly wrong.

"Because, Laura," she said in a caustic tone, "October is Breast Cancer Awareness Month. And also for domestic violence. You can't have two fund-raisers in the same month." She returned her attention to Edward. "Regardless, it doesn't matter anymore. She didn't follow proper protocol. Her event is canceled now."

But that wasn't what Laura had overheard. Getting rid of an event was one thing. Getting rid of a person was quite another. And Laura knew that people who stepped on other people's toes were often quietly escorted to the door and their names wiped from the membership guides.

Laura frowned. "No, you're right. I'm not country club material."

"I guess it could be nice," Susan said. "Pools. Tennis. Great food."

"We can't afford it. Those places are expensive!"

"True."

"Anyway, Eric's only exploring the idea right now." Laura used air quotes around the word "exploring." "They were supposed to have lunch, but they changed it to dinner. He hasn't even joined the club yet and already it's coming between us."

"One night out isn't necessarily coming between you," Susan said in a gentle tone.

"Whatever. Hopefully he doesn't buy into that high-society-image crap." Laura finished her coffee and met Susan's gaze. "I can't see me hanging out at the pool all summer with all of the other golf widows."

"No, that I can't see." Susan laughed, her blue eyes crinkling into little half-moons.

"Laura, did you prep room 303 yet?"

Laura jumped at the sound of Gillian's stern voice. "Uh, no. Not yet. I'm doing it right now."

"Doesn't look like you're doing it. Looks like you're sitting at your workstation, chatting with Susan." She didn't wait for a response as she continued walking down the hallway.

Laura got up. "Guess that's my cue. Anyway, thanks for the coffee, Susan." She grabbed the chart from the desk and started toward room 303, making certain to swing by room 310 to double-check that Chelsea had fetched the patient's pain medicine. It would benefit no one if Gillian caught wind of Chelsea's flippant attitude and delay in caring for her patient. Although Laura's initial impressions of Chelsea were poor, everyone deserved a second chance. Didn't they?

CHAPTER 12

Something was wrong. Laura couldn't put her finger on it, but she could just tell that things weren't quite right. When she had arrived for her Sunday swing shift, she had met with Susan, the assigned day nurse for her patients, in the break room for an update and to sign off on the medicine counts. Everything seemed straightforward enough. Four patients: two recovering from open-heart surgery, one from stomach surgery, and another from a hip replacement. And Geri was still there, too.

After finishing her meeting, Laura began her first rounds to check on her patients.

"Well, good morning there, sunshine!" Laura swept into Geri's dark room and immediately went to the windows. *Why hasn't Susan opened them already?* she wondered. "How about a little light in here?" Laura glanced over her shoulder at the elderly woman lying on the bed. "Yes?"

Geri lifted her arm, just a little, and motioned toward the window. "Not too much, though. I'm so tired."

After shifting the blinds so that it was bright enough to not need the overhead lights switched on, Laura turned around and gave Geri a smile. "How'd you make out last night?" she asked. "Didn't you get any sleep?"

"Oh, pshaw!" The woman rolled her head on the pillow and stared at the wall. "Who can sleep in this joint? Why, that night nurse . . . what's her name? That petite little gal?"

Laura stood by the bed. "Chelsea?"

"That's the one!" Geri pointed a bent finger at Laura. "Sneaky one. She turned on the lights and tripped over the leg of that chair. I swear it was on purpose to wake me!"

Shaking her head, Laura clicked her tongue three times in disapproval. Even when taking blood pressure and temperature, there was no reason to startle the patients awake. Strike One for Chelsea.

"I'll speak to her," Laura promised as she leaned down and gently laid her hand on Geri's foot beneath the blanket. "Now, let's get you situated and then I can give you your medicine, OK?" Laura turned to the machine with the IV drip and pressed a button on it.

"Not a minute too soon," Geri said, trying to sit up but not having the strength. "Why, after all that ruckus, you know that Chelsea didn't even give me my pain med?"

Laura paused. "Excuse me?"

Geri nodded. "She scanned my bracelet and then left the room. Woke me up for nothing."

Surely she's mistaken, Laura thought. In all of her years working as a nurse, she had never heard of such a thing. If it were true, Laura would have to report her to Gillian. Strike Two for Chelsea.

She glanced down at Geri's thinning gray hair, thankful that her patient was more interested in fussing with the sheet than looking at her. Laura backed away from the bed and went over to the rolling computer station that she had left just inside the doorway. She pushed it farther into the room and pressed a few buttons before taking the scanner over to Geri. She smiled as she lifted Geri's arm and scanned her patient bracelet.

When Geri's chart came on to the screen, Laura glanced through the notes. Sure enough, Chelsea had checked on Geri at four o'clock in the morning. And, according to the report, she had dispensed the prescribed OxyContin to Geri.

Interesting.

Had Chelsea forgotten to actually give Geri the medicine, or had she dropped it, and fearing Gillian's rebuke, decided to just toss it? Laura knew that the night shift could be crazy. Even though there were no doctors or visitors, the staffing was lighter, and that meant more work. She understood forgetting things. She, herself, had noticed that she seemed a bit off in that department these days. And she could remember a few times when she had become distracted by something or was called away from a patient in the middle of administering medicine.

Still . . .

"Well, let's get that taken care of, shall we?" Laura said with a reassuring smile.

A few minutes later, after fetching some fresh ice water for Geri, she checked on the woman with the hip replacement.

"Good morning, Mrs. Turner. I'm Laura. I'll be your nurse today." She wrote her name on the whiteboard that hung on the wall beneath the television and then turned, smiling, to face the patient.

She was an older woman and rather frail-looking. Her cheeks were devoid of color and Laura thought she saw tears in her eyes.

"Hey, are you OK?" Laura rushed to the woman's side and peered into her face. "Tell me what's going on."

"Pain." Her pale, wrinkled fingers tried to move over the white blanket toward her hip. "It's . . . it hurts."

"On a scale of one to ten," Laura said in a gentle but firm voice, "one being barely anything and ten being the worst, how bad is it?"

"Twelve."

Laura gave the woman's shoulder a reassuring pat. "Let me see what the night nurse wrote down. But we'll take care of this."

She moved to the computer cart and checked the electronic file on the patient. Hopefully, Chelsea had updated Mrs. Turner's chart. While

Laura waited for the records to appear, she wondered why Chelsea hadn't mentioned something about the woman being in an unusual amount of pain. Usually, that was the first thing a nurse would mention when the shifts switched, and the outgoing nurse updated the incoming one.

The computer screen flashed and Laura glanced through the notes. The patient's records were up-to-date. Laura double-checked that Chelsea had given the woman her pain medicine only two hours before the end of her shift. Everything matched up. And yet, the patient was crying from pain.

"You took your medicine when the night nurse came in at six o'clock, right, Mrs. Turner?"

The woman gave a feeble shake of her head.

"You *didn't* take it?"

The woman moistened her lips. "No," she managed to say, her voice raspy. "She didn't come."

Laura frowned. While she wanted to presume that Mrs. Turner had merely *forgotten* that Chelsea administered the medicine—perhaps she had still been half asleep?—what were the odds that two patients had the same complaint about the same nurse? Strike Three for Chelsea.

"Let me contact your doctor, Mrs. Turner. I'll be right back."

Laura rolled her computer cart into the hallway, leaving it near the next patient's door. But rather than go into the room, Laura headed for the nurses' station. She leaned against the counter in front of Susan, who was bent over the computer keyboard at her workstation updating her patients' charts before leaving for the day.

Drumming her hands on the counter, Laura cleared her throat. "Hey, Gillian didn't pop in today, by any chance?"

Susan glanced up. "Nope. We lucked out this weekend. No unexpected visits."

"Crap."

"Something wrong?"

Laura wasn't certain how much she wanted to share with Susan. Yes, they were friends as well as colleagues. And Laura trusted her with almost anything. Not once in the years that they had worked together had Susan been anything but honorable regarding things Laura had told her in confidence. But Laura hadn't told her anything that was as serious as this. Perhaps it would be best if she limited the amount of information she shared. And yet, if anyone would know what to do, it would be Susan.

"Well," Laura began slowly. "I'm not sure. Two patients complained that Chelsea didn't give them the pain meds they were supposed to receive when she made her six o'clock rounds."

"No one said anything to me during my ten o'clock rounds." Susan frowned. "Which patients?"

"Room 311. Geri Nussbaum. And 313, Mrs. Turner, the hip replacement."

Susan returned her attention to the computer and pressed a few keys. Laura tried to peer over the top of the monitor but couldn't see anything from the glare of the overhead lights. However, Susan quickly found what she was looking for. "Well, it says here that Chelsea administered Nussbaum's." She tapped her finger against the screen. "And I personally signed off on the narcotic count this morning when I relieved Chelsea. Everything must have checked out against the records."

"Weird."

"Yeah, weird." Susan hit the "Escape" key on the keyboard, and the screen went blank. "You know, half the time, these older patients are still sleeping. They probably wouldn't remember getting their pain meds."

"Yeah, I guess you're right." Laura gave a soft laugh, even though she wasn't fully convinced. One maybe. But two?

Was it possible that Geri had been sleeping? She had been on the floor for over a week now and was scheduled to be released in another day or two. Her pain management was less critical since her surgery had been a while back. If a nurse had consciously stolen her medicine, it wouldn't be as noticeable. But what about Mrs. Turner? Her level of pain clearly indicated that she hadn't received any medicine.

Laura frowned at the thought of Chelsea stealing their OxyContin.

Oh, she had heard of such things happening at other hospitals. But if it had ever happened at Morristown, it had been kept quiet.

Still, Laura wondered if it was possible. Could Chelsea be so ignorant as to purposefully *not* administer medicine to a patient? Was a stolen OxyContin or two worth losing her job? Going to jail? What could possibly make someone whose entire livelihood was caring for the sick and injured stoop to such a low as to steal medicine from those in need?

CHAPTER 13

"There's no such thing as being late, Chelsea. Not on this floor."

It didn't surprise Laura that Chelsea didn't appear even remotely remorseful. "I don't report to you."

"You do when you're supposed to relieve me and take over my patients." Laura did her best to check her temper. "Being late won't win you many fans on this floor, Chelsea."

She wasn't certain why, exactly, she was so irritated. But she was. Maybe it was because of the whole pain medicine situation from Sunday. Or maybe it was Chelsea's blasé attitude about being late. Or maybe it was because Laura had just finished working the night shift—again—and she was tired. Exhausted. She wanted nothing more than to go home and collapse into her bed.

"You'd better hope Gillian doesn't catch wind of this," Laura warned.

Shifting her weight, Chelsea sighed. "Look, I've got two little ones at home and it's a real pain to get them up, fed, and ready for day care. That's why I prefer the night shift, OK?"

For a moment, Laura wanted to remind Chelsea that she, too, had small children and *she* managed to get to work on time. And while she could certainly commiserate with Chelsea, Laura knew *that* wouldn't teach Chelsea anything about being responsible to her job, her patients, and her colleagues. "You haven't been here long enough to know the ropes around here. You don't arrive late to your shift, Chelsea. And don't think nights are always so easy. They're just as demanding as days."

"Yeah," Chelsea said in mock agreement. "But quieter. With fewer interruptions and fewer people breathing down my neck."

Stunned, Laura watched as Chelsea stomped away, apparently unaware that the appropriate reaction would have been to apologize. Chelsea would never make it on the post-op floor. Regardless of whether or not Mary Mason returned from maternity leave, Chelsea was passing through a revolving door and the sooner, the better.

But that was Gillian's problem. For now, Laura had a bigger issue on her hands.

One of the patients on her floor had become infected with a bacterial infection. *Serratia marcescens*. At Gillian's request, everyone was keeping it quiet for now.

"Patient safety is our number-one priority," Gillian always told everyone who worked on her floor.

Now, however, a patient had developed a hospital-acquired infection.

It happened from time to time. Laura knew that. Staph infections tended to be the worst culprits, causing serious issues and sometimes even death. But *Serratia marcescens* was different. It was one of those opportunistic pathogens that didn't always respond to antibiotics. When the bacteria was caught from the environment, it could shut down the entire floor. So far, however, only one patient had come down with the fever and chills associated with the infection.

Laura prayed that it was an isolated case.

And yet, she couldn't help but wonder how, exactly, the patient had caught it.

Besides Laura, several nurses had tended to the patient since his arrival on the post-op floor: Monica, Chelsea, Rebecca, and Susan. Everyone knew about washing hands both before and after working with every patient, never reusing any equipment without sterilization, and immediately disposing of needles in the red containment system.

What bothered Laura about the infection was not just *that* it had happened but her suspicion of *how* it might have happened. Typically, it spread from hand-to-hand contact. But there was an alternative way: a needle puncture. Laura would never have considered that option except that the patient was on morphine. Something about that had seemed to bother Gillian. She had asked a lot of questions about who had administered it and how the bottles had been disposed of. While the questions weren't out of the ordinary, the way Gillian began restricting who dealt with the patient was a red flag to Laura.

Was it possible that someone on the floor might have taken some of the morphine and given the patient watered-down pain medicine with a dirty needle?

Just the thought made Laura sick. Who would do something that went against every principle of the health-care profession?

"Hey you!" Monica walked by and knocked her hip against Laura's thigh. "I know you want to get out of here, but Gillian called for a quick meeting before the night shift leaves."

That was unusual. Laura suspected that she was going to share the issue about the patient with *Serratia marcescens*.

Laura followed Monica into the break room, where Gillian stood toward the back, leaning against the counter, a stern expression on her face. Sitting down near the door, Laura glanced at her phone. It was almost 7:45 a.m. Her shift had officially ended fifteen minutes ago. If Chelsea hadn't been late, Laura would have been gone already, probably already pulling into the driveway. *Just one more reason to not like her,* Laura thought angrily.

Standing before the team of nurses, Gillian cleared her throat. "I don't know what's going on with narcotic counts." She paused and Laura saw her eyes scan the room. "There has been shrinkage, and I will *not* have that on *this* floor."

Laura shifted her weight in the seat and began to listen more closely. Shrinkage?

"The counts aren't right." Gillian narrowed her eyes. "Whoever is misappropriating any medicine, whether for their patients' needs or some other more sinister reason, will be caught and disciplined."

One of the nurses raised her hand and Gillian nodded at her.

"Can we at least do something about getting the doctors to respond faster? They're awful about returning our calls."

Immediately, Monica spoke up. "Or not being so stingy with the pain meds? I had a double mastectomy patient last week on ten milligrams of Oxy every six hours. It was ridiculous!"

One of the male nurses, Tyler, chimed in. "I had a doctor deny a Tylenol, for crying out loud!"

Gillian lifted her hand to indicate that no one else should speak. "I don't care if the person is crying in pain. No one . . . administers medicine without a doctor's orders. Not even a Tylenol. You know the rules. You know just as well as I do that taking extra pain medicine is against so many protocols that I'm not even going to list them."

Laura tried to block out the mumbling that was occurring around her.

"And I have spoken to Human Resources."

Silence.

"Anyone caught for shrinkage will be immediately terminated. End of story. No questions asked."

From the back of the room, Laura thought she heard someone gasp.

"And I can assure each and every one of you that there will be extra scrutiny on the narcotic counts, both before and after every single shift. The incoming nurse will review the charts and ensure that the counts match the inventory, both computerized and on paper. After that nurse signs off, the outgoing nurse will sign off. They will do it together. If there is a discrepancy, it needs to come to my attention." Gillian scanned the room once again. "Immediately."

"What happens if we drop something?" someone asked.

"Notify me. Immediately."

"What if we forget to scan a patient's band?"

"Notify me." Gillian crossed her arms over her chest. "Immediately."

"What if you aren't here?" That question came from Chelsea.

Gillian looked directly at the younger woman. "Call me. Immediately." She turned her attention back to the entire room. "And if you suspect that there is a problem," Gillian said in a loud, booming voice, "notify me." One more pause. "Immediately. Again, just to be absolutely clear, anyone caught stealing medicine will be terminated. *Immediately.*"

Laura took a deep breath. Everything involved notifying Gillian and everything was "immediately." Laura got the picture and tuned out. She just wanted the meeting to end. Why couldn't Gillian have circulated a memo? Nothing that Gillian said applied to her, anyway.

She glanced at the round white clock over Gillian's head. It was almost eight o'clock now. Laura needed sleep and not just because of the night shift. Ever since the new schedule had begun, she just couldn't sleep at night. And *that* was making her increasingly irritable, which, she suspected, was contributing to the increasing number of panic attacks. If only Chelsea had arrived on time, Laura would've been home in bed already, fortunate enough to miss this meeting. Instead, she was here, feeling herself getting more stressed by the minute.

Something had to give.

CHAPTER 14

Laura stared down at the envelope in her hand. It wasn't even officially Thanksgiving yet, and Debbie Weaver already had mailed out
her Christmas cards?

Laura almost chucked it into the garbage bin. But she knew that
Eric was friends with Ryan, and God forbid if Ryan asked if their card
was received.

Some people were like that.

Reluctantly, she slid her finger under the back flap and flipped it
open. To her surprise, it wasn't just a Christmas card but also an invitation to a holiday party. Not a Christmas party but a holiday party. Since
when did Debbie become so politically correct? She was, after all, a
weekly fixture in the front pew of Christ the King's picturesque church
in Harding with her husband on her left and her four children seated
to the right, the twins tucked in between her and her oldest daughter,
Molly, while little Kristen sat at the end of the lineup. A good Irish
Catholic family (even though her husband wasn't really Irish).

She dropped the card onto the counter and glanced at the clock.
Almost four o'clock. Eric would be home any minute.

Laura had picked up the girls after her shift ended earlier. They were
already fed and dressed in comfortable clothes for the trip. With the
holiday traffic for Thanksgiving, they had a long drive ahead of them,

and Eric wanted to leave as soon as he got home from work. If only she could spend more time with them before they left.

The front door opened and Eric appeared, as if she had just conjured up his presence.

"Hey, there!" he sang out as he shut the door and removed his coat. "Who's excited for the holidays?"

"Ho ho humbug," Laura mumbled.

He laughed and kissed the top of her head.

"You seem awfully chipper."

"Trust me, Laura. I'm forcing it. I miss you already." He opened the refrigerator, pulled out a bottle of water, and started walking toward the hallway. He paused and glanced over his shoulder at her. "The girls all packed?"

"Since yesterday." She motioned with her head toward the six bags behind the sofa. "I hope you have room for your own suitcase."

"They do know that we're only going for two nights, right?"

Three nights, Laura corrected him in her head. Seemed like a lifetime to her. While she had missed numerous holidays over the years, she had never before been left behind. Not like this. She was beginning to feel that familiar tightness in her chest. She waited until Eric disappeared into their bedroom to change from his suit before she hurried to the kitchen. Once she found her purse, tossed haphazardly on the floor behind the table, she dug inside for her prescription. It was almost empty. She needed to call the pharmacy for a refill soon.

"Hey, what's that?"

She looked up, surprised that Eric was back so fast. "Just . . . you know . . . I'm feeling stressed."

He walked over to her and reached for the bottle. Reluctantly, she gave it to him, watching as he read the label. "Xanax? What's that for?" He looked at her, his eyes studying her face. "Migraines again?"

Shaking her head, she held out her hand for the bottle. "No."

"Then what are they for?"

Laura took a deep breath, feeling a sense of relief when Eric handed back the bottle. "Panic attacks."

Eric winced.

"When did that start?"

When indeed? she wondered. She didn't have an answer for Eric and merely shrugged. "I'm not sure. A while ago, I guess."

He crossed his arms over his chest and leveled his gaze at her. "Why didn't you tell me you were having panic attacks?"

"I didn't know that's what they were." It was the truth. She had thought there was something wrong with her lungs or heart. That was why she had called for an appointment with the doctor. "And, you know, both of us *have* been a bit busy." She hoped that her ironic reminder would tamp down the situation, and by not bringing up the stresses of his promotion, she was actually doing him a favor. But, deep down, she felt terrible. Why hadn't she told him? The way he looked at her, his eyes turned down just a little at the corners when he arched his eyebrows like that. She hadn't wanted him to know because she didn't want him to worry, to think that something was wrong, or, even worse, that she couldn't keep it together.

But she knew that she had disappointed him by hiding this information from him.

"So what does the medicine do?"

"I don't know. Supposed to take the edge off of stress, I guess. I . . . I try not to take them."

"Good."

The way he said the word, flat and forceful, surprised Laura.

He pushed off the counter and leaned over to give her a chaste kiss. "You're a big girl. You can handle stress without relying on drugs. Besides, you have me, Laura. You need something, just ask."

Shoving the prescription bottle back into her purse, she changed the subject. "We got an interesting invitation today." She pointed toward the card on the counter. "Your buddy Ryan is having a holiday party on the second."

Eric reached over and picked it up. He examined the Christmas card—holiday card, Laura reminded herself—and then the invitation. "Do you know if you're working that night? We should try to go."

How did she know that he would say that? "I'm off on Saturdays in December, remember?"

"Great. You want to RSVP, or should I?"

Laura gave him a look.

"Right. I'll do it." He folded the invitation and pushed it into his back pocket.

"So how was work?" she asked. The typical ease-into-the-evening conversation starter. While she cared about her husband, she thought his job sounded rather tedious. Personally, she couldn't imagine spending her days sitting through endless meetings, working on reams of financial reports, and schmoozing clients at fancy functions.

No.

Despite the unavoidable chaos and stress, Laura much preferred her chosen profession. She thrived in that environment: constantly trouble-shooting, interacting with different people, never knowing what the day would bring. It certainly made the time go by faster.

"Great. I have to go to Chicago for a few days in December."

"It wouldn't happen to coincide with that holiday party, would it?" Laura pointed toward the invitation and Eric laughed. "I take that to mean no."

"I don't get why you don't like them."

She stared at him for a long-drawn-out moment before she responded. How could he possibly ask her that? "That whole country club scene reminds me of my mother."

"Ah." He leaned forward and planted a soft kiss on her forehead. "Gotcha."

"Daddy!" Becky ran into the room and flung her arms around his waist. Emily soon followed.

"When are we leaving?" Becky jumped up and down, her sparkle sneakers lighting up in flashes of pink, white, and blue.

"Can we watch a movie in the car?" Emily asked, waving a Disney DVD in the air.

Laura watched them and felt her heart sink. How could she be missing spending the holiday with her babies? She couldn't remember ever being alone in the house for an extended period of time. Nor could she remember being away from her children. Not like this. She felt as if her heart were breaking into a million pieces.

Once Eric extricated himself from their eager embrace, he told them to carry their bags to the car. Becky and Emily did as he asked, which gave him a few minutes alone with Laura.

"You know I feel terrible," Laura started.

"Don't. It happens."

That didn't help assuage her feelings of guilt. "But this is so important. I mean you're going to share your exciting news about the promotion, and I won't be there."

He took a step toward her and pulled her into his arms. With one hand wrapped around the small of her back, he reached up with the other and brushed the hair away from her cheek. "Maybe not physically, but I know you're there in spirit."

"That really doesn't make me feel any better."

He laughed. "Can't blame a guy for trying. Look, you and I can celebrate in January when Donald is officially gone and I'm officially the vice president with a vice-presidential salary! Maybe we can do a fabulous weekend in New York City, just the two of us."

"Ooo, that sounds nice," she murmured as she pressed her cheek against his shoulder. For a moment, she savored being that close to him.

"Besides, we'll be together when we tell Sonya, and that should make up for missing Thanksgiving," he said with a teasing smile.

At that comment, Laura did laugh. She could only imagine her mother's surprise that Eric was now upper management. Sonya never had been short of comments about how his profession was lacking in career advancements.

"Well, give them my best." She let him kiss her and tried to record the moment in her brain. She'd miss him more than she had imagined she would. Just knowing that they were leaving made her feel felt lost and alone. Unsafe.

As she watched from the doorway when the car pulled out of the driveway, Laura had a sinking feeling of abandonment. Only she knew that it wasn't them abandoning her, it was her abandoning them.

Shutting the front door, Laura sighed. Already the house seemed too quiet. Her eyes fell upon the sofa and she noticed that Emily had forgotten her favorite stuffed rabbit. She walked over to it, picked it up, and carried it to Emily's bedroom.

Standing at the side of Emily's crumpled bed, she leaned over to straighten the covers. She crossed her arms against her chest as she turned and left the room. The emptiness of the house seemed unbearable, and Laura decided that she might as well go back to the hospital. Maybe she could relieve some of the other nurses, let them take a few hours to visit with family. At any rate, it was better than sitting home alone and feeling sorry for herself.

It was after six o'clock when she arrived back at the hospital. As she headed toward the nurses' station, the first thing she noticed was that there wasn't a lot of activity, probably from a lack of fresh admits. From past experience, Laura knew that doctors tried to avoid surgeries on the Wednesday before Thanksgiving. It freed them up to travel and spend time with their own families. But the hospital still had patients who needed care and usually visitors who stopped in on their way to some other holiday festivity.

But today, the floor was unusually quiet.

The trays for supper had yet to be collected by the cafeteria staff, and there was a medical cart in the hallway, blocking the door to the women's bathroom. The nurses' station was empty, and the light outside of room 312 was blinking.

After setting down her purse at her station, Laura hurried to that patient's room. She poked her head into the room. "Everything OK?"

An older man looked at her. "I need to use the restroom."

Frowning, Laura moved over to where he lay and lowered the arm of the bed so that she could help him. "I hope you haven't been waiting long," she said.

"Ten minutes." He leaned against her and Laura held on to his IV drip, rolling it beside him as she guided him to the bathroom door.

She waited patiently for him, fuming the entire time. Ten minutes? Unacceptable. What would have happened if she hadn't been there? Would he have urinated in his bed? And that would have created more work for everyone, never mind the insult to the patient's dignity.

After seeing the patient back to his bed, Laura made certain that he was comfortable. She tucked the blanket around his feet and refilled his pitcher of ice water before she left him, curious to find out where all of the nurses were.

"You're back?"

Laura glanced over her shoulder and saw Gillian exiting her office and headed in her direction.

Laura tried to smile, hoping that it didn't appear forced. "I figured 'Why not?' Nothing else going on."

"Did I just see you leave that patient's room?" Gillian gestured toward room 312.

Laura nodded. "He needed the bathroom."

Gillian glanced around. "Where is everyone?"

Laura remained silent, leaving the question lingering between them.

Gillian appeared to realize what had happened. Her eyes narrowed and she stormed past the nurses' station and headed to their break room. Curious, Laura followed her. Gillian blocked most of her view, but Laura caught a glimpse of three nurses enjoying a leisurely coffee break. While Laura was surprised to see them neglecting their duties, Gillian's reaction bordered on outrage.

"What. Is. This?"

The nurses jumped to their feet and stammered as they tried to make excuses. But Gillian held up her hand and stopped them midsentence.

"Monica, are you aware that your patient in room 312 was trying to reach you? He needed to pee! Laura had to take care of him."

"Oh, I . . ."

Laura took a step backward. She didn't want Monica to think that she had complained about it.

Gillian's hands went to her hips. "And what about the rest of you? Don't you have enough to do?"

They scattered like squirrels, slipping past Gillian and returning to their duties. Shaking her head, Gillian turned around and looked at Laura standing near the nurses' station.

"I should write them all up," she muttered, partially under her breath.

Laura pressed her lips together and remained silent.

"What would you do?" Gillian asked suddenly.

Had Gillian just asked her for advice? Shocked, Laura took a moment to respond. "I . . . well . . . I don't know, Gillian. I mean . . ."

Gillian stood there, waiting for a response, which Laura found as surprising as the fact that she'd asked the question to begin with.

"A warning." Laura hoped it was the correct answer. She certainly did not want to get on Gillian's bad side by appearing too sympathetic with the nurses, but she also didn't want her colleagues to get in trouble. Her answer was the only compromise. "I'd issue a warning. They're good nurses. Having something on their record is rather severe. A little bit of compassion never hurts."

Gillian lifted her chin and studied Laura's face. "Compassion, eh?" She took a step toward Laura and leaned closer as she lowered her voice. "There's no room for compassion in my job, Laura. Just one display of compassion toward the nurses, they'd walk all over me. Don't you get it? It's not about compassion. It's about concern. Concern for teaching them how to be the best nurses possible. And you don't get *that* with compassion."

She didn't wait for an answer. Instead, Gillian turned and headed back to her office, leaving a stunned Laura staring after her, wondering about the difference between compassion and concern.

CHAPTER 15

One of the good things about working on Thanksgiving Day was that the visitors brought lots of food, drink, and desserts to the floor. Indulging in the different dishes that covered the tables in the nurses' break room helped Laura temporarily forget about missing her husband and children. By the time her day shift was almost over, Laura couldn't wait to go home and sleep off her food coma.

And, of course, there was the fact that Gillian was nowhere to be seen. She must have taken herself off the schedule for Thanksgiving. A perk of being the nurse supervisor—she was able to spend time with *her* family.

"Laura, did you try those brownies?"

She smiled at her patient. "I sure did."

The elderly woman gave her a warm grin. "My daughter made those from my own recipe. Best you'll ever have."

Laura checked the IV machine and pressed a button on it. It beeped loudly and made a whirling sound. "I believe that. That was really kind of her to bring them for the nurses."

"I raised her well." Despite the self-compliment, there was no indication of boasting in her words. It was a moment of reflection, not pride. "Not easy raising children to be good people. I feel for you young people. What with all that technology and social media whatchamacallit stuff." After a brief pause, the woman looked up at her. "You have children?"

"I do. Two girls. Six and eight years old."

The woman nodded her head. "That's right. You told me that two days ago." She tapped the side of her head with her finger. "My personal hard drive isn't working so good these days."

Leaning down as if conspiring with her patient, Laura whispered, "Mine sometimes crashes, too."

"Who takes care of them when you're working?"

"Well, they're at school usually."

The woman seemed to consider this. "That must be hard with your schedule."

Tell me something I don't know, Laura thought. "Oh, it's not so bad. When I work the day shift, I drop them off at school and pick them up when I'm finished. When I work nights, I get to tuck them into bed and give them breakfast the next morning." She double-checked the IV line and pressed a button on the machine. "It's the swing shift that takes me away from them, but they have their father. Gives them good bonding time."

The woman sighed. "I miss those days. Enjoy them while you can." She paused, gazing out the window. It was a sunny day, even though the bare, gray trees made it look as if it might be crisp outside. "You're missing Thanksgiving with them?"

Laura nodded her head. "I am. But they're with their father visiting his parents."

The woman patted Laura's arm. "I feel for you young women. In my day, we raised our children. Today, the world raises them."

Wasn't that the truth?

After finishing her rounds, Laura headed back to the nurses' station. Susan was already there, inputting some information into the computer system. Laura sat next to her and started updating her own patients' records. The truth was that she didn't mind working a twelve-hour shift today. Without Eric and the girls at home, she was glad to keep herself occupied. What else did she have to do?

"Hey, Laura!"

She glanced up at Monica, who was walking by with a fresh IV bag in her hands.

"Susan and I are heading to the pub after our shifts. Want to join us?"

Laura hesitated, perhaps for too long. After a full twelve-hour shift, the last thing she wanted to do was go out.

"Come on! Don't say no." Susan nudged her with her elbow. "It *is* Thanksgiving, after all."

Reluctantly, she agreed. "Maybe for one drink, I guess."

She felt her cell phone vibrate in her pocket. Glancing at the phone, she saw it was her mother. Her heart began to race. Had she really forgotten to call her mother?

Excusing herself, she made her way into the break room.

"Laura!" The sharpness of her mother's voice made Laura feel even worse about not having called her. "What is this? Don't you know how to call your own mother anymore? It was embarrassing, my guests asking how you're doing and I had to answer that I didn't know!"

Leaning against the wall, her back to the open door, Laura bent her head and lowered her voice. "I'm working, Mother."

She thought she heard her mother scoff. "Why am I not surprised?"

"So"—Laura chose to ignore her mother's comment—"how's your Thanksgiving?"

"Lovely. This morning I watched the parade, and this afternoon I had some friends from the country club over for an early dinner."

The mention of the club made Laura cringe. She realized that she hadn't heard anything about Eric's dinner with Ryan Weaver. She wondered if no news meant good news. "And Rodney?"

"Oh, please, Laura," Sonya said. "You think he'd come visit me for a holiday?"

Laura couldn't blame him.

"At least he landed a new job."

"Oh? That's great news."

"A computer tutor."

Laura shut her eyes. There was no mistaking the disdain in her mother's voice. "Well, at least it's something."

"Well, I'll be sending you my itinerary for Christmas. I hope you won't be working for *that* holiday."

"No, Mother. I'm not."

"Thank God for small miracles."

It was all Laura could do to get her mother off the phone. After hanging up, Laura made her way back to her workstation and reached for her purse. She needed a Xanax to take the edge off her palpitating heart. As she waited for the medicine to dissolve and slide down her throat, she checked the time. Less than two hours until seven o'clock.

Suddenly, Laura was looking forward to joining Monica and Susan at the bar for a drink. One drink, she told herself, and then she would leave. If she couldn't be with her family for the holiday, she could at least be in her own house where she could feel her family and be near their things. Emily's backpack. Becky's stuffed animals. Eric's pillow.

Two hours later, and not a minute too soon, Laura followed Monica and Susan into the dark pub on Pine Street.

A man sitting at the bar watched as they entered and made their way toward three empty stools. With a glazed look in his eyes, he was clearly drowning his sorrows and not celebrating the holiday. "Ah yes, here come those heavenly blues!"

Laura frowned and looked down at the front of her uniform as she slid onto a bar stool next to Susan. "I hate these blue scrubs! I have nightmares about being buried in them."

Susan laughed.

But it was Monica who leaned forward so that Laura could see her. "No, he means benzos. Valium, Ativan, Xanax. You know. Heavenly blues?"

Heavenly blues? Laura had never heard that term used before to describe benzodiazepines. "Why on earth would he say that about us?"

"Oh, for God's sake!" Monica waved her hand at Laura but directed her question to Susan. "Is she for real?"

Confused by the question, Laura looked to Susan for an explanation. Her friend merely shrugged. "Twenty percent of nurses are supposedly addicted to benzos or pain meds, Laura."

For a moment, Laura couldn't quite process what Susan was telling her. Twenty percent? Addicted? "That's awful."

"Yeah, it is. But nurses have the easiest access to the stuff."

Monica gave a stiff laugh. "We probably need it the most, at least after the patients." She waved at the bartender. "And you can always count on some idiot nurse to steal it and sell it. Apparently, that guy knows someone who does just that."

"Hence the name 'heavenly blues,'" Susan added.

Laura's mouth opened. "Are you serious?"

Susan laughed. "I don't know, but it sure makes sense. Blue scrubs, you know?"

The bartender interrupted the conversation and plopped three white cocktail napkins before them. "What'll you ladies have tonight?"

After he took their drink orders, Laura glanced around, noticing that there were plenty of people in the bar. Mostly younger people. They had probably spent their days with their families and had ventured into Morristown to reconnect with old high school friends who, like them, were home for the holiday.

Laura tried to convince herself that she wasn't any different. After all, she, too, was out with friends. It certainly helped her think less about missing Eric and the girls. As the bartender set down a glass of Chardonnay in front of her, she wondered if Eric was sitting with his family, enjoying an after-dinner drink and talking about his new promotion. And suddenly she was missing them all over again.

Fortunately, Monica distracted her by lifting her glass in a mock toast. "Here's to us, ladies. May Florence Nightingale be proud of our sacrifices."

"Hear, hear!" Susan tapped her beer glass against Monica's and held it out for Laura to do the same.

As she sipped her Chardonnay, Laura tried to relax. And why shouldn't she? Work hadn't been too crazy, the patients had been occupied by visitors, and the visitors kept the nurses and interns fed, that was for darn certain. Kudos to the family who had brought in aluminum trays of sliced turkey in brown gravy with another tray of sweet potatoes!

"Hmm." Monica took a sip of her drink and glanced at the television screen. "If I can't be with my family, I'd rather be here with friends."

"So I guess you kissed and made up with Gillian?" Susan asked.

Monica laughed. "Ha! Hardly. I'd never kiss her, and I suspect she'd never make up with anyone." She toyed with the paper napkin under her glass. "Not good to already be on Gillian's bad side. She hasn't even been there . . . what? . . . two months?"

"Seems easy enough to get on her bad side, though," Laura quipped.

Monica leaned forward and looked at her. "You're still here? You're quiet as a mouse," she teased. "Hey, did I tell you she wrote us up to Human Resources for yesterday?"

Laura froze. While she suspected that Gillian might do that, she was still surprised. "Unbelievable."

Susan's eyes opened wide. "What happened?"

Monica lifted her wineglass to her lips. "Gillian caught the nurses in the break room at the same time." She took a sip. "Honestly, I thought she had left already. And we hadn't even been in there five minutes. Why does all the bad stuff go in our file, and the good stuff earns us nothing more than an attaboy?"

"If that!" Susan said.

"I don't care so much for the attaboy," Laura offered, "as long as she just leaves me alone." She glanced at the plastic clock over the mirror behind the bar. Not even eight o'clock. She couldn't help but wonder what the girls were doing. Probably dressed for bed and watching a Disney video while Eric sat with his parents. They'd be drinking coffee and talking, maybe about everything that his new job would entail. And Laura wasn't there to share in her husband's joy and his mother's pride.

Susan nudged her. "Everything OK?"

"Hmm?" Laura started from her thoughts. "Oh, yeah. Just thinking about what my girls are doing." She took another sip of the Chardonnay. It was bitter and bland. Not to her liking.

"First holiday away from them?"

Laura nodded, despite not wanting to talk about it. Even though she considered Monica and Susan more than coworkers, perhaps even friends—although, between work and family, she didn't really have time for *close* friends—Laura preferred to keep most of her private life just that: private.

"I remember the first holiday when my husband took my daughters away." Susan gave her an empathetic smile. "It's hard, but I learned that I missed them more than they missed me."

Suddenly, Laura felt every ounce of relaxation disappear. She had never thought about her absence in such a way. She had just assumed that they would miss her. Constantly. Now as she realized that Susan was most likely right, she felt the onset of a panic attack. Why wasn't she with them? Recovering from the feast, curled up next to her girls, or splitting a last slice of pie with Eric before bed? It was just all so wrong. She couldn't pretend anymore that it was OK. Her anxiety came on fast and furious, causing Laura to remove her hands from the bar so that no one could see them trembling.

"I . . . I think I best get going. I need to call them before they go to bed." She reached into her purse to find her wallet. Instead, her fingers touched the prescription bottle. Heavenly blues, the man had called them. Despite the tightness in her chest and the tingling sensation in her arms, Laura ignored the bottle and found her wallet. She withdrew a crisp ten-dollar bill and set it on the counter.

Monica looked up, a confused expression on her face. "Already? We just got here."

But Laura knew that she needed to be home, not sitting at a bar, even with friends. "Another night. I'm beat." She smiled her apologies and slid off the bar stool. "See you ladies tomorrow?"

Without waiting for a response, Laura hurried outside and practically ran to her car. She opened the driver's door and threw her purse onto the passenger seat before she got in. After starting the car, she reached for her bag to find her bottle of Xanax. But it wasn't there.

"What in the . . . ?"

She flicked on the overhead light and searched her purse. Nothing. Cursing, she slammed her hands against the steering wheel and pressed her forehead against it. Now what? She had volunteered to work the morning shift on Friday so that another nurse could enjoy an extra day off after Thanksgiving. Laura had figured that if she was already home and without the kids, she might as well work. Plus, she'd get overtime and that would come in handy next month when she had to shop for Christmas presents. But how, she wondered, would she ever get through the day without her medicine?

Slowly, she opened her eyes and tilted her head, staring into her purse. And that was when she saw the bottle of pills on the floor, the lid open and a few pills spilled on the mat. *There is a God and he still performs miracles!* she thought as she leaned over and scooped up the medicine, popping one into her mouth before she dropped the rest into the bottle. She waited a few minutes, both for the car to warm up and for the medicine to kick in. A wave of relief washed over her, and with bolstered strength, she moved the gearshift into drive and headed home.

CHAPTER 16

On Sunday morning, Laura awoke early.

Eric and the girls had arrived home at eight o'clock the night before. Both girls eagerly told Laura about seeing a real Native American and about how small the Pilgrims' houses were. Eric had remained quiet, particularly so when Becky described the special desserts Aunt Christy had brought for Thanksgiving dinner.

Hadn't Eric said his sister wasn't going to be there?

When Laura glanced at him, he had averted his eyes.

Now as she sat at the table, nursing her coffee and staring out the window as the shadows of night faded into a blue-gray dawn, Laura wondered why he hadn't told her that Christy changed her holiday plans. Had he known beforehand? Or had she simply shown up unannounced? Even worse, the thought crossed her mind that her sister-in-law had decided to make the trip to her parents when she learned Laura had to work.

Almost without realizing it, Laura found herself reaching for her purse. Only when she had taken the Xanax and started to zip the inside pocket did she realize that the bottle felt lighter than usual. When had she started taking them to prevent panic attacks rather than stop them?

"Hey you."

Quickly, she withdrew her hand and pushed her purse aside as Eric strode into the room, his bare feet brushing against the floor. He reached for her coffee cup, took a sip, and then leaned down to kiss her cheek.

"Couldn't sleep again?" he asked as he made his way over to the coffee machine to brew a fresh pot of coffee.

She watched as he threw out the old filter and soggy grounds. "Nope."

"That's been happening a lot."

She shrugged, even though he couldn't see her.

"Everything OK?"

"Yup. Just fine."

As he opened the faucet, the noise from the water pouring into the coffeepot made her cringe. It was loud, breaking the peace of the morning that she had been trying to enjoy. For a moment, she resented his intrusion.

"You never mentioned anything about Christy going to Thanksgiving."

"I forgot."

Laura frowned. *I forgot?* "When did she decide to go?"

He poured the water into the back of the coffee machine. "What does it matter?"

"It matters to me."

"It shouldn't."

She clenched her jaw and shivered. Had he just dismissed her so easily? That wasn't like Eric at all. She took a deep breath, willing the Xanax to work faster.

"So anyway," Eric began with an exaggerated deep breath, "she was very pleasant, Laura. Congratulated me on the promotion." He paused before he added, "She asked after you several times and seemed genuinely disappointed that you weren't there."

I bet, she thought.

"Did you connect with your family at all?"

His question surprised her and snapped her back to attention. "Connect with them? You mean my mother? Do I ever connect with her?"

He gave her a look of reprimand.

"Yes, Eric. I spoke to her by phone." She stood up and walked over to the sink to rinse out her coffee mug.

"And?"

"And she's still coming for Christmas. No changes there, unfortunately."

He laughed. "She's not *that* bad."

"Yeah. Yeah she is." But Laura knew better than to try to justify her claim. He hadn't lived through it. He couldn't understand.

"You know, I was thinking . . ." He leaned against the counter and crossed his arms over his chest. He was staring at her, his eyes holding her gaze, and she knew he had something to tell her, something that had, most likely, come up during his visit to his parents. She braced herself.

". . . Maybe we should consider moving. You know, in the spring."

It felt as if someone had punched her in the stomach. Her knees almost gave out, and she had to clutch the side of the counter. "Move?" *Please,* she prayed. *Don't let this be happening!* "To where?"

"Not to where but to what." He smiled at her. "A bigger, newer house, you know?"

Her throat constricted and she couldn't swallow. But it didn't matter because her mouth was dry. "What's wrong with our house?"

He turned his head and looked around the room. "It's small. Not good for entertaining. And the yard . . . well, I'd love to have a really nice yard, you know? We could have barbecues in the summer. Invite friends over."

"What friends?"

"Oh Laura! We have plenty of friends."

"Like who? The Weavers?" She made a face and shook her head. They didn't have time for friends, at least not like that. She couldn't remember the last time they had entertained people at home. Occasionally hanging out with coworkers was one thing, but between work and family, they just didn't have time to cultivate friendships. And Laura preferred it that way. "Besides," she added, "I like our house."

"It's just an idea."

"It's a terrible idea."

"Terrible seems a bit overly dramatic."

She could tell that he was trying to sound light and casual, treating the topic—and her!—with kid gloves. "Eric, you know I'm not big into change like that. You know how everything changed when we moved to a bigger, *better* house. And for what? Just to appear grander than everyone else? To keep up with the Joneses? I never saw any of my neighborhood friends again and had to go to a new school. Besides, it's added stress and expenses that we don't need." She pushed away from the counter and walked to the coffee machine with her rinsed coffee mug. Even though it wasn't done brewing, she pulled it out and poured herself a cup of coffee. She needed the caffeine to wake up. She needed the mug in her hand to stop her hands from shaking. "Wouldn't it be nice to just enjoy your promotion and raise for a while? You know, without adding more onto our plates?"

He didn't answer.

"Look, I have to get dressed. I promised the girls I'd take them to the diner for breakfast when they wake up. You want to come?"

He shook his head. "Thanks but no. Enjoy your girl time."

"Don't forget I have the swing shift today."

"How could I forget?"

She cast him a dark, questioning look. Was he sulky because she'd shot down his idea about moving or was something else on his mind? Whatever it was, she wasn't about to get into another fight with him.

"Moving? To where?"

Her mother practically glowed with joy. "Not to where, but to what! A brand-new house in Ponte Vedra Beach! One of those gated communities!"

Laura wasn't certain what that meant. Nor did she care. "Will I go to the same school?"

"What? Oh. Of course not. You'll go to a new school—a better one!—on the other side of town near our new home."

Rodney made a face. "The other side of town?"

"The nicer side of town," Laura whispered.

"Don't get sassy, Laura."

"I don't want to move! I start high school next year. I'll have no friends."

Her mother gave a little laugh. "You can reinvent yourself, Laura. They'll be curious about you."

"They'll ignore me and hang out with their friends," Laura said tersely. "Friends they've had since kindergarten because they didn't have to move. No one likes the new kid."

The expression on her mother's face morphed. From joy to indignation. "If no one likes you, Laura, it's because you don't like yourself."

Their father coughed into his hand. "Sonya . . ."

"Don't 'Sonya' me," she snapped. "Just because Laura is so determined to resist change . . ."

Two months later, just weeks after the Driscoll family moved, school started and, as Laura had predicted, she began one of the hardest, loneliest years of her teenage life.

An hour later, Laura stood with her back against the refrigerator in the break room, staring over Susan's shoulder to make certain that no one approached. She didn't want anyone to overhear their conversation. But there was no one there except several computer technicians installing new wireless routers to increase the speed of the Wi-Fi for the patients. Everyone else was busy with their patients.

Susan stared at her, wide-eyed. "Again?"

"I'm almost certain of it now," Laura admitted, her voice low. "I mean, what else could it be?"

She hadn't expected such drama at work today. After taking Becky and Emily to the diner and then for a quick visit to see the horses at the county-owned horse stable on South Street, Laura had brought them home and headed for the hospital. She had actually been looking forward to a relatively peaceful shift. Usually, the weekend after Thanksgiving was quiet on the post-op floor, since doctors and surgeons were still on holiday with their families.

When Laura arrived, Chelsea briefed her on the patients, and they conducted their now-routine narcotic counts. Everything matched. But as soon as Laura began making her rounds, she noticed that two patients were in acute pain.

When she asked the patients about their two o'clock pain medicine that Chelsea had administered, both patients said that they hadn't seen Chelsea at two o'clock.

Laura had sought out Susan and confided in her.

"How do you know, Laura? I mean, this is serious stuff."

"Two other patients told me the same thing a couple of weeks ago."

Susan exhaled slowly. "So, you think she's stealing it?"

That was the question. Laura hated having such a suspicion about another nurse. It was a federal offense and could result in serious jail time. And yet the facts remained the same: medicine was missing.

"Not outright stealing it. Just not administering it."

Susan whistled under her breath. "Wow."

"Gillian was just talking about this."

"I know, right?"

"Wasn't Chelsea there?"

Laura tried to remember, but she couldn't picture Chelsea's face.

"No, I don't think so. But I heard that Gillian had the same meeting again on Friday."

With a deeply furrowed brow, Susan shook her head. "Then why would she do it again now? Right after Gillian said something?"

"That's the big question."

"An even bigger question, Laura, is what are you going to do about it?"

Despite Gillian's speech about notifying her "immediately," Laura wasn't certain what to do. She didn't feel comfortable. What if she was wrong? What if there was a legitimate explanation? Maybe she should just confront Chelsea, speak to her privately, rather than notify Gillian of her suspicions.

There were pros and cons to both courses of action. Professionally, Laura knew that she should let Gillian handle it. However, from a personal perspective, she didn't want to hang Chelsea out to dry.

"I don't know," Laura admitted. "What would you do?"

"I can't answer that for you." Susan gave her an empathetic look. "I'm not the one whose patients are complaining."

"I guess I'll tell Gillian," Laura said slowly. "I mean, morally and ethically, that's what I *should* do, right?"

Susan pressed her hand against Laura's shoulder in a friendly gesture of solidarity. But she remained silent, and before Laura could say anything else, someone called out for Susan. "Whoops! Gotta run." She took a step backward. "Keep me posted, OK?"

Laura sighed as Susan hurried away.

Stealing medicine from a patient, she thought. Over the years, she had heard stories but never suspected that one of her own patients might be victimized. With so much medicine around, it was easier than ever to obtain the narcotics. But was it really worth someone losing their job? And why?

That was the big question. If a nurse was having problems coping or facing anxiety, why steal medication? Wasn't it easy enough to get a doctor to write a prescription?

CHAPTER 17

On Wednesday, when she arrived at work and finished being briefed by the nurse signing off from the night shift, Laura was surprised to see Chelsea still lingering near the nurses' station. She didn't appear busy with paperwork, and her shift had ended already. On the few days when they crossed each other's paths during shift changes, Chelsea tended to race off the floor, clearly eager to get home.

Today wasn't one of those days.

Susan nudged her arm as if Laura hadn't noticed Chelsea.

"I see her."

"You going to say something," Susan asked, "or are you going to talk to Gillian?"

Laura sighed. "I guess I'll start with Chelsea. I mean, I don't know for a fact that she *stole* the medicine."

Susan made a noise, but Laura wasn't certain whether or not that meant that she agreed with her decision. But it was too late now. Even if she had thought that maybe, just maybe, she might do nothing and let someone else figure it out, Laura felt obligated to do something now that Susan had reminded her. Still, she was having a hard time with the idea of reporting a colleague to Gillian. *Everyone deserves a chance,* she reasoned as she reluctantly walked over to Chelsea.

"Hey, Chelsea, you got a minute?"

Chelsea glanced over her shoulder at Laura, her large chocolate-brown eyes and plump, pursed lips making her look even younger. Though she was a pretty girl, Chelsea's cheeks were breaking out, and she looked as if she had lost weight. But she always seemed to have energy, even after her shifts.

"What's up?" Chelsea bounced over to where Laura stood, a few feet away from the nurses' station.

"Let's go into that empty room, OK?"

Once they entered the empty patient room, Laura shut the door quietly behind them.

"Is everything all right?" Chelsea asked, her dark eyes widening.

"Maybe. Maybe not." Laura bit her lip. She hadn't expected to run into Chelsea today so she wasn't prepared to confront the young woman. She tried not to stumble over her words. "I thought I'd mention this to you in private."

"Mention what?"

Laura sighed and gave Chelsea a compassionate look. "Several of my patients have complained that they aren't getting their medicine at night."

"Really? Wow. That's odd."

"And it always seems to happen during your night shift."

Chelsea narrowed her eyes. There was a darkness about her expression that, for a brief moment, scared Laura.

God, she hated confrontations! Laura couldn't help but think that she never should've told Susan. If she had kept silent, she wouldn't have to say a word to Chelsea or Gillian or anyone. No one would've known what she suspected. A wave of anxiety washed over her, and Laura wished that she had her purse with her. She needed a Xanax.

The darkness did not leave Chelsea's face. "What are you trying to say, Laura?" She pursed her lips as if waiting for Laura to say something. When Laura remained silent, Chelsea put her hand on her hip. "Are you accusing me of not doing my job?"

"No." Laura dragged the word out for a long second. This wasn't going the way she had thought it might go. But what, exactly, had she expected? "That's not what I'm saying."

"Then what *are* you trying to say?"

Laura pressed her lips together, suddenly worried that she might have made a mistake. The way that Chelsea glared at her was convincing, and Laura began to feel guilty that she had ever suspected Chelsea of taking the medicines.

"Look, I'm not saying anything. I'm just suggesting . . ." That was a good word! ". . . that you double-check when you give patients their meds, OK?"

"Yeah. Sure." But there was still anger in Chelsea's voice and a rage in her eyes that frightened Laura.

Laura realized the mistake she had made. How would she have felt if someone accused her of taking patients' medicine? In hindsight, she should have just told Gillian what was happening and let her sort it out. Now Laura feared that she had made an enemy. And that was something she didn't need.

"I mean, you know, if the complaints get back to Gillian . . ." Laura stammered, feeling a constriction in her throat.

Chelsea rolled her eyes.

". . . Well, she might think something strange was going on, and that wouldn't be great for whoever is administering the medicine."

"Got it. Loud and clear." Chelsea crossed her arms over her chest and glowered at Laura. "Are we finished here?"

"I'm . . . I'm sorry if I offended you, Chelsea . . ."

"Well, you did!"

Now she really felt guilty. "That's why I wanted to talk to you in private, rather than alert Gillian. I mean, she'd go through the roof if she thought someone on her floor was taking medicines from patients. I'm sure you can understand how it looks."

"I think we're finished here," Chelsea snapped. She stormed out of the room, leaving Laura staring after her, her heart pounding and pulse racing.

Why couldn't Chelsea see that Laura had extended a hand in friendship? That Laura had been trying to help her avoid a problem down the road? Clearly, Chelsea wasn't interested in friends or people watching her back. Unfortunately, now Laura would have to watch her own.

Her hands trembled and she shoved them into her pockets, wishing that she had a Xanax in there so she could calm her frayed nerves and release that pressure in her chest. With her head down, she hurried out of the empty room and headed toward the workstation where she had shoved her purse into a drawer.

She fished around inside for the pill bottle and realized that she had just taken the last Xanax. She'd need to stop at the pharmacy for a refill. Using an app on her cell phone, Laura ordered the refill. She wouldn't be able to stop by after work today, but she could pick it up the following day before the girls came home from school.

Twirling around in her chair, she was only partially surprised to see Susan approach her. "I saw you leave the room after Chelsea stormed away. I take it that didn't go as planned?"

Laura looked up, but once their eyes met, she averted her gaze. "No. Not really." She paused, grabbing a pen and scribbling absentmindedly on a piece of scrap paper. "I don't know what I expected. Words of gratitude? A big warm hug and a thank-you?" Laura shook her head. "I feel awful. Maybe I was just plain wrong."

"She looked angry."

"What do you think?" Laura gave a quick, hostile laugh. "How would you feel if someone accused you of not administering pain meds?" She shook her head. "I'm so stupid," she whispered to herself.

"I don't think you're stupid," Susan said in a soft voice. "You did what you had to do. That's all."

But Laura wasn't so certain. The narcotic counts matched up. Wasn't that all that mattered? Instead, Laura had acted on a suspicion. And, even if she had felt strongly about it, there was something still bothering her.

"What if I was wrong?"

Susan shrugged. "What if? Look, it's up to us to hold others accountable to the nursing practice. It's our job to advocate on behalf of our patients."

Laura rolled her eyes. "The good old code of ethics."

"That's right." She nodded her head. "It doesn't hurt to review them once in a while, you know? Sometimes we have to do things that might not feel right, but that doesn't mean they are wrong."

The cell phone vibrated, making a rattling noise next to the desk phone. Laura snatched it and looked at her incoming text. Ah! A notification from the pharmacy. Relieved that they had refilled the prescription so quickly, Laura shoved the cell phone back without even reading the text.

"Can you do me a favor?" she asked, her voice lowered so no one could overhear. "I'm fighting a migraine and need to run over to the pharmacy in town."

"Why not just take some Tylenol?"

But Laura shook her head. "Imitrex," she said, shocked at how easily she had just lied. It was as if the words simply poured out of her mouth without her brain realizing what she was saying. "I need to pick up my prescription for it. Would you cover my patients until I return?"

"Of course."

"Just keep an eye on room 315. She needs help if she has to use the restroom. The others should be fine until I get back." Laura reached on the floor for her purse and swung it over her shoulder as she stood up. "Thanks, Susan. I owe you one."

Laura hurried to the elevators. Only when she heard the *bing* that announced its arrival did she begin to feel a little more relaxed. Just the knowledge that her prescription had been refilled—and faster than she had thought!—made her feel better. Sometimes that was all it took, just *knowing* that the orange prescription bottle was in her purse.

The pharmacy was less than half a mile from the hospital. She was surprised that there was a long line of people waiting. *Of course, just my luck,* she thought. Impatiently, Laura glanced at her cell phone, suddenly worried that she wouldn't get back soon enough. She didn't want to take advantage of Susan's kindness.

Ten minutes later, she made her way to the front of the line. By the time she approached the counter, any sense of calm had dissipated.

"Laura Reese. I just got a notification that my script is ready."

The pharmacist nodded and began riffling through some bins. When she stood up empty-handed, she frowned and walked over to the computer. "What's your birthday, please?"

Laura told her and glanced at the clock. *Come on, come on,* she thought. Maybe she should have just waited to pick them up the next day. Sometimes bad ideas were followed by worse ones. This was a perfect example.

"Uh, I'm sorry. We can't refill that."

Laura blinked. "Excuse me?"

"No refills."

"What do you mean no refills?"

The young woman moistened her lips nervously. "You need a new prescription from the doctor before we can refill it."

Laura stood at the counter at Walgreens, not caring that a line of people were waiting their turn. This was the last thing Laura wanted to hear. She had already waited twenty minutes just to get this far. *With Christmas coming, everyone probably needs refills,* she thought, only half jokingly.

Laura began to panic. "Could you try to call him?"

"We did."

"Did you speak to the doctor? Dr. Barton? Dr. *James* Barton?" Laura suggested. "Could you call again and ask specifically to talk to him?" The way she was beginning to feel, she would need another Xanax just to survive getting her prescription filled. What was preventative before was suddenly becoming imperative.

The pharmacist, a young girl with straight black hair and perfectly toned skin, sighed and reached for the phone. Laura could sense the irritation of the people standing in line behind her, especially the man with the three-year-old lying on the floor, crying.

Gotta wait your turn, buddy, Laura thought. *No special favors for dads with kids.*

While the girls were older now, or at least old enough to behave properly in public, Laura remembered how people would glare at her whenever Emily cried and carried on during too-long trips to Kings Food Markets or other public places. She also remembered the first time she witnessed Emily throwing a fit in public with Eric. Laura had sent them ahead to the checkout counter while she grabbed an extra jar of peanut butter. When she turned the corner, Emily was crying hysterically in the grocery cart. Not one person glared at him. Instead, the couple in front of Eric let him go ahead of them! When Laura approached the checkout line, she heard another person comment about what a trooper Eric was to do the food shopping for his wife.

"I'm sorry, Mrs. Reese," the pharmacist said. "They said you really need to call the office and schedule an appointment. They can't write a new prescription for this type of medicine without seeing you."

"What?!" Surely this was a mistake. "That's ridiculous."

The young woman gave a slight shrug and glanced at the man with the crying child, an unspoken cue for Laura to move out of the line so that other customers could be served.

Furious, Laura hurried out of the store and to her car.

Insurance companies. Certainly that was why James wanted her to come into the office. Anything to save a buck, including prescription medicines. She wondered how many people didn't bother to get refills when told they had to see the doctor first.

Despite her racing heart and a slight twitch along her jaw, Laura knew she had no choice but to return to the hospital. She'd finish her shift, get home to have a nice supper with the family, and she'd call James's office first thing in the morning, making an appointment to see him before the night shift started. Surely she could make it through one night without relying on anxiety medicine. She'd done it before, and it appeared she had no choice but to do it again.

CHAPTER 18

Laura sat on the examination table, her legs dangling down the side as her eyes darted from her cell phone to the clock on the wall. She hated wasting time coming to the doctor's office just for a prescription refill. Why couldn't James just call it in? That's what he'd always done when she'd needed prescriptions in the past. Laura tossed her cell phone into her purse and crossed her arms over her chest.

That morning, she had contacted his office. When the receptionist informed her that James was booked all day, Laura almost considered seeing another doctor, but, at the last minute, she changed her mind. James knew her and her situation. The last thing Laura wanted was to explain everything to a stranger.

After demanding to personally speak with James—resulting in five minutes of listening to terrible on-hold music—he finally answered her call.

"I'm in a bind, James," she had said. "I need my prescription refilled, and the pharmacy said I need to come in."

"No problem. I can always find time to squeeze in an old friend."

Laura had looked upward and mouthed the words *Thank you* to the sky.

But now that she was there, sitting on the examination table and waiting, Laura felt more on edge.

She'd been sitting there for over five minutes. James was late. While she knew that she should be grateful that he had managed to fit her in, he could at least be on time! All she needed was one little prescription.

Irritated, she began to tap her fingers against her leg. She had things to do, such as pick up the girls after school, help them with homework, make supper, and then, after she put them to bed, get ready for work. Her last night shift of November! A cause for celebration if there ever was one.

The door opened and James walked in.

"Good afternoon, Laura!" He smiled at her, his dark eyes sparkling as he extended his hand to shake hers.

She breathed a sigh of relief and, just like that, her irritation disappeared. "Thanks for seeing me, James."

He looked the same as when she had first met him at Rutgers. In hindsight, Laura often wondered if during their years at school he'd had a crush on her. Despite his good looks, James hadn't caught her eye. It had been Eric, a junior when she arrived at school, who captured her attention and, eventually, her heart.

"So, what brings you in here today?"

Startled by the directness of his question, she blinked twice. Hadn't anyone taken notes when she had called and made the appointment? Didn't he remember talking to her less than six hours earlier? "The pharmacy wouldn't refill my Xanax prescription, remember? They said that I had to see you again. You know, when I tried to refill my script."

Again, James nodded. He leaned against the counter, both hands on the edge, and watched her. "That's right. I wanted to see you first."

Silence.

He had told the pharmacy she needed to come in? Laura began to feel uncomfortable under his steady stare. This wasn't like James. Something was on his mind, and he didn't seem to be certain how to broach the subject. But Laura didn't have time for a guessing game.

"How's everything at work, Laura?"

"Work?"

He nodded.

"Well, Thanksgiving was tough. I had a twelve-hour shift and Eric had to take the girls to Massachusetts for a few days without me."

James winced. "That's gotta be tough. Not being with the family for the holidays."

"Forget the holidays. It's hard juggling the kids' schedule with my work when the schedule keeps changing," she admitted. "And let me tell you, Gillian really stuck it to me in November. That might have been the worst schedule yet."

He gave a soft laugh. "How is dear Gillian? She's bothering you, eh?"

"She can be tough to work for, that's for sure."

While James wasn't a surgeon, he did have patients that he some-times visited on the post-op floor. Laura suspected that he knew Gillian or, at least, about her. "Yeah. She can be tough as nails." After a short pause, James tilted his head in a thoughtful way. "Ever think about putting in for a transfer? To a different department? Just a thought."

Another long moment of silence. Laura felt her heart begin to pal-pitate and her palms became sweaty. She needed to get out of there, fill her prescription, and fetch the girls.

"How are you sleeping at night?"

"Sleep? What's that?"

He waited for her to respond.

"Not so good. I've got a lot on my mind."

He took a deep breath and pushed off the counter, standing straight. She hadn't remembered how tall he was. Even as she sat on the exam table, he towered over her. "Here's the story, Laura. I'm concerned."

Laura narrowed her eyes and made a face. "About what?"

"You seem to have a tremendous amount of anxiety in your life. I'm sure you saw that your blood pressure was a little elevated, and you've lost a bit of weight."

"We're an obese nation. Everyone needs to lose weight," she quipped.

But he wasn't buying her lighthearted remark. "Have you thought about seeing someone? You know, like a therapist or psychologist? Maybe a psychiatrist to have a more thorough evaluation?"

Inwardly, she groaned. She didn't have time for a therapist. Between work, taking care of the house, mothering the girls, and trying to be a halfway-decent wife, there were already too few hours in the day. Was it any wonder that her blood pressure was elevated?

"I'm just on overload, James. That's all. This is the first time that I've asked for a refill."

"True, true." As he leaned against the counter, he stretched out his legs and crossed his arms over his chest. "The problem, Laura, is that Xanax is highly addictive."

And there it was. The real reason.

Immediately, she felt better. She even laughed. "Is that it? James! Please. It's me you're talking to."

"I know who I'm talking to."

She didn't appreciate the steady and stern look that he gave her. "If it makes you feel any better," she said slowly, "it's the first refill! If I was addicted, I'd have been in here long ago!"

He raised an eyebrow and studied her expression.

She tried not to react, but she felt uncomfortable. What, exactly, was he trying to say? She suspected his unspoken message and resented having to explain herself to him. "I'm not addicted to Xanax, James. I'm a nurse, for crying out loud."

"Xanax is *highly* addictive, Laura," he repeated.

"But not for everyone."

"You are under a lot of stress."

"Of course I'm under a lot of stress! I'm a nurse! I have a tough-as-nails new boss! I have a family! The holidays are around the corner! Should I continue?" Of all people, he knew what it was like working at the hospital. "Look, I really have to get going. Are you going to write that prescription for me or not?"

For a long moment, he said nothing. Instead, he remained focused on her face. Finally, he sighed and reached for his blue prescription pad. "I want you to try this, instead."

As soon as the words came out of his mouth and registered in her brain, she felt as if the walls were closing in on her.

He scribbled something on to the pad, and tore off the paper to hand to her.

She took it and looked at what he had written.

"Buspirone?" It was a different kind of antianxiety medicine, one that was not as fast acting as Xanax. Stunned, she looked up at him. "Seriously?"

He nodded. "Seriously, Laura. It's much safer in the long run and it's nonaddictive."

"Buspirone can take up to a month to work!" She couldn't wait that long. "The holidays! My mother!"

He chuckled. "Yes, your mother."

"She's coming for the holidays. Talk about stress!"

"Just give it a try, Laura."

She stared at him, pleading with her eyes. "James. You've met my mother. Remember? Graduation? You know what she's like. I can't survive a visit from her!"

He tapped his pen on the side of his prescription pad. "If it helps, I'll give you a prescription for a few Xanax. That should hold you over until the Buspirone kicks in."

She sighed. "Thank you."

"What do you think? Five?"

Her mouth opened. "She's coming for five days!"

James raised an eyebrow at her protest. "That's one a day, Laura. Sounds perfect to me."

It didn't feel perfect to Laura but she knew better than to argue.

"Fine." She hoped that her voice didn't sound as disappointed as she felt. "But I'm not addicted to them."

James scribbled another prescription on his pad. After he handed it to her, he stood up and placed his hand on her shoulder, squeezing it gently. "Try to relax a bit, Laura. And let's get you back in here after New Year's. See how you're feeling then." He paused and gave her a warm smile as he opened the door, the signal that their time together was over. "And send my regards to Eric, OK? Haven't seen him in ages. We need to get together one night. It's been too long."

Laura watched as he walked down the hallway, and then she glanced at her cell phone. As she suspected, she'd only have time to drop the prescription off at the pharmacy if she was going to get home in time to meet the girls at the bus. Then she would shift into mommy mode, helping with homework, and fixing their supper, and, after, putting them to bed. Then she'd have to get ready for the night shift. She'd just have to pick up the medicine in the morning.

Great, she thought, as she shoved the prescription into her purse and headed for the door. Already her chest was tightening. She'd have to take it on the chin and pray that the Buspirone worked. If it didn't, she didn't know what she would do.

CHAPTER 19

An hour later, Laura sat at the kitchen table, sipping at a cup of coffee as she stared at her open calendar. The month of December was filling in. Quickly. Between work, holiday gatherings, and children's parties, Laura didn't know how she'd manage to juggle everything.

The new December schedule would begin the next day. Somehow Laura had lucked out. Three swing shifts and two day shifts per week. She couldn't remember not having a night shift for an entire month. She couldn't have asked for a better schedule, except for the fact that she didn't have an excuse to miss Debbie Weaver's party on Saturday night. *Talk about bad luck,* she thought.

If that wasn't stressful enough, then there was Eric's company party, Emily's cookie swap, and Becky's Girl Scout holiday party. And, of course, she couldn't forget about her mother, who was arriving on the Friday before Christmas.

Laura shut her eyes and sighed.

Her mother.

Merry Christmas indeed.

Just the thought made her anxious. There was no amount of Xanax or Buspirone that could help her with *that* visit.

"Mommy!" Emily ran down the hallway and turned into the kitchen, a paper in her hand that she waved excitedly. "I forgot to give this to you."

"Oh? What is it?"

Laura reached for the paper and saw that it was a letter from the school. She scanned it and took a deep breath. A holiday concert. Fortunately, it was during the early afternoon on a Friday when she worked the swing shift. *Thank God for small miracles,* Laura thought. She might have missed Thanksgiving, but she drew the line at disappointing her girls for school events.

Somehow she'd have to squeeze in Christmas shopping before then.

"You'll come, right?" Emily spun around, her skirt flaring out and her arms over her head like a ballerina. "I get to dress like an elf!"

"I'm sure elves don't dance like that," Laura said.

"But you can come, right?"

Laura leaned down so that she was eye level with her daughter. She stared into Emily's face, seeing the bright eyes that waited, so anxiously, for an answer. "I wouldn't miss it for all the reindeer in the world!"

"Even Rudolph?"

"Especially Rudolph!" She hugged her daughter. "His bright nose would keep us up all night."

Emily laughed as she squeezed Laura's neck. "You're the best mommy in the whole wide world."

The weight of Emily against her chest and the warmth of her arms around her neck made Laura's heart swell. She breathed in the sweet scent of her daughter's hair, enjoying the smell of lavender that reminded her so much of innocence and purity. "Well, I don't know about that, but I sure do try." She enjoyed the embrace for another long moment before she pulled back. "Now, how about you help me make supper? Daddy will be home soon and he'll be so proud that you helped!"

"OK!"

Standing up, Laura glanced toward the kitchen doorway as she went to the refrigerator to pull out the hamburger meat she had thawed earlier that day. "Where's your sister?"

"Becky?"

Laura managed to find the energy to laugh. "How many sisters do you have? You hiding a spare one in your room?"

Emily giggled as she grabbed a stool from the counter and slid it across the floor so that she could help her mother cook. "She's in her room. Crying."

Immediately, Laura faced Emily. "Crying? What's wrong? Is she sick?"

With a little shrug, Emily crawled onto the stool and, after sitting down, began swinging her feet. "I dunno. Maybe it's that boy who keeps bugging her on the bus."

Bugging Becky? Laura hadn't heard about this. But Emily said it in such a way that it seemed like she should have known. "What boy?"

"Michael."

"Michael? Michael Dannon?"

Emily shook her head emphatically. "He moved, Mom."

Somehow Laura suspected that she should have known that. "Then who?"

"Michael Stevens."

The name didn't ring a bell. Still, if Becky was crying in her room, it must be bad. Becky wasn't a crybaby. Laura couldn't help but wonder why Becky hadn't said anything when they got home from school.

Concerned, Laura hurried out of the kitchen and headed down the hallway to Becky's bedroom. To her surprise, the door was shut. And locked.

Softly, Laura knocked on the door. "Becks? You OK?"

She thought she heard some sniffling before her daughter answered with "Uh-huh."

"We're going to make supper now." Pause. "Spaghetti. Your favorite. Want to help?"

"No thanks."

"Could you open the door, please?"

The sound of soft footsteps padded across the carpet on the other side of the door. Within a few seconds of fumbling at the doorknob, Becky opened the door, hiding her face from her mother.

"What's going on, Becks?"

"Nothin'."

Laura leaned against the door frame. "Doesn't look like nothing." She reached out and touched Becky's chin, lifting it so that she could see her daughter's face. "What in the world?"

There was a small bruise and scratch on her daughter's cheek. Laura felt her chest tighten, and she had to take several deep breaths in order to stay calm.

"I'd like to know what happened, Becky." This time, Laura's voice was firm. Neither of her girls kept secrets from her.

A tear rolled down Becky's cheek and she took a step backward. She looked down at the carpet and sniffled. "Michael Stevens hit me."

"Someone hit you?" It was all that Laura could do to remain calm. "A boy?"

"Uh-huh."

"When?"

"On the bus."

Laura clenched her teeth and felt that familiar throb in her temples. The bus. It was always the bus. "Who is this Michael Stevens?" Laura heard herself ask, surprised at how calm she sounded when, inside, she felt crazed.

Becky sniffled. "A fifth grader."

Laura grimaced. Oh, that stupid Morris School District with their combined busing system. It had been nothing but a problem for years. Even before Laura's girls attended public school, she had heard other people complain. The older students were supposed to sit in the back of the bus while the smaller children had assigned seats right behind the driver. It was an imperfect system because the bus drivers couldn't keep their eyes on both the children *and* the road. And sometimes older children picked on the younger ones.

"Why didn't you tell me?"

Becky shook her head. "I'm not allowed to tell you."

Laura frowned. "Why not?"

"Because he told me not to tell."

Kneeling down, Laura took hold of Becky's arms. "Well, *I'm* telling you to tell me. And I outrank Michael Stevens."

"He stole my backpack," Becky cried, sobbing onto Laura's shoulder. "And he took my pencil case and broke it. I wasn't supposed to go back there, but I did. He scratched me when I tried to pull it away from him."

Laura didn't need to hear the rest of the story. Every nerve in her body was on fire. How dare anyone touch her daughter! She tightened her hold on Becky and soothed her as best she could. And while Becky cried, Laura felt as if she, too, might cry. It was her job to protect her children. The realization struck her that she had been fooling herself to think she could shield her children from the evils of the world.

"I'm so sorry, Becks," she whispered.

"I don't want to ever ride that bus again!" Becky sobbed.

Even if the school reprimanded the fifth grader, they'd never revoke his transportation privileges. That was just how the school district worked: practicing equal rights for both the troublemakers and the victims alike.

"Don't worry, sweetheart. You won't have to ride the bus, OK?"

Now she'd have to drive the girls to school even on the days when they normally would have taken the bus. One more layer of logistical detail to fit into their already full-to-bursting schedule.

Thank you, Michael Stevens, she thought resentfully, still holding Becky and wishing she could erase her daughter's pain.

CHAPTER 20

The next day, Laura was just about to finish the first rounds of her Friday swing shift when Tyler poked his head around the corner of her patient's room, his hand on the door frame to support himself.

"Gillian wants to see you."

Surprised, Laura looked up. "Why?"

"How would I know?" And with that, he disappeared.

Great. The last thing she needed was Gillian on her back.

As she wheeled her cart into her last patient's room, Laura reached into her pocket and wrapped her fingers around her prescription bottle. She could feel the onset of an anxiety attack, but she knew that if she took one of the Xanax, she'd only have four left. However, the heart palpitations were coming on fast and furious. If it continued, she feared she might faint. Reluctantly, she took one of the pills, rationalizing that it was better to be prepared for the worst than to suffer. After all, when Gillian called someone into the office, it usually meant problems.

"How are we doing today?" she asked the patient.

"My hip aches." The woman looked pale with dark circles under her eyes.

Laura walked over to the bed and placed her hand on the woman's arm. "That happens when you have a hip replacement."

Looking at Laura with pleading eyes, the woman said in a soft voice, "I really could use something for the pain."

Laura felt her breath catch in her throat. *Not again.* Trying to contain her anger, she quickly ran through the charts, even though she knew what she'd find. Sure enough, Chelsea had administered the woman's last pain medicine. Only it wasn't OxyContin or Percocet, but Vicodin. The woman was supposed to get two pills.

Feigning ignorance, Laura began to put the blood pressure cuff around the woman's arm. "Didn't your last round of pain medicine kick in?"

To Laura's surprise, the woman nodded. "It did, but it wore off quicker than usual."

Hmm. This was new.

"But you took them, right? Both of them?"

At this question, the woman shut her eyes and shook her head as a single tear trickled down her cheek. "Just one. Was I supposed to get two?" She moaned before Laura could answer. "It's really bad."

Laura started the machine; the whirling noise of air being pushed into the cuff filled the room. "I'll call your doctor," she said, avoiding the question that the woman had asked. "We'll get you taken care of. The trick is to stay on top of the pain, not race to catch up with it."

Fifteen minutes later, with great apprehension, she stood outside of Gillian's office and knocked on the door. She wasn't certain how she was going to broach the subject.

"What is it?"

Laura opened the door just a crack. Peering inside, she saw Gillian staring at her computer monitor. "You wanted to see me?"

"Yes, Laura." Gillian gestured for her to enter and take a seat. "Let me finish this. One second."

For a few long-drawn-out moments, she watched as Gillian typed something, her fingers flying over the keyboard, the noise a distinct clacking sound that irritated Laura. She let her eyes wander, scanning the walls with the numerous framed awards that Gillian had received over the years. The small office was not cluttered with any personal items. Laura realized that she didn't know one single thing about the woman seated before her, not outside of work anyway.

"OK." Gillian clicked her mouse and pushed her keyboard to the side, turning her attention to Laura. "I need your help."

That startled Laura. Gillian had never asked anyone for help. Usually, she just told people what to do, when to do it, and how it needed to be done. "Sure," Laura replied slowly. "Just ask."

Nodding, Gillian reached for a manila folder on her desk. "Apparently Mary Mason was on the interdepartmental committee to organize a holiday party for the children's center." She tossed the folder at Laura. "Only she neglected to inform me that she hadn't completed her tasks for the committee before she left on maternity leave." Gillian scowled and shook her head. "I just learned about this."

Laura's surprise turned to dismay. *Please don't assign this to me,* she prayed. "And you want me to do what?"

But her prayer was too late.

Gillian gestured at the folder. "We need to organize a gift drive. Get the other nurses involved, get the patients' families involved. We only have . . ." She glanced at her calendar. Laura shut her eyes and took a deep breath. The party was almost always held the day before Christmas Eve. She didn't need to look at a calendar to know what Gillian was going to say. "About three weeks."

"I . . . I don't know . . ."

Gillian exhaled and leaned back in her chair. "I know you have your own family to deal with. This isn't exactly great timing. For either of us. But I couldn't think of anyone else on the floor who could actually get it done."

A compliment? Laura wondered if she had misheard Gillian. On the one hand, she was flattered that Gillian considered her the only one capable of doing a project like this in such a short amount of time. On the other hand, she didn't need more stress, especially now that she had to drive the girls to school every day.

As she took the folder, it felt heavy in her hand. She hoped that it wouldn't be too time-consuming or, at least, that Gillian would lighten up her patient load. She'd need to concentrate on this new assignment during work hours, and she was already up to her eyeballs in patients.

"Do what you can," Gillian said. "All of the information's in the folder. We need to supply baked goods, gifts, and a volunteer or two to help distribute the presents to the children." She reached for her glasses and pushed them over her nose. "It shouldn't be too demanding, and if you encounter any resistance, just let me know." She returned her attention to the computer, mumbling something under her breath about Mary Mason's head being in a fog.

Clearly, the meeting was over.

Laura stood up but didn't move toward the door. Not at first. She waited for Gillian to notice that she hadn't left the office.

"Yes? Is there something else?"

Nervously, Laura moistened her lips. She still didn't know what she was going to say. "I . . . I need to ask for your advice."

Turning away from her computer, Gillian gave Laura her undivided attention. But she made no motion for Laura to sit back down.

"I have this patient," Laura began slowly. "A hip replacement. She had her medicine two hours ago, but she's out of her mind with pain. I didn't want to talk to the doctor without coming to you first . . ."

Gillian pressed her lips together and shot Laura a dark look. "You need advice? On this? Laura, you call the doctor. What do you want me to do about it?"

Laura swallowed. "I . . . uh . . . I was hoping you could advise me. I mean . . . well, this has been happening a lot recently . . ."

But Gillian interrupted her. "Call the doctor. I can't do a darn thing about it and you know it. And I'm tired of hearing you nurses whining about doctors skimping on pain medicines."

"It's not just that," she stammered. "I . . . I don't think you understand. This woman is literally crying and the chart says that Chelsea administered her pain med, but . . ."

Gillian sighed and leaned back in her chair. "Look. You know as well as I do that the doctor will never authorize more Oxy before it's due. You know the protocol, Laura. If the narcotic isn't working, you contact the doctor for approval to administer acetaminophen."

That wasn't the answer that Laura had wanted to hear. She wanted to clarify that she wasn't complaining about the doctors but about something else. But Gillian hadn't let her finish talking.

"I'm surprised you'd even bother me with such a simple thing," Gillian said, returning her attention to her computer. "I consider you one of the stronger nurses on the floor."

Despite the compliment, Laura was disappointed. She had thought Gillian would have shown more interest in the patient's care, especially after her speech the other week about shrinkage and monitoring the narcotic counts. If only Gillian hadn't interrupted her, had let her finish talking. Clearly, Gillian hadn't understood that Laura was trying to alert her, that she wasn't just complaining about the doctors under-prescribing, but that the shrinkage problem on the floor had just emerged again, and this time with one of Laura's patients.

Deep down, Laura knew that Gillian cared about more than just management issues. When Laura's patient had caught that bacterial infection, Gillian's interest in and constant follow-up on the situation had surprised Laura. Hospital-acquired infections were not unheard of, but Gillian had taken a great interest in that particular case.

Back at the nurses' station, Laura contacted the doctor and received approval for the Tylenol. After updating the patient's chart to indicate the conversation with the doctor's office, Laura went to retrieve her computer cart. Even though it was just Tylenol, Laura still needed to scan the patient's armband in order to administer the medicine.

"What did Gillian say about the hip replacement?"

Laura looked up, surprised to see Chelsea still hanging around the break room. Her shift had ended over an hour ago. "Huh?"

Chelsea gave her a stern look, as if Laura should have been able to read her mind. "You know, the woman with the pain?"

Laura frowned. Had Chelsea seen her go into Gillian's office? And why hadn't she left yet? "Oh, uh . . . Tylenol."

Chelsea slung her backpack over her shoulder, the hint of a smug look on her face. "That's what I suspected she'd say. Nothing."

Stunned, Laura watched as Chelsea sauntered down the hallway toward the elevators. Her cavalier attitude was shocking. If Laura had doubted it before, she now knew exactly what Chelsea was doing. And, apparently, Chelsea was aware of that. It was just as apparent that Chelsea felt above the law, that she could get away with it. But Laura knew that she was wrong. It was only a matter of time before Chelsea's world came crashing down around her. Laura only hoped that she wasn't there when it happened.

CHAPTER 21

"Mommy! Your phone's ringing!"

"Just leave it, Becks." Getting ready for the Weavers' party had put a damper on Laura's mood, and the last thing she wanted to do was talk to anyone. She'd call whoever it was later.

Becky appeared in the doorway, the phone pressed against her ear. "Hang on, Granny. She's right here." She held out the cell phone. "Here you go, Mommy."

Laura stared at the phone and then at her daughter. Granny? Her chest tightened. "Thanks," she mumbled as she reached out for the phone.

"Hello, Mother."

There was a slight hesitation on the other end of the line. And then that all-too-familiar nasal voice. "Laura. You'd think you lived in another country. Would it kill you to call your mother once in a while?"

"Good to hear from you, too." Laura leaned against the counter, eyeballing the almost-empty prescription bottle in the open drawer. Despite wanting to take a pill, she was trying to ration them. Disgusted, she hit the drawer with her hip and closed it. "To what do I owe the pleasure of this call?"

"Christmas, Laura. It's about Christmas."

For a brief moment, Laura hoped that her mother was canceling.

"I think it's best that I stay at a hotel."

Laura almost breathed a sigh of relief. She wouldn't have to worry about her mother complaining about sleeping in one of the girls' bedrooms. Things were starting to look up.

"And not that shabby Best Western place, either."

Laura frowned. "It's not shabby. It's actually very nice."

"The Hyatt suits me better."

"Whatever works for you."

"Have you checked your schedule with the hospital, Laura? I certainly don't want to come all that way to find out you're working the entire time I'm there."

It was the tone. The tone of disapproval.

"I do have to work some of the time, Mother. I'm a nurse, after all."

"You don't have to remind me."

"Sick people need care, even on Christmas."

"There's no need to be impertinent, Laura."

She needed to cut this conversation short. She could tell her mother was in one of her moods, and that only meant the phone call would not end well. "Look, I have to run. We're getting ready to go out. To a holiday party." She hesitated before adding, "With country club people."

"Oh?"

Laura dug into her purse, hoping that by some miraculous gift from God she might find a Xanax that had fallen from the bottle. But she found nothing. Frustrated, she shoved her purse on the floor. "That's right. They want Eric to join."

She thought she heard her mother catch her breath. "A country club? I hope you aren't wearing those god-awful blue scrubs!"

Laura shut her eyes and leaned her head against the wall.

Why had James insisted on prescribing that stupid Buspirone? It wasn't helping. Not one bit. What, exactly, was he trying to prove to her? She would have paid for the Xanax out of her own pocket. Screw the insurance company and their stupid rules! What did *they* know anyway? They weren't medical professionals!

"Please, Mom. You know I have *some* class."

"You know doctors make their rounds in suits. At least they did when your father was in the hospital for his bypass. Why can't nurses dress in nice business-casual attire?"

"I'm wearing a dress, Mom. A black dress."

"Thank God!" And then her mother hesitated. "Do these people even *know* that you're just a nurse?"

"Mother!" The way her mother had stressed the word "know" had sent a chill down Laura's spine. If she had said "convicted criminal" or "pedophile," there could have been no deeper disdain in her voice.

"Well, nurses aren't your typical country club fare."

It was all that Laura could do not to throw the phone across the room. "Then I guess it's good that they're courting Eric and not me!"

"It's a wonder how either of you could afford a country club. Especially in New Jersey."

"Sorry, Mom. I gotta run. Talk to you soon." Laura didn't wait for her mother to respond. Instead, she pushed the big red button at the bottom of her phone and slammed it down on the counter.

Thirty minutes later, as Eric steered the car down a dark road lined with large houses, Laura still felt on edge from her mother's phone call.

"I still don't understand why, exactly, we have to go to this thing," Laura fussed. "Can you explain it to me again?"

"Because it's the holidays. Because we were invited." He glanced at her as he parked the car on the side of the road. "And because you look beautiful and I want to show you off."

She scoffed at his flattery. "In other words, because you told me we're going."

He smiled at her. "That, too."

"Well, you know I'm only going along with this because I love you," she said as she opened the car door. "I really despise this Weaver woman."

"*Despise* is a strong word, Laura." He got out of the car and walked around to help her out. "You don't know them well enough to actually *despise* them."

She laughed.

"Besides, you only met Debbie once and she had an off night. Give her a second chance."

They walked along the street, already lined with other cars. Laura's high heels clicked against the pavement. "By the way, I forgot to tell you that my mother called tonight."

"Really?" He sounded genuinely surprised. "What was the special occasion?"

"I'm not exactly sure. We didn't get much further beyond how I shouldn't wear blue scrubs to a holiday party hosted by snobby country club people."

She smiled when she heard him chuckle.

"I trust you told her that you are wearing a very, very sexy black dress," he said in a low voice. "With amazing heels that make your legs look like they go on forever."

She leaned against his shoulder as she walked, enjoying the husky undertone of his voice. "I left out the high heels part. She would've gone into cardiac arrest that I wasn't wearing sneakers."

"I bet!" He laughed and she joined him.

At least she was laughing. That was a good start to the evening.

Maybe Eric couldn't understand why she was always so self-deprecating about herself, but Laura did. She had always felt uncomfortable when her parents dragged her and Rodney to fancy restaurants or events at the country club. Her mother always made certain everyone was impeccably dressed. But the robe did not make the king, and Laura had never fit in with the other teenagers that her mother forced her to interact with.

But tonight, Laura knew that she could certainly stand her ground with the Weavers and their friends. Her formfitting dress showed off her figure. And the fact that she didn't spend her summers playing tennis or drinking mojitos by the pool meant that she didn't have any premature aging on her face or hands.

Half an hour later, as Laura stood to the side of the room, she looked around and realized that she didn't know one single person in the entire house except for Debbie and her husband. And, from the looks of most people who were there, Laura had nothing in common with any of them. The men congregated in another room while the women stood in small groups, laughing as they knocked back red drinks in tall-stemmed martini glasses. Cosmos. From the Lilly Pulitzer dresses to the big-name shoes that Laura doubted were knockoffs, each woman looked more pretentious than the next.

When they had first arrived, Laura had stayed by Eric's side. He had the advantage of knowing a few of the men who greeted him as they walked into the main room. When Laura was introduced to their wives, she'd smiled and wished them Merry Christmas. A few women asked her if she was ready for the holidays or if they were traveling over the winter break. But that was the extent of the conversation. Meaningless small talk among strangers she would, undoubtedly, never meet again.

But all of that changed when Eric excused himself to slip into the other room where some of the men were watching a football game.

Bored, Laura wandered over to the bar and let the bartender make her one of those fancy red drinks.

"Here you are," the bartender said as he handed her the trade-marked posh martini glass, the bottom of the stem wrapped in a red cocktail napkin embossed with a big silver W. Somehow Laura doubted that Debbie had found those napkins at any store.

"Laura?"

Startled to hear her name, Laura turned around. Debbie stood with several women and waved for her to join them.

"I want you to meet some of my friends," Debbie said in her high-pitched voice. Laura remembered far too well that the more Debbie drank, the higher her voice got. By the end of the night, she'd probably be screeching.

But, like Eric had said, Laura needed to give her a second chance. So Laura forced a pleasant greeting, despite knowing at once that she had next to nothing in common with these women.

After introducing her, Debbie leaned over as if to tell them a big secret. "Laura's a nurse."

Immediately, Laura forgot about second chances and began plotting her escape.

"Oh really?" a bulimic-looking woman said, lifting her glass to her lips for a healthy sip. Laura was glad to see that her lipstick was bleeding up her lip lines. "At Saint Barnabas?"

Strike One, Laura thought. People always acted as if Saint Barnabas was such a high-class hospital. It was always the first hospital people presumed she worked at. "No, Morristown."

The other women nodded their heads and made the obligatory noises of feigned interest.

"How do you manage that with children? You have two, right?" Debbie asked. "I mean, those shifts . . ." She left the sentence dangling in the air. But Laura knew what she was insinuating.

"I suppose I manage just as well as the other nurses." Laura forced another smile as she swallowed the anxiety that was building in her throat. "Teamwork, you know. Eric helps out when I have late shifts."

"Do your children go to Peck?"

Laura frowned. Peck? "No. Woodland." When one of the other women, Jen, made a face as if trying to place the school, Laura saved her the pain. "They attend public school."

From the expressions on their faces, Laura knew that was the wrong answer.

"We contemplated sending our son to the public school, but when I heard he'd have to attend Hillcrest Elementary . . ." Jen smacked her lips together in disapproval. "Well, we just couldn't have that. So off to Catholic school he went."

Curiosity got the best of Laura. "What's wrong with Hillcrest?"

"Kids from Mount Kemble Avenue or Burnham Park neighborhoods are zoned for that school. I don't want my son hanging out with them."

Laura took a deep breath and quickly counted to ten. She scanned the room, hoping to catch sight of Eric.

"And that junior high school!" Jen shook her head. "Such a disgrace."

"Frelinghuysen?" Laura felt her chest tighten, and she had to work hard to keep her tongue in check. "They have a great curriculum."

"It's just so . . ." Jen struggled for the right word, which Laura suspected was "diverse." Fortunately, Jen settled on "big."

"And what will you do for high school?" another woman asked, glancing at Debbie. "The drugs at that school are just terrible. I heard there's even a meth problem."

"Every school has drugs," Laura countered. "And I can assure you there's no meth problem. I'd certainly have heard about *that* at the hospital."

Conveniently, Debbie shifted the conversation to her own children and their school Christmas pageant, which was being held at the same time as the annual country club golf dinner.

"I suppose you'll have to figure *that* out next year," Debbie said, laughing gaily as she sipped her drink.

"What do you mean?"

"Why!" Debbie's eyes opened wide. "You'll be golf members and have to make those same choices!"

"Excuse me?"

Debbie linked her arm through Laura's. "You do know that Ryan and I are sponsoring you and your husband, don't you?"

Laura stared at Debbie with a blank expression. Her breath came in short gulps, despite her best efforts to remain calm.

"Why, you're the newest member! Welcome to the golf club!" Debbie lifted her glass and the other women did the same. Reluctantly, Laura raised her own, all the while feeling as if she might explode.

She glanced around the room. But Eric was still in the other room with the men, watching that silly football game. That, too, aggravated her. How could he have just abandoned her, especially when he should've known Debbie might mention the country club?

Laura clenched her teeth and took the break in the conversation as the perfect opportunity to excuse herself.

"Where might I find your restroom?" she whispered to Debbie. She needed to splash cold water on her face and take some deep breaths. She'd deal with Eric later. There was no reason to make a scene.

When Debbie pointed to the stairs, Laura couldn't ascend them fast enough.

She took a moment to catch her breath at the top. Laura had to get away from those women. Her heart was racing and her arms felt as if a thousand needles were pricking her. And she could hardly breathe.

She found the bathroom and locked herself inside. For a long moment, she stood at the sink, wondering how on earth she could escape that house as soon as possible.

It didn't bother her that she didn't fit in because she worked and her children went to public school. No, what bothered her was the air of superiority held by those women about working mothers of public school children.

She had to get out of there.

The soap bottle was empty and Laura glanced around, looking for another. When she didn't see any, she opened one of the cabinets.

Towels. All neatly folded. She shut the door and opened another cabinet. She glimpsed the orange bottles on the second shelf, and for the briefest of moments, she felt palpitations in her chest. She couldn't help herself. She just reached for one of them. She scanned the label. Amoxicillin. She set the bottle back. Hesitating, she reached for another one. Lexapro. Not even the generic but the brand. Seems like Debbie wasn't as perky as she let everyone believe. Quickly, Laura put it back and was about to shut the cabinet when she saw the word on the third bottle: alprazolam.

Generic Xanax.

As soon as Laura saw that word, it was as if everything else around her disappeared. The din from the gathering on the first floor. The brightness from the overhead lights. The tightness from her panic attack just moments before.

As if on autopilot, Laura's fingers touched the white lid of the prescription bottle. She didn't even think about what she was doing. Nothing seemed real as she picked up the bottle and cradled it in her hand. She sensed the shallowness of her breathing as she turned her back to the cabinet and stared at the bottle. And then, without another moment's hesitation, she popped off the white lid and took one of those pills.

The guilt that she felt was fleeting.

From the date on the bottle, it was clear Debbie barely took them. She had a sixty-pill supply (seems money can buy anything), and had almost thirty left with an original fill date of four months ago. Why, she hardly used these at all! Laura argued with herself.

And then, without another moment's hesitation, Laura slipped that bottle into her purse. Quickly, before she changed her mind, she unlocked the door and flipped off the light switch. Hurrying down the stairs, she avoided looking in the direction of where Debbie still stood, laughing with her friends.

What Laura needed was to put some distance between herself and that woman. And then, even more important, she needed to cajole her husband into wrapping up his socializing. But she didn't want to rush him, fearful that it would look suspicious. So when she found him, she sat next to him on the sofa and pretended to care about the Giants and Cowboys game that played out on the television screen. But nothing could be further from the truth.

CHAPTER 22

Late Sunday morning, Laura sat at the kitchen table, nursing her third coffee while the girls watched cartoons. Eric was still sleeping.

Unlike Eric, Laura hadn't slept. Her mind had raced, jumping from feeling guilty about having stolen Debbie's medicine to finding a way to justify it. Then she would think about Eric's deception and she'd get angry. Twice she had gotten up and wandered around the house before returning to bed.

How dare he, she thought as she waited for him to wake up. How dare he commit to joining that country club without discussing it with her.

She had wanted to confront him about it after they left the Weavers' party. But she knew that he'd had too much to drink and, after demanding the keys to the car, she drove home while he slept in the passenger seat.

Now, as she waited for him to wake up, her temper soared and she scowled, staring out the window and feeling as if molten lava coursed through her veins.

It was after eleven o'clock when he finally emerged from the bedroom, his hair tousled and his eyes a little bloodshot. Laura said nothing. Instead, she stood up, walked to the coffee machine, and poured him a mug.

"Thanks, Laura."

He sat down at the table and took a long sip of coffee.

"Did you have fun last night?"

She stared at him. "Did you?"

He gave her a sheepish grin. "How about that couple from Manhattan?"

She tried to calm herself. "A real riot." *Drunken idiots* is what she wanted to say.

He took one more sip and then set down the mug.

"No."

He looked up at her. "No what?"

"No, I did not have fun last night, Eric." She emphasized the word "not."

At first he appeared confused.

"You asked me that question, remember? Or are you too hungover?"

He rolled his eyes. "That's not fair, Laura."

"Let me tell you what isn't fair, Eric." She narrowed her eyes and glared at him. "What's not fair is that I learned from that snit of a woman, Debbie Weaver, that you already committed to joining that stupid country club."

A guilty look washed over his face. "I was going to tell you . . ."

"Tell me?" Laura's eyes widened. "You were going to *tell* me?"

"You know what I mean."

She shook her head. "No, Eric, I don't know what you mean."

"Laura . . ."

"Don't 'Laura' me!"

"Mommy, why are you and Daddy arguing?"

Laura turned around in the chair. Emily stood in the doorway, watching them, her stuffed teddy bear under her arm. "You and your sister play in your rooms for a little bit. Mommy and Daddy are having an adult conversation."

"You mean you're arguing?"

Laura stood up and crossed the room, putting her arm around Emily's shoulders. "Not arguing. Just big-people talk. We do that sometimes."

"Sounds an awful lot like arguing."

"Becky, take your sister into your room and play, please."

She waited until both girls disappeared down the hallway and into Becky's room. Only when the door shut did she turn back to Eric.

"You aren't the same person, Eric." She stood there, her hands on her hips. "First the country club, then the promotion, then wanting to move into a bigger house. What is it with you? Suddenly you want to keep up with the Joneses? Pretend to be people who we clearly are not?" She shook her head. "Are you *trying* to force me to relive my childhood?"

"Come on, Laura." He sounded worn-out. "There's nothing wrong with bettering ourselves."

"You say it like we're not good enough as it is!"

He rested his elbow on the table and rubbed his forehead.

"Can't you just be happy with who we are?"

"That's not the point, Laura!" he snapped. "It has nothing to do with happiness!"

His admission startled her and she opened her eyes wider. "Then what does it have to do with? Maybe you can explain that me."

"It has to do with belonging, OK? Being something. Wanting more."

Being something? Wanting more? Laura couldn't speak. When had her husband turned into her mother?

"Look, we're joining the club," he said in a flat voice. "Just because you prefer to be home with the girls or sleeping doesn't mean that I can't enjoy life a little. And the company's willing to put up the bond. Fifty thousand dollars saved and a chance for me to move up the ladder, so to speak."

"The ladder of social mobility, I presume?"

"Come on, Laura." His tone softened. "If you try to get along with some of the ladies, you might find that you actually like them. The club's pool and tennis camp is much better for the girls than the public pool. And they'll make new friends and be able to network."

Laura laughed. "Network? They're eight and six, Eric. Or did you forget that?"

He sighed.

"You know how I feel about people who put on social airs." She crossed her arms over her chest. "And there is no chance that I would ever get along with those women. They aren't just like my mother, they're worse! They don't even work and they *still* find ways to neglect their children!"

"They don't neglect their children."

"Oh really?" She made a face at him. "They'd rather go to golf dinners than their children's holiday concerts! And some of them have nannies, Eric. Nannies!" She raised her hands, palms facing up. "They don't work and their children are at school, for crying out loud! And that's the world you want Becky and Emily to navigate? It will become the benchmark for what they should have but don't. That's a terrible pressure to put on two little girls. I know because that's how I was raised. Shame on you for trying to do the same to our daughters!"

Eric stood up and faced her. "You are overreacting, Laura, and I'm done with this conversation."

He stormed out of the room, leaving Laura alone in the kitchen.

How could he just walk away? Dismiss her concerns as if they meant nothing?

She grabbed her purse and headed for the door. He could take care of the girls today. She'd just go to work early and let him stew in his own juices.

Half an hour later, Laura was still fuming when she walked around the nurses' station. It was easier to feel anger at Eric, using that to justify what she had done at the Weavers' house the previous evening.

When Laura sat down, Monica looked up in surprise. "What are you doing here? You aren't scheduled until tonight's shift."

"Thought I'd come in early to work on the children's holiday party."

"Ah."

"Besides, Eric needs some daddy-daughter bonding time." She hoped that Monica couldn't hear the anger in her voice. Shuffling through her file folder of notes, Laura gave an exasperated groan. "This whole thing is bad timing. Why did she delegate this to me?"

"The children's party?"

"They're having it on a Saturday, the day before Christmas Eve. I'm not even scheduled to work Saturdays in December!"

"Let me know what you need. I'll help any way that I can," Monica promised. "But right now I have a problem."

Laura raised an eyebrow. "Oh?"

"Maybe you can help. You worked the swing shift on Friday, right? And you admitted room 307, yes?"

"The kidney surgery?"

Monica nodded. "That's the one. Well, how did she seem?"

Laura shrugged. "For coming out of surgery, she was all right. Nothing unusual."

"So, today, two days after surgery, her pain at the incision site is off the charts." Monica pulled up the patient's electronic chart on the computer.

"Hmm." Laura leaned over and glanced at the monitor. "Says Chelsea administered Percocet at six o'clock, an hour before the night shift ended."

"Exactly." Monica scratched the back of her neck. "But I don't think the patient ever got the meds."

The color drained from Laura's face. She hoped that Monica didn't notice.

Monica leaned back in her chair, glancing around to make certain no one could overhear. "Do you think she might be . . . you know . . . stealing them?"

"Monica, I . . ."

Before she could say another word, Monica shook her head and interrupted her. "I know, I know. That's a really serious accusation."

"It's not that, but . . ."

"Forget I said anything," Monica said quickly. "Seriously. I'll just keep an eye on her, see if anything else happens. If it does, I'll talk to Gillian." She gave a nervous chuckle. "Heck, the patient could have been half asleep and didn't even remember getting it, right?"

Laura pressed her lips together and nodded. "Maybe."

"Well, that's what I have to believe." Monica hit the "Escape" button on her keyboard and stood up. "Gotta make my rounds. Don't forget. Let me know how I can help you with that party, OK?"

"Sure. Thanks."

She watched as Monica walked away. Her hands were trembling. If only she had been successful when she tried to report her suspicions about Chelsea to Gillian. And yet Laura knew that she could never report Chelsea. Not now. How could she after what *she* had done the previous night? And while she could justify her actions from a dozen different angles—*if only Eric had told her, if only James had given her a normal prescription, if only her mother hadn't called beforehand, if only Debbie hadn't been such a snob*—no excuse could change the fact that Laura had, indeed, stolen someone else's medicine.

CHAPTER 23

On Wednesday, when Laura arrived at work at a quarter to three, she heard Susan catch her breath.

"Wow! Are you OK? You look terrible."

Under any other circumstances, Laura would've been offended, but she knew that she looked as awful as she felt. Ever since the Weavers' party and her fight with Eric the following day, Laura couldn't quite get her act together. Usually, she was put together: her hair pulled back, makeup on, and her scrubs clean and pressed. But, that day, Laura knew she looked as if she were sick. Seriously sick.

And she felt it, too.

"It's just a cold," she mumbled. "I took something earlier, but I feel a bit groggy."

"Maybe you should go home."

Laura shook her head. That was the last place she wanted to be.

Almost four days had passed since that party. Laura wondered if Debbie even *knew* that her Xanax was gone. Probably not. For someone like Debbie, having an antianxiety medicine was probably in vogue, something she just did to fit in with everyone else. It wasn't like she actually *had* anything to be anxious about. She didn't work. Her husband made big bucks. And her children attended private schools where the only involvement required of the parents—outside of tuition, of course—was a donation check at the annual fund-raiser.

"I'm fine. Really," she said at last when she realized that Susan was waiting for a response.

"If you say so." Susan didn't sound convinced, but she didn't push the issue.

"How was that party?" Susan asked. "The one you went to last weekend? I haven't seen you since then."

"I know which one you mean!" Laura snapped and then, almost immediately, she shut her eyes and rubbed her temples with her fingers. "I'm sorry. Truly. I . . . I just don't feel so hot."

"No worries." But there was a hurt look on Susan's face.

Deep down, Laura felt disgusted with herself. It wasn't like her to lash out at people. Yes, the party had been a disaster. Yes, the fight had been awful. But what was bothering Laura the most was the fact that she had stolen Debbie Weaver's medicine. Even worse, she had started taking it. Stolen medicine prescribed for someone else. Truly, Laura was no different from Chelsea, who stole from patients. Maybe she was even worse.

But that didn't mean that she should behave horribly to her friends. "I'm sorry, Susan." Laura dropped her hands and turned to face her friend. "I found out at the party that Eric joined the club. And he didn't tell me."

"The country club? He joined the country club?"

She nodded. "I don't know what's worse: that he didn't tell me or that horrid Debbie Weaver did!" She felt tears well up in her eyes, which surprised her because she wasn't the type of person who cried.

"I'm so sorry, Laura."

"All my life, my mother was into keeping up with the Joneses. I know those people. Even though they're all complete strangers, I *know* them."

She blew her nose and tossed the tissue into the wastebasket. "I married Eric because he was so anti–pomp and circumstance. He was down-to-earth. The real deal. Suddenly," Laura said with a sad laugh, "he's transforming into my mother."

"It can't be that bad." Susan pushed the tissue box toward her.

"But it is! He's pushing me to do things and be friends with people that I just don't like. He even wants us to move."

Susan's eyes widened.

"That's right. To move because our house suddenly isn't nice enough." A single tear fell from her eye, and abruptly, Laura wiped at it. "He should've told me. I shouldn't have heard about it from that Weaver woman," she said, her voice suddenly sounding stronger. Somehow she forced a halfhearted smile. "Anyway, I'm sorry for dumping all of this on you. It's just been a really bad few days."

"Just take it easy tonight, OK? If you need help, just ask."

Laura was not the type of nurse who asked for help. But she nodded anyway as she picked up her charts and pretended to read through them, even though her mind was still focused on six different things at once. She felt as though she were losing her mind. No matter what story she had just told Susan, she had left out the worst of it.

After Susan walked away and the floor quieted down, Laura sat in the desk chair, staring into her purse at the pills in the little orange bottle. Once again, she felt an overwhelming wave of guilt and a cloud of shame. On Monday, her day off, she had stayed in bed, pleading sickness when it was really self-reproach that stole her motivation and weighed heavily on her mind. For the past few nights, she couldn't sleep. During the days, she couldn't eat. The guilt clung to her, making her feel paranoid that people, especially Eric, knew what she had done.

But that same guilt hadn't stopped her from taking the Xanax.

Why did I steal them? For the past few days, she kept asking herself that question over and over again. She wasn't sleeping and that was adding to her irritable mood. There was no answer to that question. No justification. And *that* only increased her anxiety. She found herself taking more Xanax, hoping that the calming effect would make her forget.

It didn't.

"You feeling OK?"

Laura craned her neck around and saw Monica approaching her from the other side of the hall. "Yeah, thanks." She wished people would just leave her alone, stop pointing out the obvious that she looked as bad as she felt.

"You look like someone just peed in your Cheerios."

Laura tried to laugh but found it difficult. "Something like that." She shoved the prescription bottle into her pocket and pushed back from the desk. "Best go do my rounds."

The problem was that she didn't want to do her rounds. What she really wanted was to go home and hide in bed. Just cover her head with the blanket and sleep. Then, if everything went well, she'd wake up to find that all of this was just a bad dream.

CHAPTER 24

"On a scale of one to ten, ten being the highest, how would you rate your pain?"

The patient in room 306 could barely keep her eyes open. She was a younger woman, maybe forty, and recovering from abdominal surgery. As she clutched at her side, she moaned. "Ten. A ten." She gave a small groan and added, "Maybe eleven!"

Laura glanced at the computer screen. She had another two hours before she could administer more Percocet, but it appeared that the patient couldn't wait that long. "Let me call your doctor. See if we can get you some Tylenol to hold you over."

"Screw the Tylenol!"

Placing her hand on the woman's arm, Laura tried to give her a reassuring smile. "Hang in there, OK? Let me see what the doctor says."

She hurried back to her workstation and paged the doctor. Working the swing shift on Friday was normally fairly low-key. But nothing seemed low-key anymore and today was falling into that same pattern.

While she waited for the doctor to return her call, Laura pulled up the patient's chart on the computer screen. Sure enough, she saw that Chelsea had administered pain medicine to the patient two hours ago. There was nothing to indicate that previous doses were insufficient to ease the woman's pain. That only meant one thing: Chelsea was back at it, and this time she had stolen pain medicine from another nurse's patient!

Laura knew that she had no choice but to inform Gillian. Unfortunately, Gillian wasn't there. Maybe that was a blessing in disguise, Laura thought. She didn't cherish the idea of being the one to notify Gillian that there was a drug-addicted nurse stealing medicine from the patients.

"Hey Laura." Monica walked up to her, a large bag in her arms. "I bought some toys for that children's holiday party. Where do you want them?"

It took Laura a moment to shift gears. Toys? Holiday party? Then she remembered. "Gee, that's great," she managed to say. "I guess just take them to the children's floor. Give me a minute and I'll call up there. See who we should give them to."

Before she could reach for the phone, her cell phone buzzed. Excusing herself from Monica, Laura took the call.

"Dr. Carter here," the female voice said. "You called?"

"Thanks for getting back to me so quickly." Laura reached for the patient's chart. "Mrs. Rainor in post-op. She's in a lot of pain."

The doctor hesitated, and Laura heard the sound of papers shuffling. "When was she given her last pain medicine?"

"Two hours ago." Laura glanced down at the notes in the chart. "Percocet. Five milligrams."

"Hmm." Dr. Carter paused as if thinking. Finally, she asked, "How bad is the pain?"

"Eleven on the ten-point scale."

The doctor chuckled. "They *always* say that."

"This time, I think she means it."

"I don't want to authorize more Percocet. Try Tylenol."

The woman's face flashed before Laura, the way her mouth had twisted and her muscles tensed. *"Screw Tylenol,"* the woman had cried out. Laura hated seeing patients suffering. There was no reason for it and, in this particular case, there was a solution. "Uh, I see a note here that the night nurse had tried to contact you." She winced as she spoke the lie. "Apparently, she dropped it and the doctor on duty never called back to authorize a replacement."

The doctor sighed. "Fine. I'll authorize it then."

"Thanks, Dr. Carter."

Before she hung up, though, the doctor added, "Seems to be a lot of clumsy nurses on that floor. Funny how no one seems to drop the non-narcotic medicine." And the line went dead.

Laura clutched the phone and shut her eyes. She hated that she'd lied. In the past week, she had done the two things she despised the most: lied and stolen. And yet, she was finding it easier to justify both.

"Did you call the children's floor?"

Laura looked up, surprised to see Monica still lingering near the workstation. The bag of wrapped toys was on the counter. "Not yet. Just leave them and I'll take care of it."

"You sure?"

One of the student nurses appeared behind Monica. "Laura, room 314 just vomited."

She gave Monica a weary smile as she pushed back the chair and stood up. "I'll take it up to the children's floor after I take care of 314." She started to walk away. "Oh, and thanks, Monica."

An hour later, Laura found a few minutes to take the package to the children's center. She needed a break anyway.

Unlike the sterile environment on the post-op floor, the children's center was bright and full of life. The walls were painted in muted shades of yellow, red, and blue. The waiting room had furniture for adults as well as children. Near the nurses' station there was a game room. Laura glanced inside, smiling when she saw a boy in a wheelchair playing a computer game while his mother sat next to him in an orange plastic chair.

"May I help you?"

Laura turned around and smiled at the nurse who greeted her. "I'm Laura Reese from post-op. We're starting to get gifts brought in for the holiday party."

"Ah." The nurse motioned for her to follow as she began to hustle down the hallway. "You need to speak with Mandy. She's organizing that."

As they passed several patients' rooms, Laura couldn't help but peek inside. She paused when she saw one child, a young girl who appeared no older than Becky, lying in the bed. The girl was pale and bald. Right away Laura knew that it was cancer.

"How do you do it?" Laura whispered as she caught up with the nurse.

"Do what?"

Laura nodded toward the patient's room. "Be around sick children."

The nurse laughed. "How do *you* do it? Being around post-op patients."

"But these are just children! That girl looks like she's my daughter's age. I don't think I could handle it emotionally."

The nurse stopped in front of a closed door. "You get used to it." She put her hand on the doorknob. "You know, everyone faces tough journeys in life. They all need support systems. Sure, it's terrible when one of our patients dies. I'm not going to say it isn't tough. It does take its toll on us. But I find it's easier to focus on the journey. What I can do to bring some sunlight into the lives of the children *and* their families while they are here. I get a natural high from that, you know? Making a difference, even if the outcome isn't what any of us want."

She didn't wait for Laura to respond as she opened the door and poked her head inside the room. "Mandy? Laura Reese is here from post-op with gifts."

After spending a few minutes with Mandy discussing how donations should be delivered, Laura walked back down the hall to return to her own floor. She passed by a couple who carried a stuffed animal and a balloon that Laura recognized as being from the gift shop. As soon as they walked by her, they turned and entered a patient's room. Laura could hear a little girl squeal in delight, whether from seeing her parents or from the new teddy bear, she couldn't tell.

Sounds of delight weren't noises that Laura often heard on the post-op floor. In fact, she hadn't heard much of them recently at all, even outside of the post-op floor. While she knew that she couldn't handle working around sick and dying children, she knew that she missed being happy. Truly happy. Maybe she needed to spend more time with the girls. Maybe she did need a job with a regular work schedule. Maybe she needed to stop trying to nurture the world and focus more on herself and her family.

If she could just get through the holidays and her mother's visit, she thought, she'd work extra hard to find happiness again. It couldn't be that difficult to find, could it?

CHAPTER 25

"Why do I have to go to this again?" she asked for what felt like the tenth time.

Eric was wearing a new black suit, perfectly tailored to fit his still-muscular frame. He leaned against the door frame as she finished getting ready. "Because it's the holidays. Because it's my company Christmas party. Because I want to show you off."

"Ha." But she smiled at him in the reflection of the bathroom mirror.

"And I promise you . . . we won't be late tonight. Not like last weekend."

She pressed the earring back onto the stud in her ear. Just the reminder of the Weavers' party made her want to shudder. She shoved away the guilty feelings that still flooded her, often triggering fresh panic attacks. She was doing her best to lock those feelings into an imaginary black box. The visual helped calm her down. Most times.

"I hope not." She turned to face Eric. "How do I look?"

His eyes gave her a drawn-out inspection, starting with her head all the way down to her high heels. "Very vice presidential."

This time, she laughed.

It had been a rough week for the two of them, and Laura was trying her best to forgive Eric about the country club. Slowly, they had worked their way out of the shadows that sometimes covered a marriage in darkness, and she hoped they were headed back into the light, even if it was only a gray-blue dawn and not a full-blown sunny day.

"You guys are going out again?" Becky whined.

"Oh stop. You love Tamara!" Laura glanced at the clock. Where *was* the babysitter anyway?

Emily looked up from her coloring book. "She gives us ice cream before bed."

Becky shot her sister a fierce scowl. "Shh, Emily! You aren't supposed to tell!"

Eric laughed and Laura tried to suppress her amusement. "Well, I suppose it's OK, but only because it's the holiday season."

"Yay!" Emily shouted just a little too loud.

"Inside voice, please." Laura walked over to her purse to transfer her lipstick to her handbag. She felt the orange pill bottle and hesitated. Should she take them or not? When she heard Emily start singing a song, Laura decided to shove the bottle in the small bag. She didn't like the idea of leaving her pills in the house. Who knew what could happen?

An hour later, when they arrived at the hotel where the holiday party was being held, Laura was glad that she had decided to bring them. She began to feel the waves of a panic attack. As the wife of the soon-to-be vice president, she'd be expected to behave differently. She wasn't sure how, exactly, but she knew that people would be watching her, assessing her behavior.

Before parking the car, Eric dropped her off at the entrance. Laura headed inside and found a private place to sit and take one of the stolen Xanax.

It was just beginning to kick in when he walked through the revolving doors.

"They had valet," he said. "I should've done that."

"Valet? Why? So you can pay someone ten bucks to park your car?"

He gave her a look. "Ten bucks. Big deal."

She stood up and brushed down the front of her dress. "Says the almost–vice president of AES Financial!"

He laughed and leaned over to press a gentle kiss against her cheek. "I love you, Laura Reese."

That caught her off guard and she looked at him in surprise.

"Look, I know things have been a little crazy recently. That's life, right? But I want you to know that I love you."

"I love you, too."

He held her hand. "For better or worse. Through sickness and health."

She smiled at his words. "'Til death do us part," she added in a soft voice.

"Well, let's hope *that* never happens." Quickly, he changed gears. "Let's go find this shindig, Mrs. Reese. I want to show you off to all of the company."

When they found the ballroom, Laura clutched Eric's hand as they entered. The crystal chandelier hung from the ceiling over an empty dance floor. A band was playing some soft music, a female vocalist singing her rendition of "White Christmas." Eric led Laura over to a group of men standing near the open bar.

"Donald! John!" Eric shook the men's hands. "You remember my wife, Laura, right?"

"Great to see you again," Donald said and leaned forward to kiss her cheek. The other man merely shook her hand.

"Merry Christmas," Laura said. She felt a momentary wave of panic over whether or not that was politically correct. Should she have said "happy holidays" instead?

"And a merry Christmas to you," Donald replied.

Eric whispered, "What do you want to drink? Wine?"

She nodded and, from the corner of her eye, saw him leave her with the men as he headed toward the bar.

"So what do you think of Eric's big promotion?" the man named John asked.

She swallowed what she really wanted to say and responded with a forced smile that she hoped looked natural. "It's great. Really great."

Donald nodded. "He's the only one for the job, to be sure."

Another man approached them, and Laura was introduced. Andrew Ellison, the CEO and the "A" and "E" from AES. When Eric returned with her drink, Andrew was still talking with the other men, Laura pretending to listen. She noticed that Eric stood just a little straighter and appeared more serious than usual while Andrew engaged in conversation with them.

For the next half hour, people continued to approach the group. Laura realized that the men were basically holding court. They were part of the upper management team, the royalty among the rest of the company. This was the one night out of the year when people could feel free to speak to them about anything they wanted, to socialize with one another outside of the office.

As she listened to them, she noticed that some of the employees took advantage of the carefree atmosphere and tried to discuss business. Laura found herself observing the body language of the other men when people did this. Occasionally, they seemed receptive. Other times, they looked as bored as she felt.

Laura couldn't imagine being a part of such a world. It made her even more grateful for her own chosen career path. Despite the stress and the chaos, the constantly changing schedules and the barrage of interruptions, she liked being her own boss. Well, not exactly. But she didn't have to kiss up to anyone, at least not like these men were doing to the AES royal court.

After an hour of listening to idle chitchat, Laura found the right moment to excuse herself. She took her time as she made her way back out to the lobby of the hotel, pausing to grab an hors d'oeuvre from a tray that was being passed around by a young man in a poorly made pseudotuxedo.

Meandering through the crowd and toward a hallway, she finally found the ladies' room. Soon the main meal would be served and then, after an hour of dining and listening to more stories, dessert and dancing. If she could make it to the dancing part, she could easily convince Eric to slip away. He hated dancing almost as much as Laura hated socializing.

"Laura? Laura Reese?"

She had just exited the restroom when she heard someone call out her name. She turned and saw an older woman approach her. Unfortunately, Laura did not recognize her.

"Carol. Donald's wife," the woman said, saving Laura the embarrassment of having to admit that she didn't know her name.

Laura leaned forward and planted an air kiss on the woman's cheek. As she did so, she caught a whiff of alcohol. "I didn't know you were here," Laura said as she pulled away. Where had Carol been hiding for the past hour? The bar?

"Donald sent me to look for you. They're sitting down for the meal." The woman looped her arm through Laura's as if they were old friends. "I hope they don't sit boy-girl-boy. I'd much rather sit next to you."

What is it about alcohol? Laura thought. She'd never been a drinker and was still nursing the first wine that Eric had brought to her. She probably wouldn't finish it. She could count on one hand how many times she had drunk too much. It just wasn't her thing. Maybe it was because she didn't like losing her self-control. That was one thing that she had learned from her mother.

"Hey Laura," Rodney whispered. "You gotta see this. Dad's drunk."

Laura had been lying in bed, reading a book. "What?" She swung her legs over the side of the bed and got up, quickly following Rodney down the stairs where they could peek, undetected, into the kitchen.

"Seriously, Edward," Sonya said. "Did you have to embarrass me like that?"

His tie was askew and a goofy smile was plastered on his face. He stumbled and reached for the counter to steady himself. "Have a holly jolly Christmas," *he began to sing. He stopped and hiccupped.*

Rodney stifled a giggle, but Laura didn't think it was funny.

"You're a disgrace." Their mother turned her back on their father and fetched herself a glass of water. "It's a holiday party and you behaved like a common lush!"

". . . It's the best time of the year . . ." He made a move to reach for her as if to embrace her, but he fell and landed on the kitchen floor.

Laura wanted to shut her eyes. She didn't want to see her father like this. But it was like watching a horror movie. As much as she wanted to look away, she couldn't.

Rodney choked back a laugh. "He can't get up. He looks like a turtle!"

"Shut up, Rodney!" she hissed.

When Sonya turned and saw him lying on his back on the floor, her face contorted. Laura had seen that look only once before and that was the night of the Titanic *fiasco. "Edward Driscoll! Get up right now!"*

He struggled to get up and, when he couldn't, he started laughing.

Clearly, Sonya wasn't amused, for she kicked him. Not once but twice. And hard.

Laura gasped and even Rodney winced.

"Stay there for all I care!" their mother shouted. "That's where drunks belong! On the ground and under people's feet. You, Edward, have no self-control." She kicked him one more time before she stormed out of the kitchen, leaving her husband on the floor as he clutched his side.

Rodney and Laura scrambled to their feet and hurried up the stairs so that their mother didn't catch them watching.

When she returned to the table, Laura noticed that Eric was deep in conversation, again, with Andrew Ellison. Even though the dinner would be served shortly, Laura knew it was going to be a long night.

This was Eric's night, his chance to shine in front of his CEO and the people who would soon be reporting to him. She did her best to smile as she made her way to his side, knowing that her support was important to him.

By the time they finally returned home, it was not quite eleven o'clock. Laura paid the babysitter and then, her feet killing her, she hurried to remove her high heels. She tossed them in the closet and said a silent prayer of gratitude that all of her fancy holiday obligations were officially over. No more high heels until the next corporate event, which, according to Carol, was more often than Laura had anticipated. Apparently, Eric would attend many more events in his new role as vice president, and Laura would be expected to join him.

No wonder Carol drinks, Laura thought as she washed her face. If Laura had been a drinker, she'd be inclined to do the same. Standing around with a bunch of executives that ran a financial services company was less than exciting, to say the least.

"The girls are sound asleep," Eric said as he walked into the bedroom. He tugged at his tie and tossed it onto a chair. "Despite the ice cream."

Laura gave a soft smile. "I should hope so. It's eleven o'clock."

Eric sat down on the edge of the bed and sighed. "What a long night."

"You better get used to it." Laura dried her face in a towel. "Carol claims it's all part of the vice president's duties to entertain people and attend events."

Eric gave a halfhearted cheer.

"She drank too much. Did you notice?"

Eric laughed. "Quite a few of the wives drank way too much. Did *you* notice?"

She flipped off the bathroom light and padded across the carpet to her side of the bed. "I might have if Carol had left my side for two minutes." She crawled under the covers and shut her eyes as she lay down. "I am dreading this week," she sighed. "Work. The girls' holiday concert. Christmas shopping."

"And don't forget I have that business trip next week."

She groaned.

He leaned over and kissed her cheek. "Thank you, Laura."

She opened her eyes. "For what?"

"For being you." He stood by the side of the bed and stared down at her. "For not being like those other wives."

"And what if I was?"

He raised an eyebrow. "You wouldn't be." He paused before he added, "Usually."

"But if I were?"

He reached down and brushed his fingers across her cheek. "Then I'd take care of you. Sickness and health, remember?"

She watched as he walked to the bathroom and shut the door behind him. For a long few moments, she stared at the ceiling. She wondered if he'd feel the same way if he knew about Debbie Weaver's pills. A momentary wave of panic flooded through her and she squeezed her eyes shut, willing it to stop. Slowly, it disappeared before it became a full-blown attack.

See? she told herself. She *did* have self-control. She didn't always *need* the medicine. Not all the time. And surely *that* made her different from Carol and all of those other people. She fell asleep having convinced herself that it was true, her dark secret about the stolen medicine conveniently locked into a little black box and tucked into the dark recesses of her mind.

CHAPTER 26

"Daddy's home! Daddy's home!"

Laura could hear Becky and Emily screaming, even though she was in her bedroom, lying down. It had been a long day, first with working the day shift and then with carting the girls around. One needed presents for her classmates while the other wanted to buy something for her art teacher. Laura had needed a moment to relax. But, as she heard the front door open, she knew that moment was now over.

"There're my girls!" she heard Eric say as he entered the house. She could imagine that his arms were immediately full of two little girls who smelled of lavender shampoo and baby powder. She thought she heard one of them ask him if he had brought them anything and suspected that Emily was searching through his pockets as if there might be some magical present tucked inside.

"Ooo! Candy!" Becky shrieked.

Laura cringed. *No. Sugar.* She wanted to shout it, but she had no energy. Her body felt as if she had been dragged along a rocky road by a truck. He'd just have to deal with their sugar high.

She heard Eric laugh. "Where's your momma?"

"She's sleeping, Daddy."

"Sleeping?"

She heard him walking down the hallway, pausing to flip a light switch—probably left on by one of the girls in their bedroom. When the bedroom door opened, he flicked on the bedroom light and, even though her eyes were closed, it was blinding.

"Laura? What's going on?"

"Hmm?" She barely moved.

He walked to the side of the bed and sat down next to her. "You all right, sweetheart?" He reached out to touch her forehead. His hand felt cool against her skin, but he said, "No fever."

"Just tired," she mumbled. She knew she wasn't sick. Not physically anyway. The pressure of the holidays was getting to her. "What time is it anyway? I took a nap and must have really been knocked out."

"Seven."

She sighed. Seven o'clock? "You're home late."

"Meetings." He stared at her, concern still etched in his face. "Can I get you anything?"

She hesitated.

"Water? Tea?"

"Sure." But she didn't say which one. Frankly, she didn't care.

Getting up from the bed, Eric quietly left the room. She could hear him moving around in the kitchen. A cabinet door opened. A glass clinked against another. Water ran from the faucet. When he returned, he made her sit up. Only then did he hand her a cool glass of water and two Tylenol. "Start with this, OK?"

Laura nodded and took the two pills, which she put on the nightstand. She drank the water. It cooled her throat. She hadn't realized how thirsty she had been.

"What happened at work today?"

Laura took another big sip and handed him the empty glass. "Nothing much. I just can't sleep. Too much on my mind."

He walked to the bathroom, and she heard him run the faucet. After turning it off, he was silent for a few long-drawn-out moments before she heard him return to the bedroom. There was a concerned look on his face. In his one hand, he held the refilled glass of water. In the other was her prescription bottle.

She felt an immediate bolt of panic.

"What's this?" He shook the bottle and the pills rattled inside.

"Give that to me."

"Answer my question."

Laura clenched her teeth as Eric wrapped his fingers around the bottle, his eyes never leaving hers. She found it difficult to hold his gaze. "You know I have a prescription for Xanax."

"Yes, I do."

She got up from the bed and walked over to him, reaching for the bottle.

He jerked his hand back so that she couldn't take it. "This bottle is full, Laura. And it looks like there are a lot more than what you were prescribed."

"Excuse me?"

He popped off the white cap and tilted the bottle toward her so that she could see all of Debbie Weaver's pills that filled it. The morning after the Weavers' party, long before Eric had finally awoken, Laura had transferred Debbie's Xanax into her own bottle. She had been careful to throw out the stolen—but empty—prescription bottle so that no one would find it. At least *that* secret had been protected. But she hadn't thought about the fact that the bottle wore the label from the one James had just prescribed to her. The one for just a few pills.

"Seems a bit full, doesn't it?"

Laura averted her eyes.

"You know, you've been acting strange recently. Are you taking too many of these?"

"No!"

"I did research, you know. Xanax is addictive." He narrowed his eyes. "Highly addictive."

"Eric, please . . ."

"Please what?"

She licked her lower lip. "Just give them to me, OK? I'm not addicted."

He snapped his hand around the bottle once again. "You're not? Well, that's good to know. Then I guess you won't be needing these."

He walked back to the bathroom, Laura at his heels and grabbing at his shoulder. "What are you doing? Eric, don't. Please!"

Without any emotion in his voice, Eric replied, "You don't need that stuff, Laura." And he dumped the contents of the bottle into the toilet. After he flushed it, he handed her the now-empty bottle and walked out of the bathroom.

Standing there, Laura stared at the empty bottle. Her chest constricted and she began to breathe in short, rapid bursts. A surge of fury rose in her and she darted back into the bedroom. "How dare you, Eric!" Laura threw the bottle at him. It struck him in the chest, but he managed to catch it before it could fall to the ground. She ran at him and pummeled him on the chest. "How dare you do that!"

"Calm down, Laura. Please." His eyes flickered toward the door.

"No! I will not calm down! That was my medicine, and if you had any concerns, you should have discussed them with me, not taken it upon yourself to just flush them down the toilet!" She raised her hands to her head, grabbing at her hair. "You just don't get it, do you? It's all about you, Eric Reese! Your big promotion. That stupid country club. And don't think I'm not aware that you spoke to a real estate agent! Charlotte whatever-her-name-is left a message on the answering machine!"

"You're getting yourself worked up for nothing, Laura."

She hated how calm he sounded when her insides raged. And when he took a step toward her, she felt like an animal cornered by a predator. "Don't come near me!" she shrieked. "Just. Don't."

"You're going to scare the girls," he whispered.

The truth was that she was scaring herself. But she couldn't admit that to him. "Leave. Me. Alone." She pushed him toward the hallway and grabbed a pillow and a blanket to throw them out the bedroom door before she slammed it shut and locked it. Only then did she fling herself onto the bed and curl up into a ball.

Her mind reeled and she could barely control her thinking. For a moment, she wondered if she was going crazy, and she didn't know why. Was all of the pressure worth it? And why, exactly, was she feeling so pressured anyway? Was it the holidays? Work? Eric? If it wasn't for Becky and Emily, she knew that she might consider her options, desperate options that sometimes floated through her mind when she was feeling so out of control. And those crazy thoughts made her begin to weep.

Nothing felt right anymore. Where she used to feel so strong, she felt as though she had been pushed down on her knees. Eric had stolen her lifeline, her only chance at sanity. He had no idea what he had done to her, and only one question continued to interrupt every other thought in her mind: How on earth would she be able to last until January now?

CHAPTER 27

On Friday, the school auditorium was filled with mothers, fathers, grandparents, and siblings. Fortunately, since Laura was alone, she had managed to get a seat close to the stage. Eric hadn't been able to attend. He had a business meeting, but he had promised the girls that he would watch the video with them after he picked them up from aftercare later that afternoon.

Laura was just as glad. Ever since their fight on Tuesday, there was a heavy tension between the two of them. She had been grateful to return to work on Thursday, and was even more relieved to be working the swing shift that night.

But, before her shift started at three o'clock, she pretended that all was well, that she didn't really feel as if she were losing her mind, as she sat among hundreds of strangers waiting for the children's holiday concert to begin.

Right on time, the principal opened the door to the side of the stage, and the children walked single file through it, finding their places on the risers. Emily grinned and waved her hand while Becky tried to hide her pleasure. Laura waved back at both of them and settled into her seat. "Laura Reese?"

Startled, Laura looked up, surprised to see a woman smiling at her. She looked to be about her own age, her short brown hair cut in a neat bob, and her wide smile far too bright. But try as she might, Laura couldn't recognize her.

"I'm sorry," Laura said after a moment's hesitation. "Do I know you?"

"Oh yes! I'm the room mother for Emily's class." She gave a light laugh. "Allison Tucker?"

How could she have forgotten her from Halloween? Maybe it was her new haircut? Or that she wasn't in a yoga outfit? "I'm sorry. I . . . I've got so much on my mind."

Allison laughed and waved her hand. "Don't think twice about it. The holidays are always so chaotic. Anyway, I've been trying to reach out to you. The class is having a little holiday party and all of the parents are bringing things. Do you think . . . ?"

A holiday party? Laura couldn't remember any mention of a holiday party. But she knew exactly what Allison Tucker wanted from her. A commitment to bring something. "What day is it again?"

"December twenty-second. We have most everything except goody bags and brownies. Do you think . . . ?"

She forced a smile. "Sure."

"Oh fabulous!" Allison clapped her hands together and, at that moment, Laura knew that she didn't care for Allison Tucker. Although they were from different ends of the social spectrum, Allison was as far removed from reality as Debbie Weaver. "Now, the things in the goody bags need to be nondenominational."

"Excuse me?" Laura frowned as she leaned toward Allison. "What do you mean? It's for the holidays, right?"

"Right!" Another big grin. "But we have Jewish children in the classroom, two girls from India, and a handful of black children. We don't want to offend anyone, do we?"

"Certainly not," Laura said, biting back the not-politically-correct answer that she wanted to say.

Holidays were based on holy days. Even at the hospital, people tended to say "happy holidays" instead of "merry Christmas" for fear of offending Jewish or Muslim or Hindu workers. Laura never understood that. Why would anyone be offended if someone wished them a merry Christmas?

"Well, count me in for the brownies, anyway."

A look of disappointment crossed Allison's face, which puzzled Laura. "Well, something is better than nothing," Allison said, forcing a polite smile. "Now remember that December twenty-second is the last day of school before the winter break. Perhaps you could chaperone . . ."

Laura interrupted her. "I'm sorry. I'm working that day." At least she *thought* she was working. If it wasn't true, she figured that God would forgive her for that one little lie and hopefully a lot of other things that she'd done recently. Besides, she had her hands full with gathering gifts for the children's Christmas party that Gillian had asked her to organize.

"I see."

But Laura knew that Allison did not see. Laura was beginning to hate that expression. *I see.*

As the concert started, Allison bade her a quick goodbye and slipped back to her seat.

Clutching her purse on her lap, Laura's hand touched the opening before she remembered what Eric had done.

With January still over two weeks away and her mother's arrival imminent, Laura knew that she'd never make it through the holidays without any Xanax.

For a split second, she felt another wave of guilt. Even though the medicine was gone, she couldn't stop beating herself up for having taken Debbie's medicine. Even though she continued to try justifying her actions over and over again in her mind, the truth of the matter was that she couldn't. And yet, what was she supposed to do? Confess to Debbie? It wasn't as if anyone knew that she had taken them. But she, herself, knew. The guilt was beginning to feel like a crushing blow to her chest. Before she realized it, she was in the midst of a full-blown panic attack.

As the students ended their first song and began their second, Laura knew that if her nerves didn't calm down shortly, she'd have to leave. The auditorium felt unbearably hot and she knew that the back of her neck was sweating. The walls began to close in on her, and she clutched the arms of her seat. Slowly and silently, she counted to ten, taking deep breaths and staring straight ahead. Her eyes focused on the back wall where the children had hung different posters to represent all holidays. Even their artwork was politically correct.

Laura wondered if Emily and Becky had been forced to paint something for Kwanzaa or Hanukkah instead of Christmas.

And *that* thought, that one small, insignificant thought, put her over the edge.

Her heart pounded and her blood raced through her veins. She couldn't breathe and knew that she had to leave the auditorium. Her head felt as if it might explode, and her vision seemed to narrow, a wall of black clouding the edges as her brain burned with a mixture of rage and panic.

"Excuse me," she whispered to the man sitting next to her. Without waiting for him to shift his legs, Laura grabbed her purse and slipped by him. A few of the parents glared at her for disturbing their line of vision, but Laura didn't care. It was better to have a few parents irritated for one brief moment than to sit there, panicking and feeling as if the walls were closing in around her.

Within seconds, Laura was free of the overcrowded auditorium and in the middle of the aisle. She walked as fast as she could toward the doors in the back, pausing only once to look behind her. Her eyes scanned the risers filled with children and she saw that both Becky and Emily were watching her. Their lips no longer sang, and the smiles had vanished from their faces. Once again, Laura had disappointed them. She had also disappointed herself.

But she couldn't help it.

She waved to them before pressing her fingers to her lips and holding out her hand. A blown kiss did not make up for a mother missing the concert.

Without another look in their direction, Laura pushed through the doors and left behind the singing children, the diversified decorations, and the pressing panic that had overcome her. She needed something . . . anything . . . that would calm her. And, frankly, she didn't care what it was or where she got it. The only thing she cared about was being able to breathe again.

Even though it was only two o'clock, as if on autopilot, she headed toward the hospital.

CHAPTER 28

As soon as she arrived on the floor, Laura knew that it was going to be a horrible day. Besides the fact that she had to work with Chelsea, Gillian appeared to be waiting for her, perched near the nurses' station and ready to pounce on her.

"There you are!"

Laura frowned. She was early. Why would Gillian act as if she were late?

"How are you doing with the children's party?"

"Fine."

"What do you mean, 'fine'?" Gillian snapped. "It's a week away and there are no gifts here!"

"I've had people taking the gifts right up to the children's floor. I know how much you like everything to be so orderly," she said slowly, "so I thought that was best."

Gillian pursed her lips and shook her head. "No, no, no. We're supposed to *bring* them to the children. All of the departments do it. Together on the day of the party."

Laura remained silent.

"How do you even know people are doing it if they aren't bringing the gifts here?"

"Mandy gets them and reports back to me. So far, eight gifts were dropped off, five for girls and three for boys."

Gillian sighed but she looked disappointed. "I guess that's better than nothing."

"We still have a week," Laura reminded her in a sharp tone that she immediately regretted. "And Susan is bringing in cookies, Rebecca's bringing juice, and Tyler managed to get Kings to donate ten gingerbread-house–making kits."

Gillian raised an eyebrow. "Tyler did that?"

"His roommate works there."

"Good work. But keep pushing for more presents, please." She started to walk away and then paused. "Oh, and I know that you aren't scheduled to work Saturdays this month, but I need you here in the morning. Just for a half shift."

"Tomorrow? On such short notice?" Laura knew she sounded indignant, but she couldn't help it. She had made plans. She had wanted to sleep until noon and then run some errands in town. Hair, nails, food shopping. As mundane as those tasks were, those had been her plans. Had. Past tense.

"I'm sorry, Laura. And I expect you here next Saturday, too, for the party. It's the least you could do since I gave you off for both Christmas Eve and Christmas Day."

Laura stomped back to her workstation. She hadn't planned on attending that children's party. She was off on Saturdays and the twenty-third was her last Saturday to prepare for Christmas Eve and Christmas. Now Gillian had snatched that away from her. And with no notice whatsoever.

As she prepared to make her first rounds, Laura tried to compartmentalize her anger. The last thing she wanted was to be grumpy with the patients. It wasn't *their* fault that she had class-A jerks for a boss *and* a husband. She glanced at her purse and squeezed her eyes shut. Tight.

The nerves in her arms felt tingly, and she had to take several deep breaths to calm down. January couldn't come fast enough.

She pushed the computer cart into the first room on her list. Arnold Miller. Seventy-eight. Recovering from a heart bypass. Laura hadn't met him yet, and he was sleeping. She turned on the overhead light by the sink so she didn't shock him awake. *No sense giving him a heart attack after all he just went through,* she thought.

"Mr. Miller?" She gently touched his arm. "I need to give you your medicine."

He rolled his head on the pillow and groaned. "Leave me alone," he mumbled. "I'm sleeping."

"I know that, Mr. Miller. But you need to take your medicine."

He swatted at her hand, but it was no more than a feeble attempt. "You nurses love to wake us up every ten minutes!"

His complaints were nothing new. Laura had heard them all before. She ignored him as he mumbled more abusive accusations against her while she scanned his bracelet and took his medicine out of the cart. She forced herself to smile as she handed him the little white paper cup that contained his pills.

"Here you go."

"If I take these, will you go away?"

"Gladly."

He mumbled something else and Laura felt her pulse quicken. She had been called names before by patients. In fact, much worse than what Arnold Miller had just said under his breath. But tonight, for some reason, it made her blood boil.

As he reached for the paper cup, his hand trembled and he dropped it on the bed. Four different pills scattered onto his blanket. Quickly, Laura scooped up three of them with the rim of the cup.

"Good aim," she lied, resting her hand on his leg and palming the fourth pill, a round white one that she knew was pain medicine. Without giving it a second thought, Laura carefully slipped it into her pocket as she handed Arnold the paper cup with the remaining three pills. *What would he care,* she wondered, *if one were missing?* She watched as Arnold Miller begrudgingly took his pills and practically threw the medicine cup at her.

As she walked out of the room, Laura felt inside her pocket. She found the pill, and a new sense of calm washed over her. Gently, she rubbed it between her thumb and forefinger, not caring that Arnold Miller with his grumpy attitude and abusive words would undoubtedly wake up in pain in two hours. He had been abusive with her. And Laura wasn't in the mood to be abused today.

In between her third and fourth patients, Laura managed to escape to the restroom, break the OxyContin in half, and pop one of the halves into her mouth. She swished the saliva around in her mouth, trying to summon enough to swallow it. Immediately, she felt the release of tension in her body, just knowing that she would soon feel the relief from the pill.

It came quicker than when she took Xanax. And it was different. Better. Almost immediately Laura felt detached, even though she was acutely aware of everything she was doing. Unlike with Xanax, Laura felt calm, relaxed, and happy, but not in a totally euphoric way. Suddenly, her problems didn't seem so bad after all. She could handle them, she told herself, believing her silent one-sided conversation.

She felt as if she were floating as she pushed the cart into another patient's room.

Samuel Ogden, fifty-two. He had just had a knee replacement. His eyes were riveted to the television. He was watching *The Ellen DeGeneres Show.* "How're you feeling this afternoon, Mr. Ogden? I'm Laura and I'll be your nurse until later tonight."

He glanced at her. "I'm in a little pain, to be honest."

"Wait until you start physical therapy." She glanced at the television screen. "Pitbull?"

"You know him?"

Laura nodded and then laughed. Oh, she was feeling much better already! "Not personally or anything," she joked with the patient. "But I like his music." She reached for his wrist and scanned the bar code. "You might want to get some sleep."

The man shrugged. "You got something for that in your magic cart?"

She laughed again. She felt light. *This* was why she loved nursing. The interactions with the patients. "I sure do. But the real question is whether or not your doctor ordered it." She glanced at her computer screen. "Well, no sleeping medicine on his list, but you have an Oxy coming your way. That should help a bit."

"Oh, great. *That* will definitely knock me out. Maybe I should only take a half. The last one made me groggy forever."

Laura scanned his wristband and dispensed the medicine from her cart. "You really aren't supposed to do that, Mr. Ogden."

He raised one eyebrow and gave her a look. "Yeah, well . . ." He split the pill in half and gave her the other half.

Stunned, she watched as he popped the half into his mouth and drank some water to swallow it. "I could get in a lot of trouble if anyone knew you didn't take the whole pill!" The irony of that statement hit her and she pressed her lips together, feeling her heart begin to race.

He held his finger to his lips. "I won't tell if you don't."

Outside in the hallway, she hesitated, but only long enough to pocket the unused half of an Oxy that her patient had refused. *Is it really that easy?* she thought, feeling only a small pang of guilt. If she followed procedure, she should have thrown it into the medical waste bin, which was locked so that no one could steal anything. She should have logged what happened, but Laura knew that no one ever read those logs anyway, so really, what difference did it make?

Feeling a little bit better, whether from the medicine she had already taken or because she had convinced herself that she *shouldn't* feel bad, Laura pushed the cart back to the nurses' station, a new calm washing over her. *Now* she was ready for her shift.

CHAPTER 29

Clinging to the edge of the kitchen counter, Laura stared out the window over the sink. She took deep breaths and tried to calm her nerves as she waited for the OxyContin to kick in.

It had been a bear of a day. The previous evening, Eric had left for his business trip to Chicago. In the morning, the girls had fought, and after a round of tears and screaming fits, Laura had hardly been able to muster them into the car. They arrived at school late, which, in turn, meant that she was late for her shift.

When she arrived on the floor, Gillian was waiting for her, a fierce look on her face as she ripped into Laura. By the time she made her rounds and dealt with one of the doctors who refused to increase a patient's pain medicine, Laura was on her last nerve.

Fortunately, she had managed to palm more Xanax to get her through the day. But that hadn't calmed her. The dose was lower than what she was used to taking. Also, two freshly admitted patients, their eyes barely opened to see what medicine she was administering, provided her the perfect opportunity to steal more OxyContin. She had broken one of them in half, taking one piece while working and pocketing the other for later. *That* had done the trick and helped her handle her shift.

And then she had been late to pick up the girls from school.

"You're *always* late," Becky whined.

"Please, Becky. I've had a horrible day."

It was true. Gillian had been holed up in her office for the rest of the morning and then gone for meetings on another floor during the afternoon. But that hadn't stopped her from assigning the most difficult patients to Laura, including not one but two admits. It was almost impossible to carry a six-patient load, especially when only two of them weren't in constant need of her care.

"Let's just leave it at 'I'm sorry,' OK?"

But Becky had crossed her arms over her chest and stared out the window. Taking her cue from her older sister, Emily did the same. But for once, Laura didn't feel moved by their pouting faces that spoke of disappointment.

After they got home, the girls still fussing, Laura had stood in the kitchen, counting to ten in the hopes that she could shake the feeling of irritation. It didn't work. After riffling through her purse, emptying half of it onto the counter, she had located her stash and finally had taken that second half of an Oxy.

Now, as Laura waited for the wave of calm to overcome her, she stared out the window. Everything looked so depressing. In the ensuing darkness from the setting sun, the grayness of the leafless trees and brown tall grasses that lined the back of their property did nothing to help lighten her mood.

"Mom?"

Laura cringed.

"What's for dinner?"

For a moment, Laura felt tense. She had given no thought to dinner. Nor had she taken anything out in the morning to thaw. Going out was the last thing she wanted. It was too cold and she hated driving at night.

"Spaghetti," she said at last, hoping that might pacify Becky.

"Again?"

Laura took another deep breath. The dinner thing. It was always the dinner thing. On the days that she didn't work, she didn't mind cooking. It was actually relaxing. Sometimes Eric would join her in the kitchen. They'd open a bottle of wine and talk about their days. But on the days when she had worked, Laura dreaded the dinner hour.

"OK then. What would you like?" The Oxy just wasn't working fast enough. She knew that when it finally kicked in, she'd feel better than she had in years. All day she had practically floated through her remaining rounds. It made her wonder why doctors were so protective of that medicine.

"The diner."

She knew it. Becky and Emily loved the Morristown Diner. Laura had no idea why. Maybe it was the free refills on sodas. However, as she began to feel the tension ebb from her body, the agitation that flowed through her veins slowly disappearing, she sighed. *Why not?* she thought. A quick trip to the diner and she wouldn't even have to clean the dishes.

Nodding, she reached for her car keys and purse. "OK, kiddo. Go tell your sister."

An hour later, as Becky scowled because Laura refused to let her have a third soda, Laura motioned for the waitress to bring their check. The girls grumbled about not having their desserts, which Becky pointed out were included in their meal.

"It's not like she can put them in to-go containers," Laura retorted sharply. She began to feel that sense of calm dissipate.

The waitress handed Laura the thin piece of white paper. "Desserts? To go? Sure. I can do that."

Great, Laura thought, knowing that she did *not* want to deal with her daughters on a pre-bedtime sugar high. Still, agreeing allowed her to get out of the diner and home faster. She barely listened as the girls told the waitress what they wanted. All she heard was chocolate, chocolate, and more chocolate. When they finished, Laura hurried them up to the front counter and began rummaging through her purse for her wallet.

"Oh, for crying out loud!" It wasn't there. Her wallet.

Shutting her eyes, she tried to think where it could possibly be. Home. On the counter. She had dumped out half of her purse looking for her pills.

The girls were pressing their noses against the glass pie display, Emily shoving Becky, in response to which Becky kicked her ankle.

"Girls! Please!"

She dipped her hand back into her purse and grabbed the other half of the Oxy that she had taken earlier. Quickly, she popped the whole thing and swallowed it with water. She needed the boost to talk to the waitress, who was smiling as she brought over not one but two bags, handing one to each of the girls.

"Excuse me, miss?" Laura lowered her voice, hoping that no one could overhear her. "I have a problem. I can't find my wallet."

The woman seemed unfazed. "You guys are in here enough. I'm sure it won't be a problem. Let me send the manager over. He'll take down your information and you can either call it in or stop by later."

A wave of relief washed over Laura, along with a slow sense of calm. *Thank God for good people.*

After speaking with the manager, Laura could hardly herd the girls into the car fast enough. She needed to get home. All she wanted to do was sleep. Get the girls to bed, even if they were bouncing off the walls. Laura wanted nothing more than to crawl under the covers and forget this day.

"Mommy, you're driving too fast."

"Is not!" Emily jumped to Laura's defense.

"Girls! You're distracting me!"

She started to slow down for the stop sign when she saw bright-red lights swirling in her rearview mirror.

"Is that a police officer?" Becky asked in a whisper.

"Just be quiet!" Laura snapped. "Both of you."

She leaned over to the glove compartment and pulled out the package that held the insurance and registration cards.

"Everything all right in here?" The police officer shone his flashlight into the vehicle, the beam blinding Laura before he peered into the back of the car.

"Yes, sir," she said as she handed him the insurance and registration. "I'm sorry but I don't have my license with me. I . . . I forgot my wallet at home."

"You been out?"

"Yes. To the diner."

There was a twitch in his eye. "With no wallet?"

She nodded. "That's where I realized I forgot it. When I went to pay at the diner."

"I see."

Do you? she wanted to ask. Do you see? Do you see that my husband is traveling? That my children wanted to go out? That my job is killing me? Do you see all of that? But she remained silent, gripping the steering wheel and staring straight ahead as the officer walked back to his car.

"Are we in trouble, Mommy?"

"No, Becky. The officer is just checking on something." But Laura's heart pounded as she waited for what felt like forever to learn why the officer had pulled her over.

"Is the policeman going to arrest you?"

Laura turned to look at Becky. "What? Where do you come up with such things?" The seed, however, was planted. What if the officer did arrest her? She had heard of it happening before. People always seemed to think that DUI meant alcohol, but driving under the influence included a whole host of medications, too. Ambien for sleep. Xanax for anxiety. Lord knows what else the law considered a negative influence on driving.

"Daddy would be mad," Becky whispered. "Where would we go if they take you to jail?"

Laura took a deep breath. "Please, Becky. I'm stressed-out enough without my wallet, OK? I don't need the commentary." She'd be lucky if the officer just gave her a ticket for driving without her license. *Please God,* she prayed.

"Could you step out of the car, please?"

Laura swallowed and shut off the car engine. Slowly, she opened the door and swung her legs out. When her feet hit the pavement, her knees almost buckled from fear. *This isn't happening,* she thought. *This simply cannot be happening.*

The officer motioned her to the front of the car and turned to face her. "The reason I pulled you over was that you weaved over the double line. Twice." The flashlight made its way back to her eyes. "You haven't been drinking tonight, have you?"

She lowered her voice as she said, "I'm out with my daughters, officer. No."

For a long moment, he studied her face with such intensity that Laura felt nervous. She shouldn't have taken those OxyContin earlier, especially the one at the diner. Why hadn't she waited until they got home? It was the wallet. The missing wallet had sent her onto the edge, a place that was becoming far too familiar to her.

"I don't know if you're on any medication, but your eyes are dilated and you were, in fact, weaving." He paused and glanced over her shoulder toward the backseat of the car.

"I . . . I'm just tired," she heard herself say. "I work at the hospital. I'm a nurse and my husband is traveling. I took the girls out for dinner. That's it."

He seemed to consider this. "The hospital? On Madison Avenue?"

She nodded. "I worked a twelve-hour shift today on the post-op floor."

"Where you headed now?"

"Home." She swallowed. "I'm headed home."

"And where's that?"

When she told him her address and he nodded, backing away from the car, she almost breathed a sigh of relief. He was letting her go. "Merry Christmas," he said to her, as if not pursuing her weaving was a gift. *Maybe it is,* Laura thought as she got back into the car and fastened her seat belt. As she drove down the road, her hands clutched the steering wheel so tightly that her knuckles began to ache.

The truth was that she felt drowsy and perhaps she shouldn't have been driving. But, then again, even having cold medication was driving under the influence. Who made these laws anyway? And she didn't think she had been weaving. Maybe she'd just swerved a little bit to avoid a pothole. The road was full of them. She couldn't remember. But one thing she knew was that she wanted nothing more than to get home, go to bed, and just forget all about this terrible, awful night.

CHAPTER 30

"Good morning!" Laura greeted Susan.

"Someone is feeling better today!"

Laura dropped her purse onto the floor near her workstation, glancing at the board to see which patients she had. "I'm feeling better, yes."

The truth was that she *wasn't* feeling better. In fact, she had a headache and chills. She had to shower twice before coming to work because of how profusely she was sweating. And earlier that morning, she had felt nauseous, barely able to keep down her coffee. She knew what it was, and she knew how to correct it. She needed to get to her rounds as quickly as possible.

Sitting down, Laura began to shuffle through the charts that had been left for her. She was picking up patients from Chelsea's shift. Laura frowned as she glanced through the charts, trying to quickly assess the level of care that they would need. Two blood transfusions, one knee replacement, and an amputee. She paused and read through the chart for the amputee. A car accident from two nights ago. Driving while intoxicated.

Laura paled as she read those words.

The accident had happened two nights ago, the same night that Laura had taken the girls to the diner. The same night the officer had stopped her. And the same night that he had let her go.

Suddenly, she forgot about her need for more OxyContin and turned to Susan.

"What's the story with the amputee in room 307?" she whispered to Susan.

"Oh yeah. Terrible, that. I was here that morning when the patient came up after recovery. Completely soused, that one. Ran into a telephone pole on James Street . . . near the school." Susan shook her head, an expression of disgust on her face. "Lucky no one was killed."

James Street? Laura felt a wave of anxiety. James Street was near her own neighborhood. And, next autumn, when the new school year started, Becky would attend third grade at the school on James Street. "What time did he come in?"

"She. It's a woman." Susan's cell phone vibrated at her hip. "Midnight, I think."

Laura took a deep breath and studied the chart. The woman's lower left leg had been amputated at the knee. Too many drinks, a bad decision, and her life was ruined. "Wow." It was all Laura could say and she felt, rather than saw, Susan look at her. "That's really awful."

"Could've been worse. She could be in the morgue with a few others besides her from an accident."

But that didn't console Laura. She could think of nothing else as Tyler briefed her on the patients that she was taking over from him. No sooner had he finished reviewing the charts than Laura excused herself and headed down the hallway to room 307.

Quietly, Laura poked her head into the room. The young woman was sleeping. The IV line to the catheter in the back of her hand was slowly dripping fluid. Pain medicine and antibiotics, no doubt. The woman's face was black-and-blue, and there was a deep laceration across her forehead that Laura knew from reading the charts had taken twenty stitches to close.

The woman stirred as Laura pushed a button on the IV machine to check it.

"How're you feeling?" Laura spoke in a low voice, not wanting to disturb the patient but wanting to let her know that she was there.

"How do you think I feel?"

Bitterness. Laura could hear it in her tone. "Horrible. No doubt." There was no judgment in Laura's voice. "Can I do anything for you?"

"Turn back the clock and call me a cab."

Laura wasn't certain whether that was an attempt at humor or if she really meant it. "You'll be able to walk again, you know." It was all that Laura could give to the woman. "And it truly could've been worse."

The woman opened her eyes and blinked as she tried to focus on Laura. The dark circles under her eyes made her look ten years older than the thirty-two years listed on the chart. Laura couldn't tell if they were bruises or just dark patches. "That's what people claim when they have nothing else to say." The woman coughed and winced at the same time. "From where I'm lying right now, it looks pretty bad."

"No one died."

"Maybe I should've died."

Laura sat down in the chair next to the woman. "Please don't say that."

"You don't know me." The woman turned her head away from Laura and toward the wall. "You don't know my life."

"No, no, I don't." There was a moment of silence and Laura wondered what she could possibly say to this woman to make her feel better. Probably nothing. What would someone have said to her if she had been the one in the car accident? If she had swerved over the line in the road and hit a car or telephone pole or something? "Do you have family? A husband or children?"

The woman turned to look at Laura, and after a moment's pause, she shook her head. "I've got nobody." She shut her eyes and turned her head away once more. "I don't want to talk. Can you just get me some pain medicine? My whole body's killing me."

Laura sat there for a long second, staring at the woman in the bed. Thirty-two. No family. Or, at least, none that she professed to have. Something stirred inside of Laura, a feeling of guilt that was mixed with anxiety. As she left the room, she walked with her head down toward the nurses' station, the tightness in her chest feeling as if a vise were squeezing her to the point that she couldn't breathe.

She needed something, anything to take the edge off.

Her next patient was due for pain medicine in two hours. But Laura figured that she could fudge it just enough to get by. She hurried into that patient's room, and after greeting her with as cheerful a smile as she could muster, Laura scanned the woman's bracelet and gave her a Tylenol. But at the same time, she palmed an OxyContin from the cart, dropping it into her pocket where she managed to break it into two pieces. She would give the woman half her dose later, when it was time for her actual OxyContin. The other half, Laura snuck into her mouth when her back was turned to the patient.

It would have to do.

Back at the nurses' station, she dialed the number for the crash victim's doctor. "Dr. Olson, please," she said into the receiver when a female answered.

"He's making his rounds at the hospital."

Well, that was a start. "Great. I'm calling about one of his patients in post-op."

"Which one?"

Laura bit her lower lip. She hadn't thought to look for the woman's name. She had forgotten, which wasn't like her. "Uh . . . the amputee from the car crash?"

The woman on the other end of the line made a noise that almost sounded like she was scoffing. "The DUI? What about her?"

"She's in a lot of pain."

"I can imagine." There was no empathy in the woman's voice.

Laura remained silent, letting her lack of a reaction speak louder than words.

"All right, all right." The woman sighed. "I'll page him to stop up there." And the line clicked dead.

Laura pressed her lips together and shoved the phone receiver back onto its cradle. *How typical,* she thought. *Passing judgment against the patient.*

Long ago, Laura had learned to compartmentalize her emotions when it came to the reason people were ill. Yet she knew that many medical professionals did not. Smokers were blamed for their lung cancer. Alcoholics for their cirrhosis. Obese people for their diabetes. It was as if people needed to convince themselves that they would never be one of those patients. It was easier to cast blame and form judgment than to see through the shadow of disease or injury to the light of the soul that housed it.

"What's the matter?"

She looked up at Susan. "Room 307. She's in a lot of pain."

Susan frowned. "The amputee? She shouldn't be. She's on a drip line and can control her own pain med."

"It's not enough."

"Check the charts. Did she get her Percocet at six?"

Laura glanced through the chart. Another nurse had administered it. "Yes, but do you see the dosage?" She pointed. "Can you believe that? She just had her leg amputated and he's skimping on the pain meds?"

"What else is new? Let me guess. Olson?"

Laura nodded. "One and the same."

"It wasn't Chelsea who gave it to her, was it?"

Laura looked at the chart. "No, Monica actually administered it for some reason last night. Why?"

"No reason."

But Laura knew that there had to be a reason.

"Have there been other complaints about Chelsea?"

Susan hesitated before answering. "There hasn't been any shrinkage."

"That's not what I asked."

Susan remained silent.

"You can't possibly suspect that Chelsea—or anyone else for that matter!—would steal pain medicine from a woman who is clearly in off-the-charts pain!"

"I don't know what to think anymore, Laura. But something isn't right around here. I know you know it, too. And if Chelsea is an addict, she already crossed the line from recreational use to hard-core abuse. Only a serious drug addict would start taking that occasional pill from patients, regardless if she justified it as the patient abusing the medicine or not really being in that much pain. What's to stop her from taking it from a patient who is really suffering? Addicts rationalize, Laura, and always in their own favor. They have an uncanny ability to justify doing things that they'd never do if they weren't abusing drugs."

Susan walked away, her head hanging down as if she bore the weight of the world on her shoulders.

Laura looked after her, her hand making its way into her pocket where she was still hiding the other half of the OxyContin that she had taken earlier. The color drained from her face and her heart began to race, despite the warming effect of the medicine coursing through her veins. Was *she* so different from Chelsea? Was what *she* had done any more justifiable? A thief was a thief, no matter how great or small the object stolen. No matter the reason.

My God, Laura thought. *What have I become?*

CHAPTER 31

An hour later, Laura stood in the hallway, staring at the whiteboard. Her jaw opened and the color drained from her face as she recognized a new name on the board.

"I've been looking for you, Laura."

She jumped at the sound of Gillian's voice. She felt skittish and anxious all the time these days.

"What's wrong, Laura?"

"I . . . uh . . . I noticed that Geri Nussbaum was just admitted." She pointed toward the board.

"And?"

"May I take her case?"

Gillian frowned. "Do you know her?"

"I've dealt with her in the past, yes."

Gillian shrugged. "I really don't care who takes her as long as someone does." Gillian returned her attention to the clipboard in her hand. "Swap it out for all I care." She started to walk away. "Oh, and I want to speak to you in private. You and Susan, before you get too involved in your shifts."

"Is . . . is there a problem?"

Gillian narrowed her eyes and shot Laura a stern look that sent a chill through her. Did she know? Had she somehow learned what Laura had done?

"Just get situated and stop into my office in fifteen minutes."

Laura felt her heart plunge inside her chest. She'd never be able to concentrate until she found out what was going on. She busied herself looking for Rebecca, who had taken Geri's case. Without any argument, Laura swapped another patient so that she could take care of Geri. It wasn't often that her patients rotated back through the post-op floor, but when they did, Laura tried to get assigned to them. At least the less difficult ones, anyway.

By the time she had been briefed on Geri and had, in turn, briefed Rebecca on her patient, twenty minutes had passed. Taking a deep breath, she headed toward Gillian's office and knocked softly on the door.

"Come in."

Something about the way Gillian looked when she opened the office door made Laura start to panic.

When she walked into the room, she saw that Susan was already there as well as the union representative for the nurses. Susan stared at her hands, which she had folded primly on her lap. The union rep scowled as he shuffled through some papers in a manila folder. The office felt too small for the four of them to be meeting there. And the fact that Susan was already there, refusing to make eye contact with her, made Laura feel all the more anxious.

"What's going on?" Laura asked. She felt dizzy. For a moment, she wondered if she might need to hold on to the back of a chair for support.

"Just take a seat," Gillian said in a flat voice.

Swallowing, Laura pulled out a chair and sat down. Every nerve in her body was on fire. She watched as Gillian shut the door and moved around the table so that she was beside the union rep. At first, she simply stood there, staring at Susan first and then Laura.

"Let me start by saying that what is discussed in this room is confidential." She leveled her gaze at both of them. "There will be no discussions around the water cooler or cafeteria. If I hear of any whispers or gossip, there will be immediate disciplinary action." She paused as if to allow both Susan and Laura a moment to digest the impact of her words. "Do you understand?"

Susan managed to acknowledge Gillian's question by responding, but Laura could barely nod her head. Her heart was beating so rapidly that she knew Susan could hear it. Her eyes felt strained as she stared at Gillian, wondering what she was going to say but, at the same time, knowing what it was.

"Pain medicine."

Just those two words spilled from Gillian's lips. She let them linger in the air, hanging there as if she needed to say no more. Those two words were more than enough to send Laura into a full-blown panic attack. *She knows,* Laura thought, glancing at the door as her flight instinct kicked in. For a split second, she actually contemplated leaving the room. Just getting up and walking out the door.

"We've been having some major problems with the benzos and opioids." Gillian's voice broke through Laura's crazed thoughts. "And not just a pill here and there. A lot of pills. And I'm not talking about shrinkage, either." She paused. "Laura, are you listening?"

Somehow she managed to nod.

"With the holidays coming up," Gillian continued, "I really don't need extra aggravation, but it appears we have a drug addict among us here."

Laura's throat felt dry and her arms tingled. She wondered if she might faint. *No, no, no,* she wanted to scream. *It's all a big mistake. It was only a few times. Just a few.*

"At first I didn't realize how it was happening. The numbers weren't adding up. We began to monitor the narcotics, doing sign-offs before and after each shift, instead of just before. That seemed to do the trick for a while. But then we realized . . ."

"We?" It was an impulse question and, immediately, Laura wished she had remained silent.

Gillian shot her a look. "Let me finish, please."

Laura stared at her hands.

"Susan came to me. She told me about some things that were happening on the floor."

A wave of panic raced through Laura. *Dear Lord,* she thought. *Susan knows?*

"Wh-what's been happening?"

Gillian leveled her gaze at Laura. "Don't play dumb with me, Laura. You should've come to me the first time. You should've talked to me." Her words were abrupt and clipped, her tone completely emotionless.

Laura glanced at Susan, but the nurse kept her eyes averted. Returning her gaze to Gillian, Laura swallowed and almost reached into her pocket for the OxyContin that she had palmed from one of her patients earlier.

"I-I don't think I understand," she whispered, even though she knew darn well what was happening: she had been caught. Maybe the patients complained after all.

"I think you do."

Everything in Laura's line of vision grew dark, from the outside in. Her throat thickened and she was having a hard time breathing. *Fight or flight,* she thought and almost glanced at the door, as if she could actually escape. But this was something that she could not run from. Not today. Not this time.

The union representative turned toward her and gave her a sharp look. "If you suspected that one of the nurses was taking medicine instead of administering it to her patients, Ms. Reese, you should have reported her to your supervisor."

It took Laura a minute to process what he had just said. "I'm sorry. What did you say?"

"We need a statement from you regarding Chelsea and the suspicions you had about her stealing pain medicine from the patients." The representative handed her a pad of yellow paper and a ballpoint pen. "Dates, times, shifts, patients' names. Unfortunately, we need this information before you leave tonight."

Laura blinked her eyes. "This is about Chelsea?"

Gillian peered at her, eyebrows raised and lips pursed. "What did you think it was about?"

Quickly, Laura shook her head. "I'm sorry. I haven't been feeling well. I'm . . . I'm not thinking straight."

The union representative handed her another form. "We also need you to sign this. It's a confidentiality form. You cannot speak about this to anyone." He reached up and removed his glasses to emphasize his point when he repeated the word, "Anyone."

"I . . . I won't," she stammered, taking a pen from Gillian's desk and scribbling her name at the bottom.

"Unfortunately, you will be written up for not having disclosed this information to your supervisor," he said, slipping his glasses back on. "That's a direct violation of the nursing code of ethics."

"And, needless to say, I'm very disappointed in you, Laura."

"I understand, Gillian. I'm truly sorry."

To Laura's surprise, Gillian leveled a hard, steady gaze at her. "I don't think you *do* understand, Laura."

For a moment, Laura considered pointing out that she *had* tried to inform Gillian, but immediately she thought better of it. No sense in drawing more attention to herself. She handed the forms back to the rep and bent her head, uncertain whether the tears she felt were from relief or shame at the fact that she felt relief.

When they finally left the office, Laura walked to the break room. She needed a minute to clear her head and process what, exactly, had just happened. For a moment, she had thought that she had been caught. She had only stolen medicine a few times and only twice after Susan's little speech to her the other day. Her paranoia had made her think that, perhaps, Susan had known and turned her in.

Her thoughts were interrupted when she felt a hand on her arm. Spinning around, she was surprised to see Susan standing there, a nervous look on her face as she began wringing her hands.

"Laura, I'm so terribly sorry," she said. "I didn't mean to throw you under the bus like that."

For a split second, Laura wasn't certain what Susan meant.

When she realized, Laura wasn't certain how to react. She had been so fixated on not having been caught that she had almost forgotten that Susan had told Gillian about those incidents with Chelsea. The truth was that she was actually relieved. As far as Laura could tell, no one knew about her transgressions, and she intended to keep it that way. Yet, if she had been completely innocent, how would she have felt about Susan ratting her out? Angry, she imagined. No, make that hurt. Quickly, Laura decided that was the emotion to display.

"Well, I'd have preferred if you had spoken to me first, Susan," she said slowly, picking her words carefully. "I seem to remember asking you what I should do. You didn't exactly push me toward telling Gillian."

"I feel awful about that." Susan glanced over her shoulder and, seeing no one was there, turned back to Laura. "I didn't mean to get you in trouble."

Slowly, Laura nodded. "I get it. And I should've gone directly to Gillian anyway." She gave a small smile to Susan.

"Friends?" Susan asked.

Another nod. "Of course."

"I'll tell you something else that I found out. Remember that patient, the one with the infection?"

Barely.

"It was from a dirty needle. Gillian told me they installed security cameras."

Laura froze. "They what?"

"Security cameras. Remember when the technicians came to install wireless routers in the ceilings? They're actually hidden cameras that point into the patients' rooms."

Quickly, Laura tried to calculate when the cameras had been installed. And then, with a lump forming in her chest, she wondered how much, exactly, the cameras could see. "How'd you find out?"

"Monica."

"What?"

Susan nodded. "I asked Monica about the pain medicine for the amputee because her name was on record as having administered it. But she had never gone into that patient's room. Monica went to Gillian and I guess Gillian pulled up the security videos. Confirmed everything. That's when I told Gillian about the other issues with Chelsea and your patients."

"They keep videos of us?"

"That kinda creeped me out, too, but it's all legal. The union rep told me that. Anyway, Human Resources has a security firm going through every single recording. Can you believe it?"

"No," Laura managed to say. It wasn't a lie. She *couldn't* believe it.

"Any suspicious activity gets flagged and Gillian has to review it." Susan gave a nervous laugh. "Good thing we have nothing to hide, right?"

But Laura couldn't even fake a laugh. She felt sick to her stomach and had to excuse herself. She ran into the restroom and locked the door before leaning over the toilet, hoping to vomit but only dry heaving. Would Gillian find out? Would she learn that Laura was, in reality, no different from Chelsea?

Laura suspected that it didn't matter that she had been stealing medicine for just a week whereas Chelsea had been doing it ever since she had transferred to their floor. A crime was a crime and, if discovered, Laura knew she'd have to do the time. After all, she already knew what Gillian thought about showing any compassion to her nursing staff.

She splashed her face with cool water and stared into the mirror. Somehow she just had to pray that no one flagged any of her activity. She made a quick promise to God that she wouldn't steal any more medicine if he gave her this one mulligan. She needed a do-over and, if he gave it to her, she'd take it and aim for a hole in one.

Still, since she already had the stolen Oxy in her pocket, she took it. It was better not to have it on her person anyway, she rationalized. Besides, one way or the other, she suspected it would be the last one that she'd have.

CHAPTER 32

Laura didn't need to look into the mirror to know that she was a mess. Her hair was disheveled and her face was pale. Sleep had been impossible the previous night, and that meant it had been especially hard to get up in the morning. But she had to make brownies for the girls' holiday party. She had almost forgotten. After all, she was preoccupied with more pressing issues. But both girls had reminded her at bedtime.

She took a deep breath and shut off the bathroom light. Quietly, she stole through the bedroom, not wanting to awaken Eric. It was barely six o'clock and, even though the tension had begun to thaw between them, Laura didn't feel like dealing with him this early in the morning.

There were a lot of things that she couldn't deal with, namely that her mother would be arriving sometime during the day, and Gillian had asked Laura to come into work early on Friday, even though she was scheduled to work the swing shift.

Her mother had told Laura that she had a ton of toys to donate for the children's holiday party at the hospital. When Sonya mentioned that she wanted to drop off the gifts at the hospital on her way from the airport, Laura had immediately discouraged her. With everything going on, the last thing Laura needed was her mother popping up on the floor.

"Don't be ridiculous, Laura," Sonya had said during their phone call the previous week.

"It's a really bad time. Lots of stuff going on," Laura countered.

"What kinds of stuff, Laura?"

She hadn't wanted to explain so she had skirted the issue.

"You seem to forget that your mother worked as the head of Human Resources for a rather large hospital. Trust me, Laura. I've seen it all," Sonya had snapped.

Despite her protests, Laura suspected that her mother would probably march right into the hospital as if she owned the place. A new panic attack overcame her and Laura began to fret, her hands trembling as she poured the brownie batter into the lightly greased pan.

"Morning," Eric said in a soft voice.

Laura jumped and spun around, glaring at him. "For crying out loud, Eric!" Instead of laughing like she might have in the past, she turned her attention to the timer on the oven. "A little warning would be appreciated!" She moved over to the sink and ran the water.

He ignored her snappy comment and stepped across the threshold, heading toward the coffeepot. But she hadn't made any yet. The way he exhaled irritated her. Wasn't it enough that she was making the brownies for their daughters' holiday party? What was *he* doing, besides making noises and getting in her way while she needed to clean up after her mess?

When he reached over, indicating that he needed to put water into the coffeepot, she shoved his hand away.

"What's wrong with you?"

She dropped the pan she had been washing. It clattered against the stainless-steel sink, the noise louder in the silence of morning. "What's wrong with *me*?" She gave an angry laugh. "What's wrong with *you*?!"

To her surprise, he placed his hands on her shoulders and forced her to face him. "Look, Laura, I'm not the enemy here. I'm sorry that you've been so wound up recently and I'm sorry that I got rid of your medicine. I was concerned, Laura. It's not like you to rely on drugs, and I thought it was for the best."

If only she could forgive him. But she couldn't. If Eric hadn't thrown out her medicine, she wouldn't have stolen anything from the patients. She was in this position now because of him. *That* realization made her even angrier.

"And I know your mother's coming and that's causing you a lot of anxiety. As well as my promotion and the country club. But those are good things and when you no longer have so much on your plate, I think you'll realize that. In the meantime, I want you to know that I'm here for you, Laura." He bent his knees a little so that he was on eye level with her. "I'm always here for you."

A little of her anger dissipated. "Are you?" Laura tried to imagine what his reaction would be if Gillian realized that she had stolen medicine from patients and fired her. "Really?"

"Try me!" he said in a light, teasing tone. "I'm not going anywhere, Laura. I only have your and the girls' best interests at heart. You can't fault me for wanting to do more for the three of you. It's not like what your mother did. I promise."

And just like that, she began to cry.

Eric pulled her into his arms and embraced her. Gently, he rocked her back and forth, just like she often did with Becky or Emily when they awoke from a bad dream or hurt themselves playing outside. It was comforting and, for the first time in a long while, Laura felt safe and protected.

"Everything's going to be fine," he whispered and pressed his lips against the side of her head before he released her. Pulling back, she saw him inspect the disarray in the kitchen. "Let me finish cleaning up in here. You get ready for work. I'll take care of the girls and brownies and whatever else needs to be done, OK? Just relax, Laura. And think . . . get through today . . . just one little day . . . and you have almost three days off to enjoy time with the family."

She stared at him, a blank expression on her face.

"Enjoy? You know the word, right?" he teased. "To take pleasure in something?"

"Ha ha," she mumbled, averting her eyes. "I might go lie down for a few minutes. I haven't been sleeping."

"I know. You've been tossing and turning more than a boat on the sea during a hurricane."

She made her way back to the bedroom and crawled under the covers. Her eyelids hurt, her eyes burning from the lack of sleep during the past few weeks. Forcing herself to ignore the aching, she shut her eyes and took several deep breaths.

"What's wrong with Mom?" Laura asked her father.

"Nothing. Why?"

Laura didn't want to say that her mother had been especially cranky lately. At first, Laura thought it was because of the letter from Rutgers and Laura's determination to attend college there. But that had been almost a month ago. Her mother's crankiness had continued far too long to still be about Laura's choice of college and career.

"She just seems . . . I don't know. Weird."

Her father laughed. "Well . . ."

"No, I mean weird weird. Not normal weird. She takes a lot of naps and I hear her prowling around at night."

Her father sobered. "She hasn't been able to sleep, Laura. She's working really hard and under a lot of stress. She's had this before. You know. Insomnia."

"Really?"

He nodded. "After the baby died?"

Ah. The rarely mentioned stillborn baby sister. The reason her mother had plummeted into depression. The reason her mother had sought a job. The reason everyone's life had changed when her mother found her career more satisfying than her family.

"Yeah. I remember now."

"We just have to be patient with her right now, OK? She'll get better eventually."

Somehow Laura doubted that.

An hour after she heard the front door shut, the girls' voices fading as Eric herded them to the car, Laura gave up on trying to sleep more. Her mind was too full of racing thoughts and fears. Even a hot shower hadn't helped. Exhausted, she drank one more cup of coffee before she headed to the hospital.

By the time she arrived on the floor, Laura began feeling nauseous. Besides the fact that she hadn't taken any medicine since the day before and was feeling shaky, she also knew that nothing good would come out of the day. When she saw that Chelsea was scheduled to work the swing shift, Laura felt even sicker. No wonder Gillian had asked her to work earlier; she'd had to juggle schedules because Chelsea's patients would need to be covered. There was no way that Gillian would let Chelsea keep working, not now that she had collected her evidence and even confided in other nurses.

Laura hated confrontations. She didn't want to be there whenever it went down.

After Tyler briefed her about her patients and they signed off the narcotic counts, the first thing Laura did was to check on Geri Nussbaum. She had developed an infection in her wound, which was why she had been readmitted. It wasn't often that Laura established such a rapport with a patient, but she felt a bit of ownership for Geri. Perhaps, under different circumstances, she could have been friends with the elderly woman. The mother she never had. One who wanted the best for her children instead of herself. One who loved openly and not with manipulative demands.

If you want a ride to the football game, help your brother with his homework.

If you want that new dress, clean out the refrigerator and clean my bathroom.

It was always like that with Sonya. If this, then that. While Laura understood that her mother hadn't wanted her to feel entitlement, she also understood that her mother had never given anything without some form of string attached. In Sonya Driscoll's world, nothing was ever freely given, especially not her love.

"How are you today?" Laura asked as she walked into Geri's room.

"Sleepy . . . You look terrible," the woman said, her voice weak.

"I suppose I could say the same to you." But Laura wasn't necessarily teasing. Geri looked gray and her eyes were watery. "You feeling OK?"

The woman tried to take a deep breath but it sounded like air rushing through the branches of a tree. She was wheezing. "I've felt"—she paused and tried to catch her breath—"better."

"Pain?"

The woman nodded as Laura scanned her bracelet before entering the information into the computer and removing the Vicodin for Geri. She put it in a white paper cup and handed it to her. But Geri waved it away.

"Can't . . . breathe," Geri mumbled.

Setting the paper cup on the side, Laura hurried over to the IV pole and checked the machine that hung from it. "Hmmm. Well, let's see if we can help you with that."

Everything looked fine. The drip was working and her fluids didn't need to be changed yet. Laura reached down for Geri's wrist, surprised to find that it was swollen. She did her best to mask her concern as she moved to the foot of the bed and casually reached under the blanket to touch Geri's ankles. Swollen. And her skin was cool to the touch.

Not good.

But she smiled at Geri. "I think I'm going to call your doctor. See about some new medicine for you. To help with your breathing," she said, even though it wasn't necessarily true. But Laura didn't consider that a lie. She just didn't want Geri to worry. Worrying was *her* job. It was her job to bear the burden of knowing that something was wrong. Very wrong. "I'll be right back."

It took almost thirty minutes for the doctor on call to arrive at Geri's room. Laura had made certain to finish her rounds with her other patients and was waiting, impatiently, for the doctor when he arrived.

"Let's see now," the doctor said, checking the latest vital signs that Laura had taken. "A bit of fluid buildup."

Laura wasn't certain if he was talking to her, Geri, or just thinking out loud. But Geri's breathing was labored. And the swelling was more than obvious.

"Let's get her on oxygen."

This time, Laura knew that he was talking to her. She did as he instructed, trying hard not to display any sense of panic that would worry Geri. But when she glanced at Geri, she noticed that the woman appeared to be sleeping. Laura peered over at the doctor but he was busy with his stethoscope, leaning over Geri as he pressed the end of it to her chest.

He glanced up. "Congestive heart failure. Does the patient have a DNR?"

"I'll check."

She knew that she should know the answer to that question. Under normal circumstances she would have. But today nothing seemed right. Not her work. Not Geri's condition. And certainly not herself.

Glancing through Geri's charts, Laura found the paper. Do not resuscitate. And it was signed. By Geri. For a brief moment, Laura hesitated, thinking about the two daughters Geri had told her about during her last hospital visit. The ones who had sent in brownies for Thanksgiving, brownies from Geri's own recipe. Brownies that weren't burnt and inedible like Laura's had been that morning. Laura knew that she could lie, pretend that she didn't see the paper. That would give her time to call Geri's daughters while the doctor began lifesaving measures. But one glance at that signature and Laura knew that she had to do the right thing.

For once.

"DNR. Signed by Geri Nussbaum two years ago."

The doctor removed the stethoscope and let it fall against his chest. "Call her family then. She's not in any pain, but it could happen at any time. Perhaps you could sit here with her? Until they get here?"

Numbly, Laura nodded.

The doctor walked over to the sink and washed his hands. "Worst part of the job," he mumbled as he reached for the paper towels. "But what's another few weeks? Maybe a few months at the most?" He tossed the paper towel into the wastebasket and looked at Geri. "She'd spend most of that time in here. Who wants to be a burden to their family?"

Laura stood at the foot of Geri's bed, staring at the dying woman. She wondered if Geri truly felt that way. Was that why she had signed the DNR? Was that what she wanted to avoid? Becoming a burden?

Ten minutes later, after having called three numbers until she reached a family member, Laura returned to the dark room. She hadn't raised the blinds earlier. Now, she did so.

Outside the window, it was a beautiful day. The blue sky seemed even more brilliant and heavenly against the skeleton-gray of the trees. But it was a sight, and a day, that Geri would most likely not awaken to see.

As she returned to Geri's bedside, her eyes fell on the paper cup holding the dispensed, but not administered, Vicodin. Without thinking, Laura reached out and covered it with her hand before sliding it off the table and shoving it into her pocket. If the day was starting out like this, Laura knew that she'd never get through it without some help. And clearly Geri wasn't going to be needing them now.

Sinking into the chair next to the bed, Laura reached out and touched Geri's cold hand. It was swollen. How rapidly she had declined! Laura wondered who had been on the night shift and whether or not they had even noticed the swelling. Probably too busy, and if Geri had been suffering in silence, they would've thought she was merely sleeping.

"Your family," Laura whispered to her. "Surely they'd want to be here, Geri. They don't think you're a burden." She gave Geri's hand a gentle squeeze. "I promised them that I'd sit here with you. They're on their way. They want to be here with you, Geri."

Laura held Geri's hand, staring out the window for a long minute. She listened to the woman's raspy, labored breathing.

While people took many different journeys during their life, death was one that was shared by all. The final one. Despite people's fear and hopes of avoiding it, no one could escape it. Death came when it wanted, sometimes unplanned or unexpected. It wasn't like the other winding roads of life where people made choices that changed their paths or even their destinations. Laura had no idea what might be brewing outside of Geri's room, and she knew that there were other patients who needed her attention, but she wasn't about to leave Geri alone. Not until her family arrived or death swept her away.

Laura returned her attention to stare at the dying woman lying on the hospital bed, practically gasping for her final breaths of life. Laura sighed and clasped Geri's hand just a little bit tighter. No one should start such a dark and scary journey without the support of loved ones.

CHAPTER 33

When she walked out of Geri's room, Laura did a double take. There was her mother, not even twelve feet away, wearing a beautiful winter coat over a simple green dress with modest heels, not too high and not too old-ladyish. In her arms, she carried several boxes, each one neatly wrapped with big, exaggerated bows on top. And her hair, although gray, was cut into a simple shoulder-length cut that accentuated her high cheekbones.

Not now, Laura thought, feeling the all-too-familiar telltale signs of a panic attack.

Her mother hadn't seen her and, from the safety of Geri's doorway, she watched as Sonya marched up to the nurses' station and plopped the packages onto the counter.

"May I help you?" Susan asked.

"I'm looking for Laura Reese." Sonya reached a perfectly manicured hand to touch her hair, correcting an imperfection that did not exist.

"Uh . . ." Susan glanced down the hallway to Geri's room and caught sight of Laura.

Laura shook her head frantically and withdrew into the shadows, peering through the crack in the door to watch.

Returning her attention to Sonya, Susan said, "It's not a good time, I'm afraid."

Laura's mother gave Susan a sharp look as if saying, *You've got to be kidding me.* "I'm sorry, I don't think I've heard you properly." Before Susan could respond, she extended her hand. "Sonya Driscoll. I'm Laura's mother."

Susan ignored the extended hand and stood up, quickly making her way around the counter. She positioned herself between the counter and Sonya. "I'm afraid this really isn't great timing." She lowered her voice. "One of her patients just . . ." She didn't finish the sentence.

But Sonya did. "Died? She just lost a patient?" The way Sonya said it, almost accusatory, sent a chill through Laura. And then, as if she hadn't just heard that someone had died, Sonya sighed. "Well, I've brought some gifts for her toy drive. The one for the children's center?"

"Ah." Susan glanced down at the packages. "I'll see that she gets those. Thank you."

Laura watched as her mother glanced around, her eyes sweeping the nurses' station, the hallways, even lingering on the open door to the break room. She seemed to be absorbing every detail. "I'd have thought it would be more orderly here," she commented, mostly to herself but loud enough so that others could hear.

Susan took a deep breath and exhaled slowly. "I'll let Laura know that you were here."

"Maybe I could wait." It wasn't a question but a statement.

Laura glanced at the clock in Geri's room. Ten thirty. Not good timing.

No sooner did she think that than the elevator doors opened and Chelsea walked out, a backpack slung over her shoulder. Simultaneously, as if she had known, Gillian opened her office door and walked out. Laura stepped into the hallway, watching as the chief of security emerged from Gillian's office, too. Together, they walked down the hallway, nonchalantly as if nothing was amiss. From the far end of the hallway, another security guard that Laura hadn't noticed before began walking toward them with Chelsea in between them.

Laura clutched the wall, suddenly in the throes of a full-blown panic attack. Unbeknownst to Chelsea, she was trapped.

To Susan's credit, Laura saw that she tried to shuffle Sonya away from the imminent situation. "Uh, maybe you could sit in the waiting room?"

But before Laura's mother could respond—and from the look of it, Sonya was going to argue with her—the chief of security and Gillian stopped in front of Chelsea, who was just a few feet from the nurses' station.

"Chelsea," Gillian said in a cold, clipped tone. "I need a word with you. In private, please."

The young woman glanced at the man standing by Gillian's side and took a step backward. She glanced over her shoulder and saw the other security guard closing in on her. "What's going on?" Her eyes widened and she had a wild look about her. "I just got here. I'm not late or anything."

Gillian reached for her arm. "Let's step into my office."

But Chelsea yanked her arm free. "Don't touch me!" she shouted.

Susan tried to guide Sonya away from the nurses' station, but Sonya's feet were firmly planted, unwilling to move.

The chief of security reached out and, this time, he grabbed Chelsea's arm and started walking, but Chelsea fought him. Her backpack fell from her arm and landed between them. As she struggled with the security guard, she tripped over it and he caught her.

"Just come with us." His deep voice indicated that there was little recourse for Chelsea but to listen. Still, she began shouting, trying to free herself from his grasp as he dragged her toward the nurses' break room. Several nurses poked their heads out of patients' rooms, wondering what the commotion was all about. The janitor stopped mopping the hallway, leaning against the mop handle, his eyes taking in the unusual scene. And several visitors watched, the confusion evident in their eyes.

When Chelsea finally disappeared into Gillian's office, Susan turned to Laura's mother. "I'm sorry about that."

Sonya started to say something as she turned to look down the hallway where the security guards had dragged Chelsea, but then her eyes fell on Laura. "There she is!" Sonya lifted her chin and took a step toward her daughter. "Laura!"

But Laura made no move in her mother's direction. She stood there, perfectly still, the color drained from her face. Her eyes traveled to the closed door of Gillian's office, just a few feet from where she stood, and then back to Susan. For a moment, they both just stared at each other. It felt as if time had frozen.

". . . federal offense . . ."

". . . confess and get help . . ."

". . . pressing charges if you don't admit . . ."

Muffled fragments of what was being said in Gillian's office filtered through the door. Laura didn't hear the specifics about Chelsea and Chelsea's crimes, just the details about what would happen to Chelsea—which she knew would also apply to her. And then there was a muffled voice replying, arguing.

Laura looked down the hallway. She saw her mother standing there, a confused look on her face. Her mouth was moving, but Laura couldn't hear her words. And when Sonya took a step toward her, Laura suddenly heard the voice of her brother, telling her that she was, indeed, like her mother.

Laura felt her knees buckle when she realized that it was true. She had indeed become her mother: angry at her husband; unable to take pleasure in her children; too involved in work. There was very little that separated what Laura had become from what she had tried so hard to avoid.

And Laura knew that she had to make a choice.

Without a moment's hesitation, Laura crossed the hallway and placed her hand on the doorknob. She thought she heard Susan call out to her, but she ignored the warning. Instead, Laura quietly opened the door and stood there, waiting for the people in the room to notice.

It took a few seconds. With their backs to the door, the two security guards, the union representative, and the director of Human Resources blocked any exit from the room for Chelsea, and they didn't immediately notice that Laura was there. Chelsea, however, glanced over their shoulders and one of them followed her gaze.

When the room quieted, Laura took a step inside.

"Laura, you need to leave," the union representative said in a warning tone.

She remained where she was, frozen to that place on the floor.

"Laura?"

That one word from Gillian broke her trance. Laura walked toward the big desk, her hand in her pocket. After hesitating for the briefest of seconds, she withdrew her clenched fist, reached out, opened her hand, and dropped two pills in front of her boss.

Gillian stared at the pills as if she didn't quite understand what they were.

Laura's eyes remained on the floor, unable to meet anyone's gaze. "I just took these." She paused. "My patient died and I knew she wouldn't need them."

The room was silent.

"And it wasn't the first time."

Laura knew that everyone was staring at her, clearly too stunned to speak.

Out of the corner of her eye, Laura saw Chelsea point at her. "She's the guilty one. Not me!"

"I'll tell the truth," Laura said softly. "I'll admit what I did." Her heart raced and she felt weak. Everything about the scene felt surreal, as if she were having an out-of-body experience. She had no idea what would happen next, but she knew that she could not let Chelsea take the blame for something that she had done.

"Bravo, Laura."

For a split second, Laura thought she had misheard Gillian's words. She had spoken them so softly that they would have been easy to miss.

Laura raised her eyes to look at Gillian, who nodded. Just once. And then Gillian turned her attention to the security guards. "As for this one," she said and gestured toward Chelsea, "she made her decision."

The security guards grabbed Chelsea's arms and, before Laura knew what was happening, Chelsea was handcuffed and being led out of the room. The commotion in the hallway of Chelsea shouting, cursing at every person she saw, shocked Laura.

Laura didn't understand what had just happened. The security guards were only taking Chelsea. But they had left Laura in the office. Why weren't they arresting her, too? She had, after all, just confessed to stealing medicine. Didn't they understand what she had just said? Wasn't that what they were after?

Blinking her eyes, Laura met Gillian's gaze. "I don't understand."

"You confessed, Laura. You admitted it. That's the first part of healing, isn't it? Admitting the disease? You cannot begin the healing process until you admit that you have a sickness." Gillian stood up and placed her hand on Laura's shoulder. "I'm proud of you."

"You knew?"

"Not at first, Laura. But once security installed cameras, it wasn't hard to uncover the truth. Chelsea was stealing medicine, used syringes, morphine, pills . . . just like we suspected. But then I noticed that you, too, were taking pills."

Laura shook her head. "Then why . . . ?"

Gillian gestured to the director of Human Resources. "I wanted to see if you would let Chelsea take the fall or, as I suspected, come clean."

"And if I hadn't?" she asked in a whisper.

Pursing her lips, Gillian studied her for a moment. Laura waited, her hands shaking. She reached out to hold the back of a nearby chair to steady herself.

"Just be glad that you did."

The enormity of the situation fell onto her shoulders. What if she had been a different type of person? What if she hadn't come clean and confessed? *My God*, she thought, sinking into one of the chairs and covering her face with her hands. The tears fell freely as she realized how close she had come to being arrested, charged with a crime that would have destroyed not just *her* life but the lives of the people she loved: Eric, Becky, Emily.

It took her a few minutes to collect herself. Gillian handed her a box of tissues, and Laura used three of them before she could compose herself enough to look up.

"Wh-what happens now?"

"We're a healing hospital," Gillian said. "We're here to help people heal. But only if they want it."

For the next hour, Laura listened to the director of Human Resources talk about what was going to happen to her. Inpatient rehabilitation for thirty days. Outpatient rehabilitation for ninety days. Ongoing counseling. Probation for a year. Therapy. Meetings. But the one term that Laura never heard was "jail time."

When the Human Resources woman stopped talking, Laura looked at her, stunned to realize that there was something else that she hadn't mentioned.

"And . . . my nursing license?"

"Suspended."

Gillian leaned forward. "You'll be supervised throughout this process, Laura. But you'll regain your license and be able to keep nursing. Eventually. Just not in a situation where there are narcotics accessible." She shuffled some papers on her desk and pulled out a single document. It was a photocopy of a letter. "I wrote this recommendation to oncology for you."

Laura took the piece of paper and scanned it. "You wrote this yesterday." If she wrote the recommendation the previous day, surely that meant one and only one thing. Setting the paper on her lap, Laura looked at Gillian. "Why?"

"I knew you'd do the right thing. You're a good nurse, Laura." Gillian reached out and touched her hand. "A very good and caring nurse. I saw that soon enough after I started here. I'd hate to see the hospital lose someone like you. The patients need people who care." And then, for the first time that Laura could remember, Gillian gave her a genuine smile. "And if there is one thing I know about you, Laura, you care." She stood up and walked around the desk, putting her hands on Laura's shoulders. "I've always known you put others before yourself. Now isn't it time for someone else to do the same for you?"

Laura felt the tears spilling down her cheeks, and she collapsed into Gillian's arms.

How many years of waiting had it taken for Laura to hear those words? And now she was hearing them, but from the most unlikely of sources: Gillian.

If only, she thought as she sobbed into Gillian's shoulder, they had come from the lips of her mother . . .

CHAPTER 34

The house was quiet when she finally pulled into the driveway. Somehow Eric had managed to get off work early and had already strung up Christmas lights on the bushes. Inside, Laura could see the outline of the Christmas tree, the white lights sparkling and the sound of laughter as music played in the background.

She didn't have to open the door to know what she would find.

The tree. The lights. The children busy decorating it with the assortment of ornaments that Laura had collected over the years.

And her mother, sipping a glass of cabernet and rolling her eyes at the lack of a decorating plan.

No, her mother would not appreciate the fact that Becky still had the ornament that she had made in preschool from a toilet paper roll or that last year's paper snowflakes with blue string hung next to red and gold balls on the tree branches. And the Mardi Gras beads from the trip Laura and Eric took to New Orleans that first year after they married would be strung across the branches: yellows, greens, purples, pinks, and blues.

No, her mother would not appreciate that tree at all.

In Sonya's house, the tree was always color coordinated: ivory, gold, and a hint of burgundy. Laura wondered what her mother had done with the ornaments that she and Rodney had made as children.

Landfill, she thought bitterly.

But Laura had bigger issues to deal with.

Taking a deep breath, she pushed open the door and hesitated, for just one brief second, before she crossed the threshold.

"Mommy's home!"

Within seconds, ornaments were dropped, forgotten in the excitement that Laura had arrived at last. Becky and Emily ran toward her, throwing their arms around her waist and legs.

Eric looked up and grinned. "I thought you forgot about us!"

Laura nodded but didn't reply. Yes, she was late. Yes, she should have been home earlier. But she had a lot of things to organize at work, considering that it was her last day for a long time.

She knelt down and hugged her daughters, inhaling the scent of their hair and fighting the urge to cry. How could she leave them for thirty days? How would Eric manage? And, even more telling, what would her mother say when she heard that Laura was going to rehab?

Eric approached her, a wineglass in hand, which he passed to her as he leaned over and kissed her cheek. "Everything OK?"

She pushed away the wineglass and shook her head. "No, not OK at all," she whispered. "But . . . later, OK?"

She saw him squint, studying her face. After all of these years, surely he knew that she had been crying. But she was just as certain that he didn't know she had no tears left to shed.

"Well, Laura," her mother said sharply as she sauntered across the room. "That was some show at the hospital today."

If Sonya expected a warm greeting from her daughter, she was sorely disappointed, for Laura walked away from her.

"What's this?"

But Laura couldn't. She just couldn't pretend that everything was all right. That her years of oppression on her mother's watch hadn't resulted in just as many years of suppression by herself. It was all that

Laura had ever known: oppression and suppression. In many ways, they were the same thing.

"Laura?" Eric followed her as she walked to the kitchen. "What's going on? I'm getting worried."

She poured herself a glass of cold water from the faucet. "It's been a really bad day," she managed to say before she downed the entire glass. Setting it on the counter, she was too aware that everyone . . . Eric, her mother, and both girls . . . were staring at her from the doorway.

"This certainly is feeling less and less festive by the minute!" Sonya said, half laughing in an attempt to not sound overly critical. Laura wondered how much wine she had drunk already.

Eric, however, did not stop studying Laura's face. His scrutiny was making her anxious.

The hospital had given her until Monday to begin rehab. That would get her through the holidays. Another small gift from Gillian. But Laura didn't know how she would manage to get through the weekend, especially with her mother underfoot, without bursting at the seams.

This is all your fault, Laura wanted to scream. But she knew that casting blame should only be done in the mirror with the finger pointed in one direction: at her own reflection.

"Girls," Eric said in a stern voice. "Go to your rooms and color a picture for Mommy. She needs a little cheering up."

Becky and Emily scampered down the hallway to their rooms.

Eric walked over to Laura and stared directly into her eyes. She tried to look away, but he put his finger under her chin and moved her face so that she had to look at him. "Now, Laura, why don't you tell us what's going on. What happened at work?"

Laura shook her head. She couldn't speak.

Sonya, however, stepped forward and responded for Laura. "I'll tell you what happened, Eric. It was chaos. Complete chaos!"

Eric gave her a pleading look and, in a sharp voice, snapped, "Sonya, please . . ."

"Security took away a nurse in handcuffs. There was a big outburst. Completely unprofessional and something you'd never see at the Mayo Clinic . . ."

"Sonya!" Eric practically shouted at her, and Laura covered her ears with her hands, but it did nothing to muffle the voices.

Laura scrunched up her eyes, willing everything to go away. *Please, please,* she begged to no one in particular. *Let me wake up and have all of this be nothing more than a nightmare. A horrible, awful nightmare. Don't they realize that could've been me?*

But when she opened her eyes, she saw that both of them—her husband and her mother—were staring at her.

"What did you just say, Laura?" Eric whispered.

Had she spoken? Had she said something out loud?

"What do you mean that could've been you?" Eric moved in such a way that he blocked Sonya from Laura's line of vision. "What's happened?"

She focused on just Eric's eyes, the rest of her outer vision blurring.

"I . . . I have to go to rehab," she whispered. "The hospital's sending me."

He didn't respond.

"I . . . I've been taking patients' pain medicine, Eric." She swallowed, wishing that she had another glass of water, for her throat was bone-dry. She must have cried out every ounce of fluid. "So they want me to go to rehab." Her lips were parched. She wished that he would say something.

His eyes never wavered from hers. "OK . . ."

"On Monday."

He caught his breath, and after that brief moment's hesitation, he nodded. Just once.

"Did she just say rehab?"

"Shut up, Sonya!" Eric snapped over his shoulder before he returned his attention to Laura. He was calm. Too calm. But that was what Laura needed. "What do you need me to do, Laura?"

Laura pressed her lips together, somehow finding the energy to shrug, like a child who had no answer to a question. "I . . . I don't know." Her eyes glanced over his shoulder and locked with her mother's. "Just be here, I suppose. Like you promised me. Help me through this," she said to Eric, even though she wasn't looking at him. "I can't get through this without you."

Eric touched his finger to her cheek and moved her face so that she had no choice but to return her gaze to him. "Hey, hey. Look at me," he whispered. "Whatever this is . . . whatever is going on . . . I'm here for you. Do you hear me?"

She tried to avert her eyes.

"No, Laura. Don't shut me out. I'm *not* judging you. I'm not even going to ask questions. I'm just going to tell you that we will get through this. Together."

A sob escaped her throat and she felt Eric crush her against his chest. With her cheek pressed against his shoulder, she realized that this was the second time that day that, despite the terrible, awful situation she was in, she felt safe. It was the second time that she had heard those words, an acknowledgment that she was not alone in this. She had people behind her, supporting her and loving her.

If only . . .

When Laura finally calmed down, she managed to pull away from Eric. "I'm so sorry," she whispered. She glanced at her mother. "I'm sorry," she repeated.

To her surprise, Sonya took a deep breath and said in a soft voice, "I'm sure that you are." She cleared her throat. "It isn't as if I'm surprised. I've dealt with this before when I was working, you know."

Laura hung her head, hating the surprisingly neutral tone that her mother had taken.

"You aren't the first nurse to take patients' medications. And you won't be the last. It's just the nature of the job. Too many opportunities and too much stress." Sonya paused long enough for Laura to look up. Only then did her mother add, "And don't think it's just the nurses."

Laura blinked.

"You are not alone, my dear girl. But you should know that your hospital's being rather kind to you, Laura." Her mother exhaled. "Drug laws are much more stringent today than when I ran Human Resources. Be thankful."

"I am," Laura managed to whisper. "Oh, how I am."

And then her mother did something unusual and unexpected. She stepped forward and took Laura into her arms. Stunned, Laura let her mother embrace her.

"You will get through this, Laura. I promise you. You're strong. Like me." She hesitated before adding, "And I got through it when I had some issues with Valium."

Laura gasped. "What did you say?"

Sonya released her and held her at arm's length. "You heard me."

"You?" Laura thought she saw her mother's cheeks redden.

"It's not something that I advertise, Laura. But yes, I relied just a little too much on Valium for a while. Juggling family, work, and social obligations . . . it's very stressful. Why do you think I always wanted you to be a doctor and not a nurse?"

To Laura's amazement, she realized that she had never asked herself that question.

"It was because I saw many nurses, Laura, who couldn't handle the pressure. Some doctors, too, but a lot more nurses. I wanted you to avoid being in this very situation."

"But why then? Why did you push yourself so hard?" That, too, was a question that Laura had never thought to ask. Perhaps it had lingered under the surface, a question she *wanted* to ask but had been too afraid to actually do so.

A darkness passed over Sonya's face, and she took a moment to breathe deeply. Her eyes looked troubled, and Laura knew it wasn't because of her own predicament. "It was the baby, Laura. Your sister."

Those two words, "your sister," struck Laura with such force that her knees almost buckled. In all those years, no one had ever spoken about the stillborn baby. And Laura realized that she had never given much consideration to the impact of that unspoken tragedy on her mother.

"Thank God you'll never know the pain, Laura, of losing a baby. I . . ." Sonya paused and lowered her eyes. "I felt like a failure. Looking back now, I know that is ridiculous, but you can only connect the dots backwards."

"A failure?"

"I couldn't protect her, even when she wasn't yet part of the world. Work became a way for me to regain my confidence and help others. To prove that I was *not* a failure. But, like you surely know now, that drive to succeed comes with quite a hefty price tag attached to it."

Eric cleared his throat and reached out, taking one of Laura's hands in his and giving it a gentle squeeze. "I'd like to suggest that, maybe, your mother take the girls out for dinner. Give you and me a little time to talk. I'd like to better understand what is happening exactly." He looked at Sonya. "Would that be all right with you?"

Laura was about to decline on behalf of her mother, but Sonya nodded. "That's a good idea. You and Laura need to sort through this." She gave Laura a reassuring smile before she left the kitchen and walked down the hallway to the girls' bedrooms. "Girls, Granny wants to take you out to eat. A special treat!"

From inside the bedroom, Laura could hear the girls cheer. She turned her back to the doorway, not wanting to have them see her. Not yet.

But she didn't have to worry.

Shutting the door behind himself, Eric came to her, wrapped his arms around her shoulders, and pulled her to him, her back pressed against his chest. He held her like that, long after the noise of the girls running down the hallway and out the front door had faded away.

"Don't worry," Eric whispered. "We're a team, Laura. A team. No matter what's happened, we'll get through this. I promise you that."

With a loud, sorrowful sigh, Laura gave herself over to the care of someone else. Just as Gillian had said, it was time for her to let others help her. Her time for being so strong for so many was over. Now, at last, she had to concentrate on one, and only one, thing: herself.

EPILOGUE

Laura hurried down the aisle, smiling at the patients seated in the mauve reclining chairs that lined the wall. Outside, the sun was shining against a perfectly blue spring sky. She carried an IV bag in her hand as she headed toward the chair in the back corner.

The corner office. That's what the patients always called it.

"OK, Madeline," Laura said as she hooked the IV bag to the pole and began pressing buttons. "Let's see how we do today."

The older woman waved her hand. "This is the easy part, Laura," the woman said. "It's that awful red juice that makes me so sick."

"The Adriamycin *is* rather strong," Laura said before quickly adding, "Or so I'm told." She always tried to empathize with the patients, but there were some things she had never experienced firsthand. She knew better than to say things that sounded as if she had.

Bending down, Laura gently patted Madeline's hand. "But if you take that anti-nausea medicine and the steroids, well, it helps, you know."

"Bah!"

Laura chuckled and shook her head. "That's why we prescribe it!"

"You doctors and nurses with all of your pills and medicines! Why, it's probably all of you causing cancer in the first place! Keeps you busy."

"Ha. Ha. Ha." Laura gave her a stern look. "Not funny."

But inside, she wasn't angry. Madeline had been a patient at the Chemo Cocktail Lounge for two months already. Laura was used to her teasing comments.

"Laura?"

She looked over her shoulder and saw one of her colleagues walking down the aisle. But it was the man walking behind her that made Laura smile.

"Eric!"

He stepped around the other nurse and approached her, a smile on his face and a brown bag in his hand. He lifted it and jiggled the bag. "Time for lunch?"

Madeline sighed and coughed into her hand.

Laura glanced at her and laughed. "Don't worry, Madeline. I won't leave you hanging."

"Good!"

Laura gestured toward one of the empty seats next to her patient, indicating that her husband should sit there. "Why don't you keep Madeline company while I get her prepped for her chemo?"

"Oh, joy," Eric teased and winked at Madeline.

"Sit right down next to me," Madeline said. "It's been a long time since I've had such handsome company."

Laura hurried to the supply station and pulled out the kit she needed to clean and attach the needle to Madeline's Port-a-Cath in her chest. She paused, just long enough to look at her husband, seated next to Madeline and sharing a sandwich with her.

She loved Thursdays. It was the day when Eric always left work at lunchtime and brought her something to eat. Sometimes, if it was busy, Laura might not have more than five or ten minutes to spend with him. But she loved the fact that her new schedule permitted such regularity in their relationship. It wasn't always like that, not seven years ago when she worked on the post-op floor. But working in oncology had changed her life. Gone was the stress of erratic schedules and dealing with too many patients. Now she worked Mondays through Fridays from seven o'clock until four o'clock, sometimes a bit later if a patient needed extra care. And while it still stung to realize that a patient had succumbed to his or her cancer, Laura had learned to cope with it in ways that she never thought possible.

Thank you, Gillian, she thought as she carried her supplies over to where Madeline sat.

"And look," Madeline was saying as she pointed at the window. "The robins are busy at the bird feeder today. Chasing away those little sparrows, they are!"

Laura glanced at the bird feeder. "Looks like it needs to be refilled soon."

"Better get on that, Nurse Laura! Kill my cancer first, though. Patients before birds."

Both Eric and Laura laughed.

"I'll let maintenance know," Laura said as she put on the purple gloves and ripped open the swab to sterilize Madeline's port. "OK, you know the drill. On the count of three . . ."

"Just push it in there, Laura. You know I don't feel it anymore."

After connecting the needle to the port, Laura flushed the line, wincing when she saw Madeline make a face. She knew the exact moment that the metallic taste would reach her patient's tongue. Usually, it was on the count of three, sometimes four. But almost as quick as it was there, it would disappear. She connected the lines and pressed some buttons on the IV machine.

"There you go. Now you sit back and relax while I get your cocktail."

"Two olives this time, dear."

Eric followed Laura as she walked away from Madeline.

"You look busy. I'll leave your lunch at your desk."

Laura smiled at him. "Thanks. And I'm sorry. It's busier than usual today."

He leaned forward and planted a soft kiss on her lips. "No worries. I'll see you tonight at home." He started to back away. "Hey, it's steak night at the club. Want to take the girls?"

She hesitated and then nodded. A family dinner at the club, sitting outside on the terrace and overlooking the golf course, actually sounded pleasant, especially since her mother was coming to visit. The girls had spring break and her mother had volunteered to spend time with them while they were off school. "Sure thing, hon. A night of calm before the storm arrives?"

He laughed. "It won't be that bad."

"No, it won't, I suppose." She gave him a knowing look. "But a whole week?"

He raised an eyebrow, taking another step backward. "She's softened enough. We'll survive." With a glance at his watch, he seemed to contemplate time. "How's seven o'clock?"

Laura nodded and then watched as he walked out of the chemotherapy center, passing by the oncology desk to set her lunch at her workstation before he disappeared through the double doors.

It hadn't been easy to get to this point in her life. For far too long, she had relied so heavily on herself for strength. But she had remained steadfast to her recovery throughout the transformation process. Of course, Eric had been by her side through every step, even attending meetings with her, and when she had started speaking at different events about the danger of narcotic addictions among hospital staff, he never once complained about watching the girls.

Perhaps it was the second chance that she had been offered. Or perhaps it was the fact that Laura had discovered that it was possible to find beauty among the very people facing death. But she had learned to appreciate both health and sickness, joy and sorrow, life and death. And what she now understood was that her problems, both real and imaginary, were insignificant in the scope of the big picture. There was no magic pill that could help her cope, unless that magic pill was her own willingness to face the dark storms of adversity, to admit her frailties, to lean on her loved ones, and to rest until she could once again enjoy skies that were colored a new shade of heavenly blue.

ACKNOWLEDGMENTS

No author can truly claim ownership of a novel. You see, it takes a team of people. From the inception of the idea to the final pages of the proofed manuscript to the bookshelves on which the book sits waiting for someone to pause, peruse, and (hopefully) purchase it.

This book was one of the hardest novels that I have written, for many reasons. The topic, the research, the style of writing . . .

I've always loved a good challenge. But it sure makes it easier to have a good team behind me.

This novel presented me with special challenges since the only thing I know about nursing is from having been a patient. I couldn't have written this book without the input of Lori Ann Zayatz and Susan Conceicao. Their input about the nursing industry was invaluable to me.

Besides striving to be an accurate storyteller, I also strive to be a really good storyteller, one who captures the readers' interest and pulls them into the story, regardless of what the story is about. This novel was particularly hard for me to map out, and I want to thank Lori Vanden Bosch for her guidance with outlining the manner in which the story should be told. I've learned more from her about the craft of writing than I should probably admit.

And, of course, I want to acknowledge Amy Hosford and the entire Waterfall Publishing team for continuing to push me into new, unchartered territory. I always knew that I should have been born a pioneer woman, leaving the comforts of home to explore new lands. They have proven me right!

ABOUT THE AUTHOR

A former college professor, bestselling author Sarah Price began writing full-time after she was diagnosed with cancer in 2013. *Heavenly Blues* is her second foray into women's fiction, following *The Faded Photo*, yet she has written more than twenty novels, including the Amish Christian novels *An Amish Buggy Ride* and *An Empty Cup*. Drawing on her own experiences as a survivor of both breast cancer and domestic violence, Sarah explores the issues that touch—and shape—women's lives. She splits her time between living in Morristown, New Jersey, and Archer, Florida, with her husband and two children. Follow her at www.sarahpriceauthor.com, at www.sarahpriceauthor.com/journal, on Facebook at fansofsarahprice, or on Instagram @sarahpriceauthor.